THE ENVELOPES

A Novel

Hasu August

The Envelopes

By Hasu August

Trade Paper: 978-988-8843-96-1
Digital: 978-988-8904-10-5

© 2025 Hasu August

FICTION

EB224

All rights reserved. No part of this book may be reproduced in material form, by any means, whether graphic, electronic, mechanical or other, including photocopying or information storage, in whole or in part. May not be used to prepare other publications without written permission from the publisher except in the case of brief quotations embodied in critical articles or reviews. For information contact info@earnshawbooks.com

Published in Hong Kong by Earnshaw Books Ltd.

China, February 2012

Part One

1

I am an ordinary woman who has spent her whole life so far living in an extraordinarily big city. I have a full-time job. It determines the daily path of my life and the places where I'm seen the most—my home, the location of my employment, and the moderate commute in between. But it hardly defines the evidence of my life. Probably if I go west today, there will be nothing left behind in those places to demonstrate that I once lived...

Why am I ruminating over the evidence of my life? Perhaps I could start by telling you about gridlock. I don't want to make it a big deal, but neither is it merely a digression—though digression is a tactic I'm prone to using, I'll admit, when I'm tense, afraid, or hurt.

It was a month ago, on a Monday evening, that I found myself trapped in the traffic that, I suspect, contributed to my act of folly in bed later that night.

The office work had been murder. By the time I'd gotten through the long, exhausting day and finally emerged from the building, the rush hour should've been over. But in the car, the radio announcer was spouting on about the traffic clogging the motorways. As I drove, I couldn't get a nightmarish image out of my mind: an aerial view of a boundlessly sprawling giant, a supine figure made up of elevated motorways. Bumper-to-

THE ENVELOPES

bumper traffic trickled up the on-ramps onto this gargantuan body, their red taillights blurring into crimson lines as they crawled along, blocked arteries spreading slowly, threatening to snuff out the giant's life. Then the sea of red taillights morphed into a scene out of Hayao Miyazaki's anime film *Nausicaä of the Valley of the Wind*: an enraged herd of thousands of Ohm, mutant insects turning red and marching on their way to destroy mankind. (Even though I'm Chinese born and bred, and I've never lived abroad in my thirty-three years, I've watched every one of the Japanese animator's films.)

Most evenings, I hardly notice heavy traffic on my way home, my mind still taken up with office matters at BrightLife China. The day had been a series of unnerving office dramas that had left me torn between tears and an odd desire to laugh. Somehow I'd managed to remain calm as I grappled with it all, but I was no Nausicaä. I did not want to be part of the fatal clot I imagined, or one more inflamed Ohm. Switching off the radio, I decided to take an alternative route, the road that everyone used before the motorway was built.

The road was almost empty. As a taxi driver said to me once, the city's workers have no patience with traffic lights anymore; they expect speedy, uninterrupted traffic flow. Some never used the road in the first place; the motorway had already been built by the time they learned to drive, and they've never thought to look for a different route.

I drove along that deserted road, taking a gamble that the first traffic light to meet me would be green, imagining the light at each successive crossroad turning green too just in time. But that evening, of course, the first traffic light was not green. Then, predictably, I hit seven or so red ones in a row, mashing down the brake pedal over and over. Each time I pulled up at a red light, the distressing images I thought I'd exorcised popped into my head again, one after another. Daisy Sweet bade me farewell, leaving a hole in my heart; Waits Bernard hit me with the news BrightLife had just been taken over by a conglomerate new to our industry, asking me to join a small secret task force that would terminate many employees over the coming six months before I myself, very likely, faced the ax. Then there was the nameless couple in their late fifties who dodged the receptionist, charged into the personnel department, and demanded to see the human resources manager—unfortunately, me. Apparently I'd turned down their son's job application. He was, they claimed, a "dedicated senior expert" in the numerous companies for which he had previously worked. I had no memory of this son—being not more than ordinarily gifted in the ability to recall every job application I'd ever seen—but with a fixed sympathetic smile, I finally cajoled the pitiable couple out of BrightLife. The last turn of the screw was the news that Zhengting Dai, who is my father-in-law, had just been released from prison on medical parole, because of a sickness we'd known nothing about until early that morning.

It was a day when everything went athwart, and every light turned red.

As by fits and starts I inched toward home, all these things came to my mind in turn, and then sank into my chest and became a little orb, then snowballed—although the growing orb wasn't white as snow but ruddy as fire. Finally I parked the car and trudged toward the elevator, the blazing orb still filling my chest.

Braced for the doleful atmosphere that would surely permeate our apartment upon the return of my father-in-law, I opened the door. But instead the first thing I saw was our maid Taohua, buzzing around setting the table, humming to herself as usual, and emanating joviality just as naturally as before. Somehow, as I looked at her, my mind's eye saw a red traffic light turning green.

Taohua, who'd been widowed at a relatively young age, had just come back from her mountain village, vowing never to leave my ailing father-in-law again. Bubbling over with a vitality that I envied and appreciated—for the last nine months, our spacious apartment had been dour and our dining dull without her cooking—she prattled on about happenings in her village. Felix, our family's young friend, and his friend were still there in the village, she told us, cleaving to their ideals. My father-in-law listened, as taciturn as ever, chewing his food even more slowly than I remembered. Life behind bars, as well as his illness, had turned his gray hair silvery and slowed his speech and movements. But when Taohua brought up the topic of Lianhua, in whom she took great pride, he seemed to rouse himself, asking about the girl's life in school. His eyes glistened as he said, "I wish I could live to see the girl and her little friends again."

These words fell heavily, silencing everyone at the dinner table. In hindsight, they must have lingered meaningfully in Taohua's mind; in turn, we actually all ended up in her village for the Spring Festival of 2012.

Later that night, we helped my father-in-law settle into his bedroom, which had been unoccupied for half a year. Taohua, as in the past, went to the study we'd converted into a bedroom for her, and was soon absorbed in her soap operas as she hand-knit a cardigan for our old man. Finally my husband Deping Dai and I made ourselves snug in bed.

I felt drained of energy, yet wide-awake, the red orb subsiding in my chest. Under the duvet, Deping lay flat on his back, arms by his sides. Even in the dark, I could sense that he was staring at the ceiling.

"I'm glad Taohua is willing to come back," I said. "And she looks all right now."

HASU AUGUST

He made a small noncommittal sound.

"You told her Father had been diagnosed with terminal cancer?" I turned my whole body toward him. I couldn't really see his face.

"She's a warm-hearted person. She said she'd like to care for Old Man. I hope it isn't because she feels obliged to." He let out a slight sigh. "I hope being here again doesn't just remind her of what she's lost... She's coped. Grieving for her losses has never stopped her from living on."

I wriggled closer to him, thinking about how Taohua's daughter, who was an exceptional student, might be the only prop in her life, and yet I'd never seen her prostrate with sorrow. "She always said she'd rather choose to live every day happily, and missing the dead doesn't make her a happy day."

"But I miss those late ones... as if they'd just gone yesterday." Suddenly his voice was choking. "Jade, I'm... I'm a useless wreck." Turning toward me, he threw his arm around my waist and buried his head in the valley of my breasts.

My hand slithered across his arm and, with a steady rhythm, caressed his back. I wanted to say something like "Don't talk nonsense, Deping. You've been of great use to many people." But queerly, the orb in my chest was now swelling up to clog my throat, just as the red taillights clotted up in the motorway's veins.

"Tell me, Jade. Tell me how I can pick up the pieces. How can I hold our family together?" His voice was muffled by my pajamas, but I could hear the edge of self-reproach. *He'd had a hard day too, full of anguish,* I thought, *just like my day of red lights.*

"But today you've brought back Father and Taohua." I swallowed hard. "And you said Taohua's daughter was coming for Spring Festival. We're going to have a merry, noisy New Year's holiday."

THE ENVELOPES

"We all know Old Man is back to die." His voice was barely audible now. "It will be the last New Year for him. I just can't hold our family together... I'm *useless*."

I heard a faint whimper—his first whimper in our seven-year connubial life—stifled between my breasts. Feeling his back quiver, I moved my hand up along his spine to stroke his thick hair. My six-foot-tall husband, who had always been my stalwart defender, now clung to me like a baby. I rubbed the nape of his neck, my other hand sliding around to hold his shoulder. Both his arms came around to clasp my torso; his leg clamped mine. I rumpled his hair, the orb heating up in my chest. His breath between my breasts became quicker and warmer, making my head spin. My eyes narrowed into pinpricks, tears gathering into drops and rolling out of the corners... Then the orb inside me detonated like a bomb...

Hold on here! Describing the details of my wild sexual arousal that night still feels as if it will disgrace me. "Sex is the dross of love," my parents impressed on me all through my rather cushy upbringing. Hayao Miyazaki's animations, too, left their mark on my adolescence—even today, as an adult, I'm still a fan of Miyazaki's young ladies, compounded of pure love and heroism.

When I grew old enough to judge for myself, I learned my parents, among their generation, were not in a minority. But I became skeptical of their attitudes toward sex, which they passed on to me in good faith. I sometimes wonder about the real reason my parents are childless, suspicious of their claims that either my father is sterile or my mother barren. Oh, haven't I mentioned that? They kept the truth of my birth a secret as I grew up, but by the age of twenty, I'd figured it out myself. When I challenged them, they admitted my aunt and her husband were my natural parents, meaning I've grown up calling my actual aunt "mother" and my real mother "auntie." They'd given me away the moment

HASU AUGUST

I was born, they said, 'in everyone's best interest'. What, then, was my own best interest? Even then I never asked. The answer wouldn't have changed my life a bit.

My upbringing colored my attitude toward sex, but it failed to turn me into a puritan, thanks to the education I chose for myself. As I pursued a degree in nursing, it was gradually evident to me that I could not stop growing up into a woman. I would have little chance to become one of Miyazaki's heroines, either in my pedestrian life or in days lit by red lights. I'm by no means sexually repressed, nor do I worship asceticism, but I still feel discomfort in describing sexual intercourse.

Anyway, let's skip the minutiae of that night. Suffice it to say that with my body and soul together in the same place — our connubial bed — I went on an orgy of sex with my husband, achieving orgasm as I had not had for almost five years...

The next morning the arms I'd pillowed and the chest I'd nestled against were gone; the sweet, husky susurration had faded away. I woke up, naked, as if from a distant dream. It was the height of folly, I told myself, getting dressed. It wasn't Deping who'd initiated my throbs of pleasure; it had been my own whim . Having both my soul and body joined in sex had been a rare thing...

But I was in a hurry. I went off to work, refusing to think.

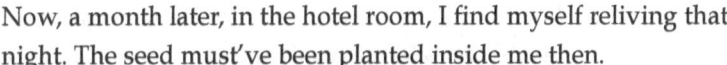

Now, a month later, in the hotel room, I find myself reliving that night. The seed must've been planted inside me then.

When I was in nursing school, listening to a lecture on the process of fertilization, an image formed in my mind (more evidence of the effect of animations on me): a little thing, a personified, cutely tailed sperm, swimming through a dark, tangled world to seek the darling egg patiently waiting and

THE ENVELOPES

pining for him. They might come across each other and unite into one. But an unfortunate fellow might just brush past a hiding egg—or they might at most manage a few smooches and then part.

About eleven years before, I'd been working in the women's hospital when I met a woman in the maternity ward. She was in her late thirties, an executive in a foreign company, and it was her first birth. Her labor pains were severe. To comfort her, I described to her the sperm as I'd imagined it during that long-ago lecture, hoping it would help her tough it out. Surely the sperm and egg's once-in-a-lifetime encounter and its most beautiful fruit in the temporal world were worth the pain, I said.

I'll never forget that woman. She had to have a caesarean, but she was finally delivered of a healthy baby boy. Resting in her hospital bed and cradling her tiny prince in her arms, she said to me, "Nurse Bai, it's a pity you don't work in personnel. You're good at watching and learning connections among things and people. You've got a talent to bring one's strength out. It's a pity you're hiding your light under a bushel. Inspiring people in a company is much more fun."

This comment from a stranger led me to eventually leave nursing profession. I enrolled part-time in business school, working toward a career in human resources management.

Two years later, in 2003, I had a patient who'd needed a laparoscopic surgery to treat a tumor in her ovary. In her late fifties, she was a cultured, learned woman, teaching English in a high school. She talked in a tender voice and always looked at me kindly. "Young lady," she would say, "has anyone ever told you your smiling lips and dimples communicate your geniality *so* irresistibly?" Right before she was discharged from the hospital, she told me that both she and her son, who had often come to visit her, adored me, and she asked on his behalf whether he had a chance with me.

This request from a stranger, named Jingwen Sai, made my toes curl at the time, but it was to take me on a life voyage I had never imagined: two years later, Madam Sai became my mother-in-law. Incidentally, she was also one of my last patients. At twenty-four, I walked away from my nursing job and began my work life as a personnel professional.

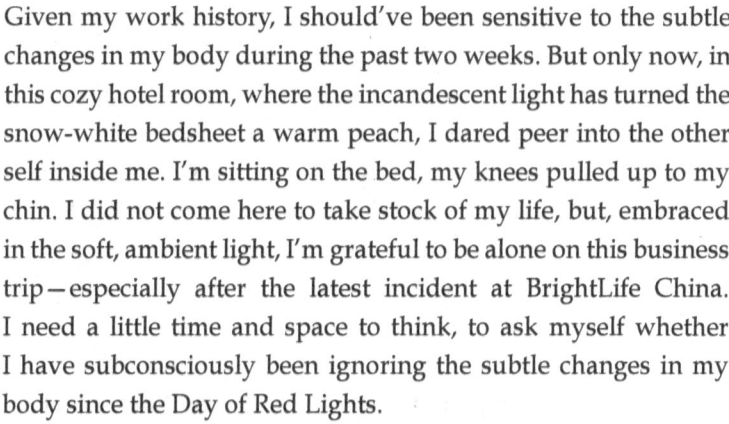

Given my work history, I should've been sensitive to the subtle changes in my body during the past two weeks. But only now, in this cozy hotel room, where the incandescent light has turned the snow-white bedsheet a warm peach, I dared peer into the other self inside me. I'm sitting on the bed, my knees pulled up to my chin. I did not come here to take stock of my life, but, embraced in the soft, ambient light, I'm grateful to be alone on this business trip—especially after the latest incident at BrightLife China. I need a little time and space to think, to ask myself whether I have subconsciously been ignoring the subtle changes in my body since the Day of Red Lights.

If only Daisy, our former Asia-Pacific finance director, with her reputation for sangfroid, were still with BrightLife. I would have sat with her in a café and bent her ear—in my natural voice, not the taut voice I usually find myself involuntarily falling into with my other bosses—about my problems over a cup of my favorite herb tea. But she's gone. "Jade," she told me when she left, "I'm bound for greener pastures, taking myself off the battlefield in a war of little meaning"—and I'm on my own now. I feel again like the 'damsel in distress'. Daisy called me soon after she joined BrightLife, four and half years ago. As a matter of fact, I've counted myself, up to now, as a clear-headed married woman for seven years. Well, maybe not quite as clear-headed at times...

THE ENVELOPES

———∞———

The incident that threw even Wings Zhan — our finance manager, mercurial and tough as nails — into a fluster had occurred a few days earlier, on the first workday after the Spring Festival, or Chinese New Year of 2012, in late January. The office was upbeat that day, as people chatted about what they'd done over the holidays. Waits, the hedonistic French head of BrightLife's Asia Pacific operations, was still swanning around a ski resort somewhere in France and wouldn't reappear for a few days. Walking past the finance department, I glimpsed accountants and clerks, their heads buried just as usual among their piles of paper, their laughter and arguments about the work at hand accompanied by the brisk tapping of their fingers on computer keys. Wings kept her staff on their toes at the beginning of every month, public holiday or not. Closing the monthly financial books on the correct day was to her a law cast in stone, even though she complained it was "inhumane" that our Boston headquarters set up cut-off dates without taking Chinese holidays into account.

I noticed one vacant seat, Jenny Chen's. I didn't feel called on to mention it, though. It wasn't exactly that Wings wouldn't want me to interfere, it was more that, partially thanks to Daisy's mentoring, she'd proven herself more than capable of managing her team effectively. Besides, in the latest employee satisfaction survey (for which I'd been chiefly responsible), the finance department had been scored especially high in "consistency of management" and "employee involvement" — well over the industry benchmarks — while as a whole, BrightLife China's average ranking in these criteria was below par. So, not wanting to interrupt their work with a New Year's greeting, I went straight on to my office without stopping.

I was on the phone, nagging my compensation and benefits specialist to send me the latest market salary survey report for review, when Wings appeared in the doorway, enveloped in the sweet scent of eau de toilette as usual, but looking oddly gloomy. I smiled at her. "Happy New Year, Wings. You look a bit down in the dumps."

"Jade, I'm in a real tizzy."

"Oh, no, don't tell me you smell a rat again. Spring's just started."

"Not a rat." She sighed. "The situation is impossible. I don't think I can handle it on my own."

"Will wonders never cease? It's rare to hear you need me," I said, only half-joking. "Is it about Jenny?"

She narrowed her catlike eyes. "You already know?"

"Oh, no, it's just a guess — her chair was empty when I passed your department. But I guess she's been on my mind, it's true. Before the holiday, I noticed that she looked like she was putting on weight. It seemed cruel to say anything right before the festival, when eating is one of the big pleasures, so I held my tongue, but I'd hate to see a young woman following in my footsteps. Look at me — I've lost my street cred, forced to wear these so-called smart-casual outfits. I used to be thinner than you, can you imagine?"

"Your clothes look nice on you." Wings could be smooth-tongued. "Daisy was right about you, Jade. She said you're a sharp observer. But I don't know how much you've guessed. Could you come with me now?" She tilted her head toward the door.

I followed her out, puzzled and uneasy. There'd been a time when, with airy self-assurance, I'd assumed nothing could escape my eagle eye, but the incident nine months before between my father-in-law and Taohua had delivered a shattering blow to my confidence.

Wings led me to the reception room. Inside, a man I'd never

seen before sat stiffly, wearing a navy sweater, arms propped on a round table in front of him, stumpy fingers interlaced. Wings sat next to him, and I pulled out a chair on the other side of the table. After Wings briefly introduced me, the man declared that he was Jenny's husband. I remembered that Jenny had given me wedding sweets about two years before — doling out candy in wrappers imprinted with the words "Double Happiness" is the customary way to announce a marriage here. But I'd never met Jenny's husband or heard him mentioned otherwise, until then.

The man's face wasn't exactly glum, despite his stiff posture. In fact his eyes, flicking from Wings to me, seemed to gleam with a hazy joy.

"Mr Wang," Wings said, "Manager Bai needs to know what's happened to Jenny. To avoid any misunderstanding, could you repeat what you've told me just now?"

"Yes," he said quickly, leaning a bit forward. "Manager Bai, no, no one expected it." He stopped speaking abruptly, his chubby face suddenly flushing under its few days' growth of stubble.

Wondering what had made this poor man's words stick in his throat when a moment before he seemed to be suppressing his delight, I said, "Go on. Relax and speak at your own pace, please. I'm listening. Then we'll see what we can do."

"Manager Bai," he resumed, clearing his throat, "the thing is: my parents came to stay with us for the festival. On the second day of New Year's, my wife complained of a pain in her stomach. We all thought she'd eaten too much of my parents' food. My wife has never been a picky eater — all food is worth trying. If she gets a little tubby, that's not a problem to me at all... Sorry, sorry, I'm wandering from the point. Yes, the pain... The pain in her stomach was getting worse. She started sweating like mad. We had to send her to the emergency room. Then, then..." He trailed off.

I wondered whether he'd had this much trouble telling the story to Wings.

"Jenny got pregnant?" I ventured, cutting things short.

"Er, how do you know, Manager Bai? You... you knew before?" His eyes snapped up to meet mine, as if he felt he'd finally found an audience receptive to his unspoken sore point.

"I didn't know, but I used to work in a women's hospital. Based on what you've described, I think Jenny is pregnant, isn't she?"

Eyes turning down again, he sighed. "Actually, miles beyond that."

"You mean something's wrong with her pregnancy?"

"The doctor checked on her and straightaway bawled us out for... for being negligent. It wasn't about her stomach. It was that she... she had a baby..."

"As I've just reasoned," I pointed out.

"Actually, Manager Bai," he murmured, looking up at me again, "a baby girl was..." He paused. "She was delivered then and there."

"Huh?" None of my experience in the women's hospital had prepared me for this. "What do you mean? She gave birth to a baby right then?"

"The, the doctor said we were lucky," he muttered, as if to himself. "At least the hospital where we rushed her has an obstetrics department."

"How is the baby? Is the baby all right?" A brief wave of anxiety washed over me, my own question ringing in my ears. "Is the baby all right? Is the baby — ?"

"Yes, yes. My baby girl was born two months early, but she's doing fine." He spoke more loudly now, his glee halting the whirring in my ears.

THE ENVELOPES

His happiness about having fathered a baby girl had been flickering through his nervousness at the shock, I realized. With an effusion of relief, I cast a glance at Wings. She was goggling at me in surprise. What was going on?

Squirming uneasily in my seat, I said, "I hope Jenny is doing fine too."

"She freaked out. The doctors performed a caesarean. But she's now on the mend, back home."

"She freaked out?"

"Let him finish the story," Wings cut in.

"Manager Bai, I—I had no inkling of her pregnancy." Tiny beads of sweat had sprung up on the ridge of his roundish nose. "Our parents don't live with us. I have lots of one-day business trips. I leave home early in the morning and return late at night."

"Are you saying your family doesn't see Jenny much?" I interrupted. Patience is not one of my virtues, even after a career in nursing. Though some might see my chronic impatience as rudeness, most seem to interpret it as quick wit, so I've never been very motivated to grapple with this flaw.

"Jade," Wings broke in, displaying a little impatience herself, "Jenny came and went in front of our eyes every day. But *we* didn't notice she was eight months gone, did we?"

Wings hadn't meant this as a barb, I reminded myself—it was just the way she was. But I had to admit that though I thought of myself as very observant in the office, I'd proven pretty dense when it came to family affairs. Jenny's normally roly-poly figure was no real excuse.

"Well, even if you don't get to see each other much," I said, "Jenny could've told you about it, couldn't she?"

"Manager Bai, the thing was..." He paused, reddening again. "The thing was, my wife herself didn't know she was pregnant."

Wings shrugged. "That's why she freaked out in the hospital," she said, with her usual gift for logical analysis. Uncharitably, I suspected she'd been less blasé when she first heard the story. With an effort I pushed the issue of how Jenny could possibly have been unaware of her own pregnancy from my mind, trying to focus instead on the new father's comic and pathetic situation. On behalf of BrightLife, I assured him that we would offer full support to Jenny and her daughter and clarified our benefits and welfare policies and procedures, closing with the usual cliché, "Mr Wang, please tell Jenny to rest assured that her work will be handled by others during her maternity leave. Meanwhile, we look forward to her return."

Looking much more relaxed, the brand-new father left, showering us with thanks. We watched him plod out of the office, headed for home, where an ignorant—if you chose to believe that—wife and an innocent new life awaited him.

Wings turned to me once his footsteps had faded away. "Does that story ring true to you?"

For some reason I found myself reluctant to answer directly. "That Jenny knew nothing about her pregnancy?" I parried.

Wings nodded. "I know some women sham pregnancy for various reasons," she mused as we walked back down the corridor. "But not even to suspect a pregnancy, right up to the birth? That's the weirdest thing I ever heard. Come on, it is 2012, not the 1200s!"

I could think of a reason, but yet again I found myself unwilling to say that. "She was probably vexed by something."

"But she's seemed content with her work here." After a second, Wings added, "She always looks happy."

"Job satisfaction doesn't equal life contentment."

"So she was so discontented, she didn't notice she'd had no period for over six months? Too deep for me." She shook her head. "She must've known in her heart of hearts."

THE ENVELOPES

"Ssh, turn down the volume," I said under my breath. "When I was nursing, I met a woman with a regular menstrual cycle of six months. The obvious logic doesn't always apply."

"Okay, I'll grant that special cases exist," Wings said, stubborn as always, "but there must've been plenty of other clues she was pregnant."

"It isn't that difficult to neglect messages coming from your body," I said, then realized that Wings was no longer beside me. I looked back to see her planted in the middle of the corridor, arms crossed, eyes narrowed in suspicion. Hastily I added, "I mean, those messages can be weak, easily not noticed by some women."

But I felt uneasy all the rest of the day. Somehow, Wings' aggressiveness had unsettled me.

Two days later, I went to see Jenny and her baby girl by myself, choosing a time when I knew Wings was busy. Visits to congratulate an employee in postpartum care were normally the combined duty of a department manager and the company's human-resources management, represented by me, but I told myself that I felt personally interested in Jenny's condition. The truth was, I was afraid that Wings' nosiness might make the visit awkward.

A short, sturdy woman answered the door, introducing herself as Jenny's mother-in-law. She led me to Jenny's bedroom and closed the door behind me, leaving us alone.

It was the first day of February, cold and wet. Despite the grayness of the day, no lights had been turned on, and the room was gloomy. A huge print of Jenny's wedding photo, mounted on the wall above the bed, was the only spark of life. Jenny herself, looking glum, was propped up against the headboard under her likeness, a book in her hands. Without the sweet smile that usually creased her eyes into a pleasant pair of tiny crescent moons, she was almost unrecognizable.

As solicitously and cheerfully as I could, I asked how everything was.

Jenny responded flatly, forcing a smile. The apartment seemed strangely quiet, given the presence of a newborn, and I wondered if Jenny's mother-in-law was holding the baby in another room. When I asked if I could see the child, Jenny merely turned her head and pointed her chin toward the cot I'd glimpsed when I entered the room, set under the window, where the curtains were drawn back. The infant was asleep there, swaddled in layers of quilt, her head wrapped in a cotton cap so that only her tiny pink face was exposed.

As I gazed at her fine, tender features, my eyes grew misty, and I felt my heart shudder. During my years in that women's hospital, newborn babies had always turned me happily loquacious. But this little girl looked so fragile that I was afraid to touch her, yet so strong that I was moved almost to tears for this great survivor. Inside me, ineffable feelings welled up, mixed, and churned.

Finally I managed to produce a few words. "She is so quiet."

"She's been quiet all the time." Jenny seemed to pick up on my real meaning, though her voice was still emotionless, as if it belonged to a stranger. "Since she was in my belly... as if she'd known she wasn't wanted."

I had succeeded in visiting without Wings physically beside me, but at that very instant I could hear her snorting in my ears. *What did I say? Of course, she knew she was pregnant!* I took a deep breath, trying to get a grip on myself. My back was still toward Jenny, but my eyes shifted from the infant to the window and the street outside.

THE ENVELOPES

"You didn't want your baby?" I said quietly.

After a long silence, Jenny spoke languidly. "I don't know... Maybe the baby has known much better than I what I've been thinking and feeling."

Hear that? Wings' voice intruded again, as if she were right there, missing no opportunity to lay into me. *She's ducking out of the whole thing. Selfish people shirk. Listen to her — she said "the baby," not even "my baby". Even now she doesn't want her little child.*

"If you didn't want a baby for some reason," I said, still looking out the window at nothing in particular, "couldn't you have taken measures to prevent it?" It felt as if I was talking to myself, not Jenny.

"Like I said, I didn't know what or why or whether. I didn't know anything... I don't know."

Come on, Jade! I could hear Wings shrilling. *Wake up and smell the coffee!*

"I think I understand," I said finally, unsure whether I was speaking to Jenny or to Wings.

"You do?" Jenny's voice actually rose a little at that. But then the door squeaked open, and she broke off.

I spun on my heel and saw that Jenny's mother-in-law was poking her head in. "It's time to feed the baby," she said.

It seemed like the perfect moment to put an end to my visit. I uttered some words to assure Jenny of our company's support, and then made my way out, the phantom Wings still tagging along behind me all the way to the parking lot. *Jade, so what do you understand?*

"That's enough!" I said aloud, almost shouting. "All right, I understand — Jenny hid her true self away, and pretended to forget it! Yes, and so did I! We all have our crosses to bear, don't we? Now, are you satisfied?" Feeling like a lunatic, I got into the car and slammed the door shut.

2

I've had no further exchanges with Wings about Jenny's situation. Nevertheless, it has only made me more conscious of my own. Reclining on the bed in this hotel room — away from Deping — I have time and space to ponder what is happening to *me*. In hindsight, I realize why I really went alone to visit Jenny, who had not wanted to be a mother. It was myself, not Wings, with whom I was crossing swords when I met Jenny's quiet but tough baby. And when I left Jenny's flat, it was as if I was fleeing the reality now facing me.

I cannot deny it. It's been half a month since I first noticed my delayed menses, my swelling breasts and darkening areolas, my aching back — all the early signs of pregnancy. As a matter of fact, Wings' usual contentiousness might have irked me, but it also compelled me to face up to my own evasion.

It's true that my working relationship with Wings has been a love-hate one: hatred of her peremptory bluntness, sometimes bordering on bullying; love fostered by Daisy, who always reminded me of the positive power in Wings' approach. But Daisy would've enlightened me with gentle questions. *Jade, why do you say it is the height of folly to make love with your soul and body dedicated to your husband? What has made a beautiful thing foolish to you? Are you still on the cusp of fear and desire?*

THE ENVELOPES

I met Daisy for the first time on May 25, 2007 — a day imprinted deeply in my memory as the first anniversary of my great loss. I'd been working for BrightLife, a sizable multinational company chomping at the bit to expand in the Asia-Pacific region, for about seven months then. Daisy and Waits had both just arrived, sent to BrightLife on a mission to institute the regional organization in our city — one of the cities taking the lead on economic dynamism in China — and drive the company toward its goal. Daisy wore a jazzy knee-skimming, three-quarter-sleeved cotton dress in a delicate floral print, with white collar and cuffs. Her chic, gamine look and purely Asian face, in piquant contrast to her Western name, instantly set tongues wagging in our office. Cathy Hu, the beady-eyed secretary to Fred Cheung, who then had been our general manager of China operations for two years, sniped, "Bowl me over! Didn't Fred say they were sending an experienced American finance director over here? She's so young, and she's Asian."

"Believe me, Cathy," I said sternly, "she may look like an Oriental ingénue, but that doesn't mean she's not a real professional."

Still, I was probably just as astonished by Daisy's looks as Cathy was, given the little I knew about her. She was thirty-seven then, nine years older than me. Prior to joining BrightLife, she'd had a proven track record in financial management in a renowned US-based multinational company, and had been on several assignments in Asian countries. As a personnel professional, I'd always kept in mind the motto, "Judge not according to appearance," while still listening to my instinct for *feeling* people, but Daisy played havoc with this balance of intellect and intuition. The pizzazz and youthful femininity she projected, as well as her riveting sartorial style, so sharply contradicted all our expectations that I was drawn to *feel* her. In the orientation meeting, suddenly aware of our own dowdy outfits, I recognized in her a keenness of mind that nothing I'd heard or read on paper had prepared me for. Despite her innocent air, her gaze felt as sharp as a knife.

Waits was also a surprise. Seeing him in the flesh, I realized how deceptive a photo could be. The image I'd seen of him showed a salt-and-pepper-haired man standing against a blank wall, with no objects nearby to indicate scale. I was expecting a Westerner of average size, but in reality, he was as slight as a small Chinese man — the antithesis of the tall and burly (though Chinese-featured) Fred, whose gracious, soigné demeanor also contrasted sharply with Waits' physical liveliness and brisk speech. My sixth sense told me Waits and Daisy would make root-and-branch changes in BrightLife China.

That evening, there was a dinner to welcome the newcomers, with Fred, his four functional managers (including me), and Cathy. After toasting Daisy and Waits, Fred started to recount his team's heroic struggle to win business for the company. Most of us listened with impassive faces. I was sitting next to Daisy, and could hardly see her face, but I knew her sharp eyes were sizing us all up.

"As a result of plugging away at sales," Fred finally concluded, "we are now profitable enough to move our office soon to a decent area, which will be better for business." He turned toward Daisy, showing his glossy, regular teeth in a broad smile. "As I told you before, my finance manager left us a short while ago. Daisy, I need your help to find a good replacement. Meanwhile, I would appreciate it if you could work out how soon we can make the move, from a financial perspective."

"Sure," Daisy said crisply. "Your finance manager had bad timing, didn't she? If she'd stuck around, she'd be working in a much nicer area."

A perfect silence fell over the table for a few seconds. Then, as if released from a spell, everyone broke out in lively discussions, in pairs or small groups — what the best location might be, how the new office would be designed... Even Waits and Fred were exchanging whispers.

Daisy leaned toward me. "If Waits wasn't here," she said quietly in Mandarin, "Fred would be the only man, surrounded by a little harem of female managers." It was the first time I'd heard her speak that language, and her clear articulation and mellow intonations surprised me.

"Oh, yes." I grinned. "And the finance manager who ditched her opportunity to sit here among us was a woman too." It was a pleasure to speak in my native language, the words sliding off my tongue so naturally. We'd been speaking English like aliens almost all day. Waits, who was fluent in English despite his heavy French accent, spoke no Chinese at all, though he'd lived in the country for years. I wished he could converse in Mandarin, even if only like Fred whose spoken Chinese was comical and whose written Chinese was frightful.

"That is interesting. I don't know about the departed finance manager, but everyone looks happy enough here," Daisy murmured. Then, throwing me a gentle look, she added, "Except you, Jade."

The grin felt frozen on my face, but I managed to keep composed outwardly. "Lucy," I said, sidetracking. "That's the old finance manager's name. She got a job she likes better, so it seems, in a company nearby."

"Good for her." Daisy lifted her water glass and took a sip. "But how about you, Jade?"

I smirked self-consciously. "I'm fine."

"But why am I seeing grief in your eyes? Despite your smiling lips..."

Just for an instant, I saw her face transfigured into my mother-in-law's, and I could say nothing.

Two waiters walked by, carrying serving dishes. I seized on the distraction, taking up my chopsticks. "Let's eat, Director Sweet."

"Call me Daisy, please. It's been making my skin crawl, hearing 'Director Sweet' all day."

"It's the respectful way to address a leader here. When in Rome, do as the Romans do, and all that." I lifted some greens to my mouth.

She plied her own chopsticks with impressive efficiency. "Depending on what the Romans do. I doubt it would be wise to take that too literally. But it's true that using chopsticks and speaking Chinese are doing me a lot of good."

"Ah, yes, I've been curious about your surname. 'Sweet' doesn't sound very Chinese."

"I was born in Taiwan, but orphaned when I was only one year old. An American couple adopted me and took me to the States. They gave me their family name and raised me there."

"Your adoptive parents told you where you came from?"

"Sure, they never made it a secret. They told me the truth as soon as I was old enough to understand."

"Well, if they hadn't, I suppose you would have eventually wondered why you looked so different."

"Sure, I'd have guessed eventually, but my parents were happy to tell me about my history. They like China very much, and they speak some Mandarin. They've always encouraged me to study things associated with China, even Asia. And they did their best to create an environment in the States where I could practice the things I'd learned. I was lucky."

"You *were*," I said, a little envious. I'd had to dig the truth out for myself, and that still stung.

"Excuse me, Daisy—" Waits, who was sitting on Daisy's other side, broke in, his voice hushed. "Have you reviewed the BrightLife China financials I emailed to you?"

"Sure." Daisy's own tone was subdued as she turned her head toward Waits. "I've done a little analysis. I'm afraid those figures don't look too rosy..."

As the two of them became engrossed in almost inaudible conversation, I could feel the edginess provoked by Daisy's question flattening out. I looked around. People at the table were drinking wine, chewing food, and chatting in twos or threes. Fred was in full spate, mixing English and Chinese as he expounded on samba music and Latin dance to Rose Huang, the cherry-mouthed sales manager, and curly haired Pearl Yang, an attentive audience of two. Cathy and Edith Tong, the exquisitely featured supply chain head, were exchanging confidences. And I myself chatted and smiled, playing the role of a cheery young woman. I thought I'd managed to fit in. I thought I looked like one of them. I'd rather pretend to be a winner than be seen as a pitiful underdog—that had been my mantra ever since I got back on my feet and started at BrightLife China. But on this grim anniversary, its significance unknown to anyone in BrightLife, this newcomer had seen through my camouflage.

Daisy and my late mother-in-law Madam Sai looked nothing like each other, neither was their deportment nor poise at all alike. But Daisy's caring tone, and even some of her words, reminded me of my mother-in-law, who'd brought many things to me, but never grief. Nine years before, when my "smiling lips and dimples" attracted the attention of my patient Madam Sai and her son, I'd been wary at first. When she set up our first rendezvous, I suspected that she was acting the matchmaker— that she, and not her son, had chosen me. Seeing how much she seemed to depend on his daily visits, as if she'd had no husband, I jumped to the conclusion that she was possessive of him, and that he might have some tendency toward an Oedipus complex. I wanted nothing to do with that. It didn't help that Deping, in the ward, had had little to say.

Still, I agreed to meet him. It was hard to say why. Was it because I was young, with a little vanity, and he looked quite dashing in his suit? Or because it would give me a chance to turn him down officially once and for all? Madam Sai embraced my suggestion for the meeting place—by the pond in Youth Park, in the center of the city—and even praised me for not following the mainstream by asking for dinner in a posh restaurant.

———∽∽———

My first official date with Deping was on a Sunday afternoon in the early summer of 2003, not long after I turned twenty-four. I was half-surprised and half-relieved not to see his mother, but I still suspected she might be within spitting distance. We strolled a little in silence, but that didn't bother me; I already knew he was quiet. From a mobile vendor, he bought me an ice cream cone and himself a bottle of water.

We settled on a wooden bench under a giant willow by the pond. "So where is Madam Sai today?" I asked.

"Huh?" He glanced sideways at me. "She's at home..." he said slowly.

"Oh, I just thought she'd come here with you." I nibbled at the rich vanilla ice cream. It was cool and refreshing. "What a beautiful day!"

"It *is* a nice day. But why did you think my mother would come?" He sounded a little tense. "It's a date between you and me."

"There is no why. I just thought..." I kept licking the ice cream to cover my embarrassment, my brain working fast. "Well, I thought you two were very close. I mean, I never saw your dad come to visit your mom in the hospital. And it was you who signed the papers for your mom's surgery." *Oops*, I thought. *That sounded a little heartless.*

But he didn't seem to take offense. "My father – well, I usually refer to him as Old Man – was overseas on a government assignment. I went to the hospital every day on his behalf."

"I see. You don't work?"

"I teach, so the schedule is flexible."

"You're a teacher too?" I glanced at him. My ice cream was starting to thaw, and I licked a stray drip off before I went on. "Your mom told me she teaches English in a high school. What do you teach?" I felt my eyebrows knitting, despite myself. "Oh, don't tell me. You work in your mom's school."

"I teach pedagogy in City Normal University," he replied, looking at me seriously. "And as to what you're hinting, yes, in a way, my mother influenced my choice of career. Miss Bai, your ice cream is dribbling down your skirt."

I sprang to my feet. Frantically I lapped at the ice cream, trying to eat it before it all dripped down over the cone and my hand. He rose too, more calmly, handing me his handkerchief. I took it with my free hand, but didn't know what to do with it while I tried to finish the ice cream, which by now was almost gone. Emitting a suppressed laugh that sounded more like a cough, he plucked the handkerchief out of my hand and dropped to one knee. "Let me help to wipe away the drips." He gently lifted the corner of my skirt over my shin with one hand, while with the other he used his snow-white handkerchief to blot the melted ice cream.

I stood frozen to the spot, all thoughts of Deping's mother swept away by this unexpected tenderness. The willow branches fluttered in the breeze before me. They almost seemed to be playing with the water, which had seemed unruffled up until then. After a short, serene while, I heard him say, "That's the best I can do. You'd better try to wash the spot off later."

"Don't bother with it." I looked down at my skirt, where only a light mark was left. "But thanks," I said, sitting down again. "Oh, right, where were we?"

"I just told you my mother fed into my career decision," he answered calmly, folding the handkerchief and jamming it in his jeans pocket before sitting down again beside me.

"So how did your mom's passion for teaching rub off on you?" Now I dawdled over my empty, crispy cone, biting it little by little.

"Hmm... Let me first ask you a question: Can you name any great teacher you've had in your life? Think hard about it."

I thought hard, as he asked, but drew a blank. Shrugging, I confessed, "I regret that I can't even remember all my teachers. But I can repeat some of almost every teacher's pet phrases, especially the ones in high school. Let's see... 'Keep practicing these questions, students! Good for the soul! I bet they're going to appear on your exam papers.' Or 'None of you students are stupid, but you're lazy!' or 'Doing anything other than studying is wasting your life. Keep up on studying, and you'll be freed once you enter a university.' Oh, there's another one. 'You students don't come to school for me. Even if you don't study, I couldn't care less—I still get my salary. Keep in mind you are here for your own good.' And so on, and so on. Do any of these sound familiar?"

"And how! I'm six years older than you, but I still heard the same things over and over again all through high school. It's awful, though, if that's all people can remember about their teachers."

THE ENVELOPES

Madam Sai must've told him my age, I thought, but I just said, "You're right about that. And most of what I learned in high school has gone from my head. Well, I do remember the ABC of some subjects, as well as most of the things I learned in nursing school—probably because I apply them in my working life. I think that's the school's value to me, not really much."

"'Not really much' often sums it up," he said. "Teachers these days seem to believe that helping their students pass exams is their main mission, though it's easy to pin the blame on the education system. I was fortunate, compared to you. My mother always drilled it into me that a teacher's job is to help her students explore the world, and teach them real values. 'Don't expect me to tell you what questions will be in the exams,' she would say. 'But you can count on me to find you the tools you'll need to learn all you want to about the world. If you just master those tools, you'll find exams a piece of cake.' The students in her class were asked to read much more often than to do exercises. Reading and writing helped them not only learn English but also develop their own academic interests and their own worldview. To this day, I'm still reaping the benefits of the tools she gave me, the keys to a wider world."

"I've never come across a teacher like your mom, but I know her school is known for its high performance in the exams. There must be many teachers like her there."

"You're right that the school is famous for its high exam scores, but it doesn't follow that it has many other teachers like my mother. In fact, its focus on exam scores is at odds with her teaching style, but she'd rather risk the school's displeasure than teach to the test." He paused, his brow creased in thought. "Well, my geography teacher there inspired me, too. His clothes were always creased and covered in chalk dust, but he kept the textbook closed, scribbling all over the blackboard instead. When he did open the textbook, it was often only to point out an error in it, or warning us of information he'd found there that was false or obsolete. Just as my mother often tries to use her own resources to give students opportunities to practice English, he encouraged us to go to the countryside with him during school holidays, at his expense, where we'd study various landforms. To him, passing exams — or even imparting knowledge — was just a secondary product. His main goal was to foster in his students an enthusiasm for studying, a respect for truth, and an interest in seeing the world."

"I think that's true," I broke in eagerly, "that arousing someone's interest is crucial to keeping them learning. I've never had a teacher that inspiring. Hayao Miyazaki's anime films taught me more about morals than school ever did. Their ideals are embedded in my brain now, a sort of life compass for me…" I grinned at him. "But I might've escaped all the detours I've ended up taking in my education, if only I'd also been lucky enough to have great teachers…"

He chuckled. "I can see the impact of Miyazaki's animations on you, though I've watched only a few of them. And it's not easy for one to keep the spirit of learning, but you've kept it."

As a matter of fact, I'd been studying for the past two years, and was now close to getting my diploma and embarking on a new personnel career. I didn't feel ready to share that plan with him yet, though. Instead I returned to the topic of his career.

"Back to your own work," I said, "it seems that you're taking a leaf out of your mom and your geography teacher's book."

"Teachers like those two are few and far between in secondary school. Even if I became like them, I wouldn't change the minority into a majority. We need more and more great teachers at all school levels to have any real impact on our coming generations, which are the future of our country. I believe the way for me to make it possible is to teach in a normal university, which, you know, is the place to mold students into teachers. That's why I chose to stay in City Normal University. I've clocked up about seven years there since my graduation." He stopped, and smiled at me. "Miss Bai, you just wolfed down your ice cream, but now you're nibbling on your cone like a mouse. You'll never finish it at this rate."

"I—I've been listening to you..." I hadn't realized how wrapped up in our conversation I'd become. Feeling uneasy, I fired off another question while I started to chomp away at the remains. "Your dad teaches, too?"

"No. Old Man works in a totally different field. He's in the Bureau of Energy." After a pause, he said, "Miss Bai, am I under police interrogation here? Who's replaced the nurse who always answers her patient's questions with sweet smiles?"

"Oh, nurses catechize too." After a final crunch, I swallowed the last morsel of cone. Then, smiling at him, I said, "Mr Dai Deping, I now have an important question for you: Do *you* like me?"

"Thank heaven! We finally got there. I thought we'd never get past the subject of my mother." He paused, his face flushing slightly. "Yes, certainly, I'm attracted to you."

"Then why was it your mom who asked me out?" I said, unable to let it go. Digging out the truth had become a reflex, a defense against the vulnerability I'd felt ever since I learned the truth about my birth.

"I wanted to. But my mother was too impatient—she beat me to the punch. She thought if she missed a second, you could've run away. She likes you very much."

"I'm flattered. Maybe she likes me because I'm as impatient as she is."

"No, I don't think so. My mother—"

HASU AUGUST

"I'm kidding!" Though amused by his eager voice, I cut him off, becoming serious. "Now, let's forget about your mom. Why do *you* like me?"

I'd been called the prettiest nurse in our hospital; admirers were constantly heaping flowers and chocolates on my desk. It had even provoked a little envy in my peers, I suspected. But not even the gallantry of handsome, promising young doctors cut any ice with me. I distrusted all declarations of love, still wounded that my real parents had given me away "in everyone's best interest" — an argument they'd made only after I myself found out the truth. Since they had no children of their own, my adoptive parents had said, they could give me all their love. But if that was truly the reason, why hadn't they told me the truth?

Deping sighed, bringing me back to the here and now. "I've wondered too." He straightened and turned toward me, gazing at me with ardent eyes. "But it's a conundrum I would like to solve. I know it's important to you to dig out the truth, but I have nothing to hide. I just hope very much to see you every day. I even like the messy way you ate your ice cream, and the ladylike way you nibbled the cone. You have no coy, silly shyness. And I saw in the hospital that you're no poseur at work. You laugh, you yell, you smile, you grunt, yet you are patient as often as impatient, and grow prim and proper when a suitor is slobbering over you. To me, you're just as genuine a heroine as the ones in Miyazaki's animations."

His words weren't the truth I was seeking, yet I felt my eyes growing moist.

He noticed, just as he'd noticed far more than I'd suspected in the hospital. "Miss Bai, I don't know why I'm so attracted to you," he said. "Does what I say upset you?"

"No, I'm not upset," I said. "I'm just a little moved, even though what you were saying is hardly a compliment. And you

THE ENVELOPES

forgot to say I'm a fool, to be so easily moved." Surprised at my own honesty, I laughed despite the tears in my eyes.

In his mother's ward, except for courteous greetings, Deping had been reticent. He'd seemed stingy with words of comfort, even as he kneaded his mother's arms or massaged her legs. But on that bright and breezy Sunday afternoon, I could see his sunny charm. Talking with him was like playing a piano. *If I hit all the right keys,* I thought, *he would return me the melody.*

As I watched him walk away in his white shirt and blue jeans that afternoon, I knew I was embarking on a voyage that would bring vistas I'd never yet imagined.

3

Deping and I knocked around together comfortably enough over the next two years. His mother Madam Sai never played matchmaker, though on occasion his parents invited us to dinner in their apartment, and we all relished the dishes Taohua cooked. Starting my new career from scratch, I realized that the rudimentary English I'd been taught in school was inadequate, and asked Madam Sai to help me improve my command of the language. This allowed me to gain a foothold in a multinational company, where my foreign colleagues called me Jade — the literal meaning of my Chinese first name, Jve, which they couldn't pronounce. Deping began to use that name too, saying that it sounded better to him than the Chinese form, though his father still called me Little Jve.

Madam Sai took on the role of private language coach with an immense zest, though I was not yet officially a part of her family. With her expert advice, I made rapid progress in both oral and written English.

Our lessons sometimes took place at the school where Madam Sai taught. There I became acquainted with Felix Lee, a British man three years my junior. With his buzz-cut blond hair and his nearly constant ear-to-ear beam, Felix exuded efficiency and confidence. Throughout his childhood, his parents' work had kept the family moving from place to place. He'd grown up in

THE ENVELOPES

many countries, seeing many things: arid plains and hills lush with crops; the rich living in opulence and the poor struggling in indigence; culture preserved and civilization ruined... This experience gave him a clear objective in life—to travel around the world, helping people in need. In Cambridge, apart from reading East Asian studies, he became interested in the Chinese language, seizing every opportunity to learn it. Upon graduation, he took the first step toward his goal by applying for a teaching job in a Chinese school. Having read Felix's résumé, passed to her by the school's head teacher, Madam Sai was convinced he was a real gem, a man who would devote himself to projects that opened up new horizons for the students and unlocked their imaginations. By the time I met him, he had been working for almost a year with my mother-in-law-to-be.

More and more often, though, I studied with Madam Sai at her home. As a result, I saw more of Deping's father Mr Zhengting Dai, as well as their maid Taohua. Deping's parents had very different dispositions, I soon learned. His father was a scholarly man, quiet and reserved. His gravity made a sharp contrast to his wife's upbeat exuberance, which he was in the habit of dampening with sober reflections. I found myself somewhat in awe of him. Deping was somewhere in the middle, neither as lively and outgoing as his mother nor as grave and quiet as his father. Deft-handed and fleet-footed, Taohua brightened the apartment with her infectious spirits, singing constantly as she did the housework and cooked delicious meals.

———∽∾∽———

In the spring of 2005, Deping and I were married, though there was discord caused by my family regarding our wedding plan, and a discovery of his family status. I could trace our unadorned ceremony back to that occasion when Deping discovered the small scar on my forehead, which was hardly visible on account of the fringe I had worn since my escape.

On the day Deping and I went to the marriage registrar, after we'd finished with formalities and were on the way back, we were caught in a sudden shower. We scurried into the subway station, and as we stood on the platform, waiting for the train, Deping got out his handkerchief. Pushing back my bangs as he attempted to dry my hair, he noticed the small scar on my forehead. "How did you get this mark?" he asked.

"It was left by a knife cut years ago," I said.

He leaned closer, studying it. "Ouch. It looks like it barely missed your eye. Was it an accident? Even given the way you eat ice cream, I don't think you could have cut yourself like that."

"I kind of got into a tussle," I said.

He stared at me in disbelief. "*You* got into a fight?"

"Oh, don't worry—I'm not usually pugnacious. But you used to say I was like a heroine in Miyazaki's animations. All his heroines have been fighters for a cause."

"For what cause did *you* fight?"

"Oh, just for the first cash pay I got in my life." Seeing his look of bewilderment and mute appeal, I dissolved into a grin. Turning sideways to him, I put my arm around his waist and stared down at the track disappearing into the dark tunnel. "It was my first payday ever. On the way home, I had to walk down a narrow alley. It was twilight. A short, dark figure lunged out of the shadows at me and tried to snatch my handbag. I clutched it to my chest for dear life." For a moment I felt my hand involuntarily grip my briefcase tight, as the other one clasped the back of Deping's jacket. "He started pulling at the bag, and it set me off. In hindsight, I think it was a bit strange, the way I reacted. I wasn't crying for help, but yelling at him, 'You don't give a damn how hard I've worked for this pay! It's unfair you're grabbing it like this!'"

"Wow, that was audacious. What happened? Was nobody else around?"

"No, not a single soul emerged from any of the houses along the alley. I was ranting and raving, grappling with him. I didn't even see him take out the knife or feel it hurt me. But he flinched a little, and I wrenched free. I cut and ran. My brain went blank until I reached home and heard my mom screeching, 'For heaven's sake, you're bleeding! What have you done?' Then, feeling the warm fluid streaming down my face, I came back to Earth. All I could think was that I still had my money."

"Wow, Jade, you, you are... you..."

Jutting my chin out, I looked up over my shoulder toward Deping. How odd he looked! You'd think a viper's bite had curdled his blood.

"What's wrong, Professor Dai Deping? Am I scaring you?" Bridling, I looked at him archly, trying to crack him up.

A rumble announced the arrival of the train, preceded by a gust of wind that seemed to blow the stunned look off Deping's face. We boarded the train and settled into a corner of the carriage, swaying a little with the motion.

"An average person would just chuck the bag and take flight," Deping said finally. "I didn't know you loved money so. No money is worth losing your life over."

"I got a scolding from my mom, too. 'You idiot,' she said, 'how could you choose a handbag over your life?' But in the cold light of day, I realized that it wasn't really about the money. It was about defending something dear to me."

"But you were almost killed. What could you hold dearer than your life?"

"I was fighting cold — I didn't even think about that. I've spent so many years making my first-time-in-life list — buying the first real present for my parents, renting a tiny flat that's all my own ... I couldn't let some hooligan scupper all those dreams."

"But Jade, your whole future wasn't riding on your first month's salary. There would have been a second paycheck, a third one... And anyway, you have to be alive to make money."

"That list was symbolic, not just about money. It was a symbol of the independence I'd always yearned for. Finally, after years of studying, I'd hit my stride. There's no way I'd let some hooligan take that all away!" The train's brakes squealed as it rattled into a curve of the track, and the carriage shuddered. I staggered, losing my balance.

Deping flung out an arm and deftly caught me. "My valiant wife! You're no one's mug," he said, steadying me and fondling my back.

"Still," — I leaned into his arm, feeling safe and snug — "I must confess I was wiser after the event. If it happened now, maybe I'd just plead with him. 'Take whatever you want,'" I said in a falsetto. "'Please, please don't hurt me.'" I flashed him a grin.

"I'm not so sure about that," he said, grinning back. "But now I dare say whatever you might do is not for money."

"You can say that again, my clever husband."

As the train clattered over the track, he segued into another subject. "Actually, I wanted to talk about our wedding, now that we've completed our marriage registration."

"What about it?" I was expecting nothing particular. It was just that we were obliged to make our marital relationship public in one way or another.

"Would you object to having just a wedding dinner for our two families?" he asked, with a strong suggestion.

"I know you aren't just saying that to tease me," I said, my mind working fast. His suggestion, I had to admit, was a little unexpected, but it didn't upset me at all.

THE ENVELOPES

"I promise it has nothing to do with money." He looked at me seriously.

"Oh, don't gild the lily," I said, half in jest. Then, in all sincerity, "You know I'm not fussy. I want very much for us to live a good life, and a life we can afford. A wedding ceremony doesn't mean anything to me, now that the registration has announced us husband and wife. That's given us permission to live under the same roof, and that's all I want."

"Speaking of roofs..." He hesitated. "Would you consider moving into my parents' apartment?"

I shot him a quizzical look. "Why, so you can carry out your filial duty properly?"

"No, it's nothing to do with that—even though I'm the only child in my family. Yes, I know, there was no one-child policy yet then, but my mother was too weak to carry a second child..."

"Get to the point, Professor."

"Well, here's what I'm thinking. The apartment is roomy enough to allow us our privacy. And sometimes my father can't be at home—we'd be on the spot, if my mother's health deteriorated."

"Doesn't Taohua keep her company?"

"Taohua's only there in the day. She has to go home and take care of her family at night. Her husband and daughter live with her."

"I see. I thought she'd left behind her family in the village to work alone in this city." I realized that I had not yet spent even one night in Deping's home.

"On the other hand, since we're both birds busy catching worms, it would be smarter to share our resources rather than pay twice for everything, including an apartment, at least until it becomes necessary when our own small family grows. What do you think, Jade?"

HASU AUGUST

For a few seconds I found my mind wandering. I could picture all too vividly my own parents' faces when they heard about this idea. Noticing my silence, Deping said hastily, "This is just an idea. But if living with your in-laws would make you feel awkward..."

"Look, your mom is wonderful to me. But your dad has been a little difficult to get to know... somehow elusive. I'm not sure how he'd take to having me around all the time."

"You're definitely in Old Man's good books, I promise. You should hear him. Your heart is a crystal-clear brook, he says."

"Really?" I made a face, faking disbelief.

"Really. He can even count the number of fishes swimming in it."

I laughed at the idea of Deping's taciturn father saying any such thing, but quickly grew serious again. "No sweat—I can give living with your family a try. But now that we're talking about the wedding, I do have a wish to fulfill. It's like a little woman's dream..." I cocked my head and looked straight into his eyes.

"What is it?" He gave me a big grin, but a furtive, flickering light in his eyes betrayed his anxiety. "You're whetting my appetite."

"Oh, Deping, I want to take our honeymoon overseas, in some affordable romantic place, and hang the expense. I know it's an extravagance, but I have money saved up. I hope you—"

The flicker of misgiving disappeared from his eyes as he broke in, "That's a terrific idea!" His loudness abashed us a little, and we looked around, but no one seemed to be paying attention. Deping added, more quietly, "But keep your piggy bank intact."

"My piggy bank?" My chin went up and my lips curved down. "Don't turn up your nose at my savings."

"That's not what I meant... You have a proud, delicate chin,

Jade." He fixed me with a tender look. "But I see no dollar signs in your eyes."

"Don't get off the point. Hear me out. I've been working and saving for five years."

"Well done, my industrious and penny-wise wife. Your pedagogical husband is not rich, but he's still got savings he can draw on to fulfill your simple wish. And don't worry, your money won't be going begging. We will have our child and maybe someday set up house together in our own place."

"Oh, with my savings, we have other fish to fry, you mean," I said with a triumphant flourish, putting his long-winded sentiment in a nutshell.

"You're spot on." He patted me on the back.

"Deping, I'd like to make one thing clear beforehand. To me, it's about casting my lot in with you, about *our* life, which I want to share with you in joy and misery, materially and spiritually." My face felt hot as I delivered this little speech. It had been too much to hope for the marriage blessing I'd seen in Western films from the dreary-faced officer in the marriage registry, snowed under with paperwork for couples either raring to get spliced or desperate to get separated (though the office was called a marriage registry, and nowhere in its name did the word divorce appear, on that day couples breaking up seemed to greatly outnumber those cementing their bond). Subconsciously, I had felt the rite incomplete without a blessed vow, I realized, and jumped at the opportunity Deping had just offered. In a rocking subway train, I'd created my own nuptial oath.

Deping smiled a little at my sheepishness, but he picked up on my subtext. "Ah, yes, equality between the sexes," he assured me. "I've learned it from my parents by osmosis. Believe me, I'm a doer of it too."

I took that to be Deping's commitment to our forthcoming

HASU AUGUST

new life.

———∞———

It was only to be expected that my parents would pour cold water on our wedding plan. I was my mother's only child, and naturally, the apple of her eye. The man who wooed me was obliged, in her eyes, to demonstrate his esteem for me with a grand wedding banquet and a new apartment for the bride and groom—the essential dowry that my mother Meili Guan had learned from the prevalent practice in our city. Only these two things could crown with a perfect full stop her lifelong mission of raising me to be married off in style.

"I knew it!" she said when I told her our plans. "The moment I met Deping, I knew we couldn't bank on him."

"What do you mean, 'we?'" I asked, glowering at her. It was just as I had suspected: my parents, like so many people in this city, coveted the wealth that their daughter's worth, perceived by an interested man, could bring, wealth that they in turn could flaunt.

"I mean that *my, Meili Guan's, daughter* doesn't deserve such shabby treatment."

"It's not shabby at all to me, Mom."

"Humph! He can't even give you a roof over your head."

"We'll have a roof over our head, Mom."

"His parents' roof, not your own."

"But I'm perfectly fine with that, Mom."

"You idiot," she said, "you even gave them a blank check for a wedding dinner—and for a measly ten people. It's your wedding, you idiot! Once in a lifetime. It's as if you're slinging a crystal out of the window, thinking it's only a piece of glass. Look at your cousin Mei Mei's wedding! Over three hundred people attended the feast. She married a man from the family

THE ENVELOPES

of a municipal official, full of savoir faire, and he's bought her a flat in the center of the city. It must've cost them a pretty penny. Did you see how your uncle behaved in our Guan's family, with his nose in the air? I can't think of any way in which you're not a better catch, yet I had to watch your uncle sashaying around like a peacock, as if his daughter had been made a queen. You have a prettier face than hers, and a decent job in a big foreign company. And now you're throwing away all of that, and all the effort we've made to bring you up right! With the best will in the world, I can't understand you, you idiot. Why do you want to marry that fellow?"

It was hard for me to fathom that the person who'd reared me on Miyazaki's strong young women and this version of my mother Meili Guan—with her longing for an ostentatious wedding and her irritation at the fact that I'd chosen to marry a proletarian—could be one and the same. Cynically, I thought once again that my parents' motivation in encouraging me to watch Miyazaki's films could not have been to inspire me to pursue the ideals of love depicted in them; it must have simply been their way of avoiding discussions about the birds and the bees.

"I'm marrying Deping for love," I said, holding my head high. I never enjoyed flouting conventions. They just had no place in the most critical decisions of my life.

"Then why do you love him?"

That put me on the spot. In two years, I had not given serious thought to the reason I loved Deping. Was it for his hair, with its classic taper cut? For his resonant voice he'd inherited from his father? For his broad shoulders and slender hips? For his always fashionably shod feet? For his exceptional academic achievements in City Normal University? Or even—the irony of this struck me—for his mother?

I bit my lip and gave the only answer I knew for sure. "Obviously, *not* because he's going to buy me an apartment or throw a fancy wedding party. Mom, he is from a family of intellectuals. They're rich in wisdom, not money."

"Yeah, the salt of the Earth." She sniffed. "Bully for them!"

I ignored that. "And he's been fast-tracked to become the youngest associate professor in his university."

"Can the title of professor fill your belly?"

"I've been fending for myself since I was twenty-one." I sighed. "Look, Mom, so many words burst from you, but I know your bark is worse than your bite. I know you just want me to live a life free of worries. Deping and I probably won't live in the lap of luxury, but I assure you that we will be able to keep our own little family in comfort. Please trust that I'm happy for what's upon us. You do feel happy for my happiness, right?"

"You idiot, is there any mother in the world who isn't worried about her baby? I only hope you have a better life than your father's and mine." Her voice quavered a little. "You're going to be taken so far from us now..."

"I'm not going far away, Mom." I took her in my arms. "I may be in the east of this city while you're in the west, but I'll see you as often as I do now. Cross my heart. Oh, and this may perk you up—Deping and I are going to have a fancy honeymoon in France. I don't mind your telling your friends about that, if it makes you feel better."

4

After all their huffing and puffing, my parents reconciled themselves to our wedding as we'd planned it. Nevertheless, a couple of days after I managed to persuade them to give us their blessing, my obtuseness manifested itself: one of the 'facts' that I'd used to convince my mother turned out to be my own misconception. It had never crossed my mind that Deping had any motive beyond a down-to-earth approach to life for his desire that our wedding be a very low-key affair, until March 8, 2005, which happened to be International Women's Day.

That afternoon was a quasi-public half-holiday for working women, so Madam Sai and I had agreed to meet for an English lesson. When I arrived at the apartment in the early afternoon, Taohua was preparing, of her own accord, a slap-up dinner to "reward us women for being hardworking," she said. Madam Sai wasn't yet home, so, as was my wont, I shut myself in the study to practice reading English essays aloud.

I hadn't been there long when the ring of the doorbell interrupted my recitation. Expecting Taohua to answer the door, I remained where I was, and had started again when the bell chimed for a second time. I could hear noises coming from the kitchen, as if Taohua was cooking, so I expected to hear her walking toward the door at any minute. Instead, the bell sounded again. Suddenly thinking that Taohua must be in the middle of some kitchen operation too pressing to set aside, I rushed out of the study to the living room, still clutching the English book in my hand. I'd only gone a few steps when I saw Taohua darting across the kitchen doorway, wiping her hands on the apron she wore. "I'll get it," she muttered, frowning slightly. "Who is it at this hour in the midafternoon?"

The apartment's tiny entrance hall was divided from the living room by a translucent inner screen, which Taohua deftly slid closed while she opened the outer door. The screen obscured my vision, but I could hear her say, "You are…?"

"Hello, my name is Gao." The man who spoke sounded gentle and middle-aged. "This is my business card. I am here for Chief Dai."

There was silence for a few seconds. I imagined that Taohua had taken the card and was poring over it. Finally she said, "Mr Dai Senior is not in."

"I know—" The man let out a quiet, dry laugh. "Pardon me, I know Chief Dai is not home now. May I come in?"

I'd been on the point of going back to the study, but an odd note in the visitor's tone caught my attention and I froze. Whatever his intention was, it didn't seem to be visiting the householder. Shadows moved across the dividing screen, and I realized that Taohua must've let him into the lit entrance hall. "Mr Gao," she said courteously, "what can I help you with?"

"You must be Chief Dai's housemaid."

"Yes, I am."

"You look like a nice person. Could you do me a favor? Just a small favor." He cleared his throat. "Could you pass my business card and this envelope on to Chief Dai?"

"I'm sorry, Mr Gao," Taohua said instantly. "I cannot take the envelope."

Again silhouettes moved across the screen, as if in a shadow

THE ENVELOPES

puppet play: two figures pushing something back and forth toward each other in silent battle. Finally the man grumbled, "You're not very helpful. In fact, you seem kind of strung out. See, I heard Chief Dai's son is getting married. It's a joyous event, and I only want to contribute to the festivities. Why don't you just relax and help me?"

"Mr Gao, I don't know what you're talking about. I'm just a bumpkin—I have no idea what you city folk's game is." Taohua's voice grew louder. "But Mr Dai Senior left strict orders. I cannot accept anything but a name card for him from anyone. Rest assured I'll forward your card to him."

The man wouldn't budge. "Please keep the envelope, please! I've come from a long way away to bring it. I'm only asking for a small favor."

Taohua was no less mulish. "I cannot. I don't want to lose my job. Mr Gao, I'm sorry, but I'm very busy. I have to go back to work. If you really must deliver this envelope to Mr Dai Senior, please take it to the bureau yourself."

There was a rustling sound, and one of the figures disappeared from the screen. Not wanting to be suspected of eavesdropping, I pretended to flip through my English book as the door clicked shut and the screen swished open. Taohua stepped back into the living room, looking flustered. "Aya!" she exclaimed. "Is my pot burning on the stove?" She seemed to be talking to herself, but then she noticed me.

I glanced up casually from my book. "I haven't smelled anything burning."

She started back toward the kitchen, heaving a sigh of relief. "I was worried sick about my pot. Aya, he's finally gone. Good riddance."

"Who was that man?" I put down the book and followed her into the kitchen. "Want me to give you a hand?"

HASU AUGUST

"You could beat the eggs if you have time." She beckoned me over to the worktop. "The man who just called? I have no idea."

"But Mr Dai Senior expected him? I heard you say he left orders for you."

"About not taking packages? Mr Dai Senior warned me about that on my first day here, three years ago." She handed me a pair of chopsticks and the bowl. The whites and yolks were already in it. "Beat them until they're foamy."

"Oh, I see. So he foresaw this sort of visit. I suppose this visitor was not the first one of that kind."

"It's happened quite a few times since I started working here, mostly during festival seasons. But it's strange," she said slowly, "there's no festival today. Oh! It's because of your ..." Her voice trailed off.

"Come again?" I stopped whipping the eggs. The chopsticks I was using made quite a racket, and I thought that the noise might've cut off her sentence.

"Never mind," she said, bending over the sink to scrub the vegetables clean, so I couldn't see her face.

It was clear she didn't want to talk about the visitor any more, but I just couldn't let it go. "Do you know what's in the envelope?"

"No idea. And I'm not allowed to ask about it." She turned toward me and shrugged. "Sometimes the visitors even bring a briefcase."

"And you've been able to stop them from leaving it every time?"

"Almost. But I failed once last year. The guy said the briefcase contained work-related materials. He was quick. After a lot of fast talk, he just dumped the briefcase at the door and ran off."

"Then how'd you get rid of the briefcase?" I pursued.

"Mr Dai Senior had the sulks and hardly spoke at the dinner

THE ENVELOPES

table. But he didn't blame me at all. The briefcase sat in the entrance hall until I went home that day, but I never saw it again. How are those eggs coming? Let me have a look at them."

I shifted toward her to show my work.

"Good, keep on," she said briskly. "Make more bubbles."

I shook my hand. "Aah, my wrist's getting stiff... I'm wondering what those envelopes could've contained." To my delight, the froth in the bowl finally seemed to be getting thicker.

"I once told my man about it. He said the thing in the envelope could be—" She stopped.

"What could it be?" I stopped whipping and stared at her.

"Never mind. Mr Dai Senior is an upright man." She leaned over to look at the eggs. "Good job. I'm impressed—it's not as easy as it seems! Thanks for your help, Miss Bai."

"Oh, don't mention it," I said, giving up. My probing wasn't getting me anywhere, and I sensed that Taohua knew nothing about the contents of the envelopes or briefcases.

Anyway, I was still an outsider, and I didn't want to mislead Taohua to think that I was trying to ferret out a mystery in the family.

———∞———

Still, I could not delude myself. Something was going on in Deping's family that I didn't understand, and the small episode I'd witnessed was probably just the tip of the iceberg. That night, as we all sat round the dining table, eating the ambrosia made by Taohua (with a little help from me), I couldn't help shooting furtive glances at Deping's father. And I began to realize that until then, though I'd found him a bit intimidating, I had not fully perceived his mental nor his physical power. Now even his commonest gestures and words felt somehow different. Without giving it much thought, I'd pigeonholed Deping's father as 'scholarly', but now, for the first time, I saw him as imposing: a man of strong build, firm and erect, brimming with power. Even as he approached sixty years of age, he was not running to seed, though the suit he always wore made it hard to tell whether underneath his clothes, flab might've replaced some of his muscle. In contrast, my own father rarely donned a suit, and the jackets and shirts he wore, which were often bought on sale, always exposed his middle-age spread. Deping's father sounded forceful, though his voice was deep and mellow. By comparison, my own father spoke in a feeble, tentative voice, always sounding a little uncertain.

I spent dinner musing about these things. My mind wandering, I imagined Deping's father as a character in one of Miyazaki's swashbuckling stories, sometimes a genial anime who bolstered the heroine's morale, sometimes in a more forbidding role, an austere man who tried to undercut the heroine's brave determination to save the world.

As the meal was drawing to its end, Taohua passed him the business card the visitor had left. "Mr Dai Senior, I'm sorry I forgot. A man asked me to give you this."

"I thank you again for staving off the trouble, Taohua," Deping's father said, bestowing on her an avuncular smile that carried just a touch of regret, and slipped the card into his pocket without glancing at it. No one else at the table seemed curious about it at all.

After dinner, Deping walked me to the subway station. I was agog to get at the truth behind the afternoon's incident, but he forestalled me. "What was wrong, Jade?" he asked as we strode out of the lift on the first floor.

I slackened my pace and turned to look at him. "What makes you think something's wrong?"

"The way you sneaked looks at Old Man during the dinner."

THE ENVELOPES

He looked baffled, frowning slightly. "As if he were a dangerous wanted criminal you'd stumbled across, and you were trying to identify him."

"Oops, did I really act that badly? Did everyone notice?" I felt more humiliated than worried.

"I think your husband was the only one who couldn't tear his eyes away from you," he said in a softer tone. "What's up?" He had the knack of taming my emotions.

I was silent for a few moments. Side by side, we walked along a meandering path that traversed a huge lawn in the community park beside the subway station. Colorful ground lights lined the path, so walkers wouldn't trip or fall or wander onto the grass. There were no lamps over our heads but the waning moon. We proceeded, our feet brightened while our faces became lost in shadow.

Drawing a long breath, I said, "It's related to the man who left his business card, the one that Taohua just now passed to your dad. I was there when she bundled the man off..." I told him the details of what I'd overheard, and my conversation with Taohua. "Look, Deping," I went on, "I'm marrying *you*. But still, I'm going to be living with you *and* your parents. I think I know your mom very well, and I do love her. But a visitor just tried, by a dodgy means, to press something on your dad. That seems fishy. Now I can't help asking myself. Who is your dad? And why do people keep trying to slip him envelopes and briefcases?" I stopped on the path and waited while a small group strolled past us, then took a deep breath and gave it to him straight from the shoulder. "There was money in the envelope, or the equivalent, wasn't there? Am I right about it? Don't underestimate me. When I was as a nurse, we all knew about how doctors took red packets of money from patients angling for preferential treatments."

One step ahead of me, he stopped too, spun round, and, in

the dim moonlight, looked me squarely in the eye. "I don't know exactly what was in that packet, and neither do you. But you're right—the man who came this afternoon was surely trying to offer Old Man a sweetener in the name of congratulating him on his son's wedding."

"What does your dad really do? The man called him Chief Dai."

"Old Man is the chief of the Bureau of Energy." He said this lightly, as if referring to any Tom, Dick, or Harry.

"You mean your dad is at the helm of the Bureau of Energy, in a city with a population of around twenty million?" I found that a little hard to swallow, but he nodded firmly.

"Your dad is a bigwig?" I said, taken aback. "I got the wrong end of the stick. I thought he was a scholar."

"You're not that far off. My mother and I see Old Man first and foremost as a scholar. It was his outstanding academic achievements over thirty-five years that raised him to eminence in the field of energy." Now he was speaking like the proud son of a father with extraordinary accomplishments.

For two years, I realized, I hadn't had the foggiest idea what kind of family I was marrying into. How was it that I'd never learned, in all this time, that my father-in-law-to-be was a high-level government dignitary? "Why didn't you tell me about it?" I asked.

"I should've explained to you earlier, I know. But I started thinking that I'd rather let nature take its course. You're a rare type, having so little interest in my family background—not like all the other girls. I can only remember you asking about Old Man's job once, in all the time I've known you. Remember that?"

I shook my head, trying in vain to recall.

"On our first date, you teased me about whether Old Man taught, too."

"Oh, that." My mind went back to the day of our first date, when we sat together by the pond, the day of the melting ice cream. "I wasn't teasing. In fact, I was fumbling for something to say. But it's so very true that you're the only one who matters to me in our mutual life."

"You're telling me! Thank heaven, you're not too angry with me." He mopped his brow in theatrical relief.

"But it wouldn't have changed anything if you'd told me." I wasn't exactly angry at him, but I felt he was being a little smug about it, all the same.

Seriousness returned to his face. "Pardon my thoughtlessness, Jade."

"Probably I was being a bit dim-witted, not realizing what kind of family you're from," I mused. "But your family just doesn't look like other powerful ones." It came to my mind how my cousin Mei Mei's husband had made my parents so envious of her.

"What do you mean, Jade?" he said, with an innocent expression.

"Oh, I'm just thinking out loud. Normally, a prominent family like yours lavishes money, even if it's filthy lucre, on its children's weddings. I'd expect something very showy, especially when the family has only one child, as in your case…"

"Jade," he cut in, "about our wedding… I've always wanted to get it off my chest. And now it's easier for me to spell it out. The menace who came this afternoon must've snooped around and found out we're going to get married. A flashy wedding attracts flies. If we have an open ceremony, I bet we're going to have uninvited guests and unwanted surprises."

"Oh, I can imagine that," I said, nudging him forward again toward the illuminated station entrance.

"As you probably can see now, a honeymoon in France works

out perfectly for me." He grinned. "We can stage a vanishing act during our wedding."

"Oh, your naïve wife's little wish did the trick."

"It's just because my wife's soul is connected with mine." He took my hand in his, brushing aside my mocking tone. "Jade, I'd like to talk a bit more about Old Man."

"I'm all ears." I felt the sureness flowing from his big hand, dry and warm, into mine.

"Old Man's had clean hands for his entire career up to now. The big apartment where we live was allotted to him by the bureau based on seniority. He has a car and driver—you've had no chance yet to see them—assigned to him for his work needs. My mother and I have never used them, even when my mother was ill."

"I dare say officials like your dad are rarer than hen's teeth," I interrupted. "Your sick mom wasn't even admitted to the best hospital in our city." If Madam Sai had had her surgery in what locals call the 'bureaucrats' hospital'—the man and woman in the street have to line up for months to see a doctor there—destiny probably would have not brought Deping and me together.

Deping's thoughts seemed to be running along the same line. "My mother mentioned that," he said. "She called it a blessing in disguise, since it led us to meet you." He gave a gentle squeeze to my hand. In the faint light, we smiled knowingly at each other.

"But doesn't your dad feel lonely among those who don't have any qualms about enjoying the fruits of their dishonest behavior?" I asked.

"Well, Old Man didn't have to become an official. But he was disinclined to be among the chattering classes, only criticizing the prevailing venality and its impact on our nation's future. Given an opportunity, he chose to lead. By setting himself up as a whiter-than-white role model, he's trying to make a difference in the bureau."

"It must've been very hard."

"It's been much harder than he predicted. People keep coming to knock on our door, trying to bribe him. Anyway, at least he has us on his side."

"Is Taohua aware of your dad's status?"

"Yes. Taohua may be a country woman, but she's smart. It's a pity she was too poor to get into high school. But she is upstanding. She has never asked Old Man to use his power inappropriately for her, and she's steadfast in turning down bribery. I think she knows what's in those envelopes, though she's never asked about it. Before her, we had to dismiss two maids, one after the other, for reasons I'm sure you could imagine. We're lucky to have Taohua."

"Taohua's husband is here too, you said before."

"Yes, he works on construction sites. He's luckier than Taohua — at least he finished high school. He's a diligent worker too, keen to learn. He's worked hard to raise himself from carpenter to supervisor, and to learn new techniques. He can even draw blueprints and work with professionals on them."

"And what about their daughter?"

"They actually have two daughters."

"They defied the one-child policy?"

"Well, they're just one of millions of families who had more than one child, defying the policy. But at least they coughed up the fine and got the second daughter registered legally."

"I have to say, as a woman and a child who grew up all the way lonely, I can sympathize with their desire to have another child."

"Then let's have two children," he said, suddenly enthused. "It's lawful for us, since we're both from one-child families."

Still walking, I nuzzled up against his shoulder. There were moments when I felt my lifelong ambition was as simple as being Deping's puppy, showered in his love. But then my curiosity got the better of me again. "But going back to the main subject— what about her daughters?"

"The elder daughter, who's in elementary school, is with them here. But they had to leave the younger one behind in their village, with her grandparents."

"That must be heart-rending, for both the children and the parents." I sighed, sincerely moved.

"It is a sad situation. Taohua is bent on giving her daughters a good education, but it's so expensive here. For the time being, they can afford fees for one child only."

"Why don't they all stay together in their village, so that their daughters can go to school there?"

"Oh, what a babe in arms you are," he said, poking me playfully. "It boggles my mind. You don't know that many of the villages in our nation no longer have schools these days? Many country folk have left their land for cities, because there they can get jobs that urban people don't want to do. They have to scrimp and save to send their children to city schools, though. They worked hard for metropolitan treasures, but they're hardly immune to the dregs in a big city."

"I've never been to the countryside," I said defensively. "And you don't get this kind of news via national media. I know some villages have no medical facilities, but it's hard to believe there can be places without schools. And anyway, you just told me that Taohua and her husband went to school."

"It's rather late. Let's not get into an interminable discussion about a very complicated issue just now," Deping said. I looked up, and saw that we were approaching the station "Before I forget," he hastened to add, "when I conferred with my parents on our wedding plans, I realized I might not have given enough

THE ENVELOPES

consideration to your parents' feelings. Have you squared it with them?"

I quickened up my pace. "Oh, they're fine with it now."

"Thank heaven! Hurry up, Jade, the train's coming. Hear that rumble?"

Hand-in-hand, we were already hurtling down the stairs into the bright station.

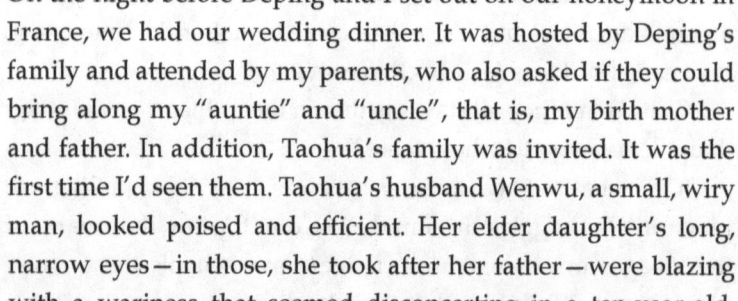

On the night before Deping and I set out on our honeymoon in France, we had our wedding dinner. It was hosted by Deping's family and attended by my parents, who also asked if they could bring along my "auntie" and "uncle", that is, my birth mother and father. In addition, Taohua's family was invited. It was the first time I'd seen them. Taohua's husband Wenwu, a small, wiry man, looked poised and efficient. Her elder daughter's long, narrow eyes—in those, she took after her father—were blazing with a wariness that seemed disconcerting in a ten-year-old. She mostly stared silently at her food or at the people who were talking all around her. At times, my mother-in-law managed to make her laugh a bit, but her smile died quickly.

I myself was keeping a watchful eye on my mother, working hard to entertain her. Especially after Taohua's family was introduced at the table, her face made her surprise and contempt all too clear. While Taohua and Wenwu entertained us all with stories about village wedding customs in their days—entrancing even my "auntie" and "uncle," whose questions showed their lively interest—my mother alone remained uncharmed. She sat staring at the couple as if she were watching a slightly crass television show, breaking her withering silence only to mutter under her breath about how loud they were. While the others at the table lamented the way that rural customs were being lost, overwhelmed by city mores, I ladled soup into her bowl, spooned dishes onto her plate, and regaling her with tales of romance in Paris, hoping to distract her. Something was clearly brewing in her mind, and I was afraid that her disdain would erupt in remarks unbecoming of a bride's mother.

Finally the dinner came to an end, and I could breathe freely again. My mother-in-law thoughtfully urged me to say a separate farewell to my parents, so I accompanied them to the taxi stand. There, just as I'd anticipated, my mother couldn't hold back any longer, and it was unbridled. "What a weird family!" she said. "To invite only those country cousins to their son's wedding dinner—my dear! Twittering, twittering, and bolting their food. They don't even have any relatives or friends in town? They must've had a village root for their family tree too." It was as if a theater critic—of a particularly savage type—were blasting a subpar show she'd just seen.

"They're just another kind of people, Mom," I said soothingly, soft-pedaling the difference between our two families, though privately I thought they were like chalk and cheese.

"You think I'm deaf?" she said peevishly. "I know I heard you say they were intellectuals. Intellectuals, really?"

"Hmmph, bully for them," my father remarked out of the blue. It was such a loyal imitation of my mother, I couldn't keep a straight face and had to turn away. Voicelessly I swore to myself that I would never correct the impression of Deping's family that—in the interest of cajoling her into accepting my marriage—I'd given to my mother. Intellectuals, I'd said, and intellectuals they would remain.

The three of us stood there stiffly, not speaking, until finally a taxi crawled into the stand. My father started moving toward it, but my mother turned to me and said in an undertone, "You little idiot, you've had a tiring evening, haven't you? Waiting on me

THE ENVELOPES

and trying to please me throughout the dinner. You little idiot, you deserve a good rest... and a happy life ahead. And, your birth parents have just witnessed you happily married the man you chose. Hope they're happy too." She stretched out her hands and cupped my face.

Overwhelmed by her affectionate touch, and on the verge of tears, I floundered for a moment. Finally I squeezed out a single sentence through clenched teeth, "Mom... thank you for raising me."

Murmuring "You little idiot...," she released me, ducked her head, and got into the cab in which my father was already seated.

I gazed after the taxi until its taillights were swallowed up by the dark night. My mother Meili Guan might not be a noble woman, yet she not only did no harm to anyone but also might have loved me in her own way.

Later that night, the first of my new life with his family, Deping and I packed our suitcases while listening to my father-in-law talk about all the East-meets-West culture clashes he'd experienced on his previous overseas trips. I had never seen him that effusive before. "You've had a few at dinner, Old Man," Deping joked, but he just talked on as if he hadn't heard Deping at all.

My mother-in-law made a fruit platter and kept handing her husband a piece of apple or a strawberry from it, jollying him along. "Papa, eat it," she kept saying, "It's anti-inebriation, good for your stomach. Eat it, Papa," until, his patience strained, he jumped up from the settee, saying "Mama, I think taking a shower is better than anything else to sober me up." It was all sweetness and light. My heart began to fill with warmth, roughing out a picture of this new life. The stress of my day would peter out when everyone came home; we would be chewing the fat and

HASU AUGUST

laughing out loud, even if there was neither a sumptuous meal nor good wine on the dinner table...

By the time I too had showered, everyone had quieted down. My mother-in-law volunteered to do my hair. Having me as her daughter-in-law made her feel as if the sky had been dropped into her palms, she said. She wanted to make sure that I was a beautiful, blithe bride on my honeymoon. I closed my eyes, enjoying the gentle warmth of the dryer and the feeling of her fingers running through my hair, brushing across the scar on my forehead. "My girl, my boy told me about your heroic act during that robbery. It made me wonder what kind of parents had developed such bravery in you. You are one in a million."

"Well, now you've met them," I said. I was eager to hear her impression of my parents, but at the same time afraid that their worldliness had been too glaring.

"Concerning our gathering, I would like to let you know, tonight, your family graced our table with their presence. I must say, for a wedding, the dinner was skimpy, even with the dainty food. However, Papa and I respected the decision of you and my boy. I hope you do not think your new husband is too parsimonious."

"As Deping said, it was *our* decision. Probably I'm just as mean as he is." I gave her a mischievous grin.

"Your lovely elfishness and dulcet tones! My girl, I can understand why my boy is so in love with you. How fortunate Papa and I are to have you as our daughter-in-law! Alcohol did not make Papa tipsy, but he is drunk with felicity." She looked at me, her eyes glowing with exultation, the dryer in her hand suspended over my forehead.

"I feel my face burning, Mother," I said, changing the subject a little self-consciously. "The hot air is blowing on it."

"I beg your pardon." She joggled the dryer hurriedly and

THE ENVELOPES

then moved around behind me. In the mirror I could see her other hand using the comb to lift my hair, blow-drying the roots.

When she turned off the dryer, I took up the subject again. "My parents are quite different, are they not?"

"All parents are unique." Picking up the curling tongs, she returned to stand in front of me again, making light waves with my fringe. I raised my eyes and saw the motherly smile I'd grown to know so well surfacing on her face. "Yet they are all the same in their love for their children. It does not necessarily take the form of their saying they love you. Sometimes it may come as impatience, anxiety, or even anger, especially when they could not steer things to the direction they have wished."

Speechless, I was associating her words with how my parents had comported themselves. As if reading my mind, she went on, "For instance, your mother might have felt helpless when you left her to marry my boy. And she might be fighting a battle against herself, trying to convince herself that you are capable of finding happiness. Try to understand, my girl, that you might have been the evidence of your mother's life. While you were growing up, every day she lived for one purpose—to bring you happiness. But we parents can hardly handle the changes that growing up brings in our children. When she could see the day you'd leave her coming, when you seemed to be melting away from her daily life, your mother might have doubted whether she had even really been existing. She might suffer the loss of the evidence of her life, as well as of the control over life she had been so used to. How harrowing it might be for your mother, to see you going out of her sight. And her sadness needed an outlet. Venting her spleen might be one of her ways. It probably disconcerted you because you thought she was just cantankerous, but she was not angry with you. She was angry with herself, for not accepting the fact that you have a larger life than the one she tried to show you.

Try to understand, my girl."

Tilting my head to make her styling work easier, I thought of what to say. "I think you, as a mom, must've experienced moments when you felt helpless like that yourself."

"Certainly," she said. "Shame on me — sometimes I have even lost my temper when I thought something wasn't going as fast as I had hoped."

"Really? I find that hard to imagine. To me, you've always been kind and optimistic. I'm curious about what would make someone like you throw a fit."

"Well ... for instance, I used to get antsy when my boy did not yet have a girlfriend to plight his troth to. We quarreled, although my boy said nothing wrong. "There's nothing else to do but leave it up to fate," he said. And after we met you, he fell for you instantly, yet did not do anything about it. He was shy. He is a very different person, mind you, when he is standing on the dais and lecturing to an audience. I was like a cat on hot bricks, urging him to grasp the opportunity while he could, but he just said, 'Mother, if it's destined to be, Jade and I will be together in time.' I paid no attention to him and bounced you two into your first date. What a thick skin I had!"

She giggled in a way I found adorable, as if she'd been restored to childhood, but I couldn't resist prying more.

"Mother, why did Deping's cool-headed attitude toward marriage make you so twitchy?" I said. "He's young, after all. Don't you believe in the saying 'Marry in haste, repent at leisure'?"

"I might have given you the wrong impression, my girl. No, having him marry in haste was not what I wanted. But I admit that, in a way, I am a selfish mother. I just hoped to see my boy start a truly happy family in my lifetime."

"But you'd have plenty of time to see that happen. You have

THE ENVELOPES

a long life ahead of you."

"Well, I have had time to see him take a wife, but now I am avid for more."

"Undoubtedly you'll see our children grow up, Mother. You're very sprightly."

"It looks that way, I know, but looks sometimes deceive. Things do not always turn out just the way they should."

I frowned. "What does that mean?"

"You must not be nervous, my girl." She gave my arm a brisk up-and-down rub while she deftly released my hair from the curling tongs with her other hand. "Now, you can put the finishing touches on your hair yourself. Look in the mirror. Aren't you beautiful?" While tidying up the hairdressing tools, she went on in a more serious tone, "I have wondered why I am so fortunate to have Papa and my boy... and lately, Taohua, plus my daughter-in-law, now. You all seem like wonderful gifts from heaven to me."

"Then why are you so fortunate?" I asked, reaching for a tube of hair gel. I met her eyes in the mirror, feeling slightly troubled, as I rubbed the gel between my palms and applied it to the strands of hair that lightly brushed my shoulders.

"Relax, my girl," she said, smiling serenely. "Well, I do not believe in blind luck. There always must be a reason a person is blessed with great good fortune. You might have earned it with past good deeds, or it might be recompense for the unjust way that life has treated you. In my case, very likely, it is because the devil has deprived me of physical health since my youth. None of the major organs in my body are functioning well. I can never know which one may just shut down someday. In the past two years, I have spent a lot of time in hospital wards." She shrugged, as if the illness she was talking about had nothing to do with her, and carried on stowing her hairdressing tools in their case.

HASU AUGUST

"It can't be that bad, Mother. I assumed you were in the pink of health. Look at all the energy you have for your work and the children in your school! And even for coaching me in English."

"I may not have good health, but I won't let that get in the way of my work. It is dedication to my job that helps me forget my illness — that is always been the best way for me to grasp the nettle."

"But Deping never told me you had health problems in these two years."

"No worries, my girl. We have gotten so used to my frequent visits to the hospital that we do not think it unusual anymore. Sometimes we do not put Papa in the picture, either. He is so often away on business trips, and as you may be aware, he bears a heavy load on his shoulders at work."

"Yes, I know that. But who's been looking after you when you were sick?"

"I owe a great debt of gratitude to Taohua and my boy. I am ashamed to admit that sometimes a terrible thought would strike me — I would imagine that my life might be over in the very next minute, and I would get ruffled by things not going my way. I created so much trouble for them." She shook her head with a rueful smile, looking down at her hands as she closed the case of hairdressing tools.

"No worries, Mother." Emulating her tone, I finished styling my hair, turned to her, and took her hands in mine. Suddenly I saw her in a new light. So many things that had bothered me before were clear to me now. I felt ashamed of the way I'd misjudged her, seeing her as a meddling, impatient matchmaker who'd pushed Deping into his first date with me. She had been racing against illness; of course she hadn't wanted to let a single wasted minute slip by.

"We'll band together now," I said. "You with your

THE ENVELOPES

determination and me with my nursing know-how — we'll be quite a team."

She stretched out her hands to grip my arms, her face radiant. "My girl, look at you. How beautiful you are, standing at the portal to a brand-new life! You are ready for it, I know. Tomorrow, you will be on the way to Paris — open the door and go! Seize the day, for you can never know how long you will walk arm in arm with your beloved one."

5

The hotel room was quiet and warm, glowing with gentle light. It seemed a perfect place to meditate on what to do with the embryo already implanted in my uterus. But, usually, if I lie on the bed in a hotel room — no matter how comfortable the bed is — the quietness begins to feel eerie. I often find myself hearing every sound that comes through the closed hall door, no matter how quiet or far away. Somewhere, people are talking loudly, something I have an aversion to. My ears can't help following the sound of distant footsteps. Something somewhere is rustling, and that tiny sound triggers a surge of fear. I even get up to check the lock. It seems ironic — I've been called "intrepid" for fearlessly confronting a mugger, yet kipping in a hotel alone, I can't overcome this groundless dread.

Tonight, an in-depth review of employee data with the local manager kept me in our factory in this small town until almost 9:00 p.m. Afterward I grabbed a burger from the McDonald's next to the hotel, gobbling it down on the spot — though not without mixed feelings. McDonald's has been a poster child for foreign corporate success in China in the last two decades, its tentacles sprawling over the countryside to the remotest places and blankest minds, much more efficiently than books and knowledge have reached them. Many peasants probably feel proud that they can take their children to a McDonald's

THE ENVELOPES

as a special treat in county towns where there is no library or bookstore—though they wouldn't likely be interested in them, even if they did exist. And nowadays most children with pocket money to spend would choose a McDonald's meal rather than a book. The familiar golden arches M magically make their mouth water, while they regard "Knowledge is power" as a hoary cliché.

Having finished my burger and crumpled up its wrapper, I returned to my room at the hotel. There I sat in a brown study, brooding on my unexpected pregnancy. After a while the silence began to feel eerie, and I turned on the television. It's one of the coping mechanisms I've resorted to, a distraction from the uneasiness I've felt in hotel rooms ever since my honeymoon seven years ago, which was the first time I had ever stayed in a hotel. I'd rather share a room with a female colleague on the same trip, but since I became the head of human resources for all of BrightLife China, I've traveled so much on business that inevitably I've often forced to stay alone.

I've been flipping through channels mindlessly, looking for a news program with talking heads, whose babble can be tuned out. But there seemed to be nothing but soap operas on at that time, all with a similar theme: a married couple in a big city—sometimes city natives, sometimes migrants—enslaved to their desires to own a prestigious apartment with a mortgage-noose around their necks, entangled in incessant strife with their in-laws, their life revolving around twin gods, wealth and their only child. Watching those shows, I've wondered whether they reflect a national economic and social trend that seems to have spared my family. Since my honeymoon in Paris, and the almost flawless consummation of my marriage to Deping—well, except that I didn't get pregnant during those nights in France—discussions in our apartment have sometimes been impassioned, but the subjects have never been trivial.

HASU AUGUST

I cast my mind back to the time when Taohua's elder daughter Meihua made an unexpected visit to our flat, less than two months after my honeymoon, in 2005. It was June 1, Children's Day, when youngsters below age fourteen have the afternoon off from school to enjoy with their parents. In the usual way, Deping's parents would've given Taohua the half-day off, to spend with Meihua. However, my mother-in-law had been sick for several days, and Taohua insisted she stay to take care of her and make her a healthy dinner. Since Taohua's husband was working, my mother-in-law invited Meihua home that afternoon, so she could be with her mother.

As it happened, I'd been attending an out-of-office seminar on employee management. The meeting ended ahead of schedule, and I got back home around four that afternoon, after dropping by a bakery en route to buy a box of assorted cakes for Meihua. As I walked into the living room, Meihua was crouched over a pile of books and papers on the coffee table in front of her. Thinking she hadn't noticed me coming in, I sang out cheerily, "I'm home."

Meihua lifted her head and gave me a look so glacial that it startled me. Then she turned her eyes toward the kitchen, where Taohua had poked her head around the door.

"Miss," Taohua said, smiling, "you're back very early today."

"I felt like having a holiday too," I quipped, and waved to her daughter. "Happy Children's Day to you, Meihua."

Lowering her head, the girl returned to her books without a word.

"You hear that?" Taohua yelled at her. "Aunt Bai is talking to you. Behave yourself!"

"Ssh…" I raised a forefinger to my lips. "It's all right, Taohua. How is Madam Sai?"

"I'm sorry for my loudness." Taohua apologetically stuck out

THE ENVELOPES

her tongue. Turning back to her worktop, she said, "Madam Sai is in bed but already doing her work."

"I'm going to see her," I said, setting the cake box down on the dining table.

As I walked past Meihua, whose head was still bent down, I heard her bleating feebly, as if to herself, "I have nothing to be happy about..." It cast a shadow over my mood, but I silently moved on to tap on the door to my parents-in-law's bedroom.

My mother-in-law was already out of bed, combing her hair at the dressing table. As I padded in, she said without turning away from the mirror, "Professional nursing has indeed put the roses in my cheeks. I feel great now. I hope you are not back early because of me."

I explained briefly. "Mother," I suggested hesitantly, "it might be better if you rested a little longer."

"I would love to take your advice, my girl. But I am expecting Felix, our friend. His class is closed this afternoon for Children's Day, and he is on the way over here. It is very kind of him to make use of this time to visit me, and I would love to hear about the progress of our school project. Come, let's move to the living room. Is Meihua already here? I heard some sounds just now."

"Yes, she's been here a while, I think. She looks like she's doing her homework." I crossed the room to neaten up the bed. "I was the noisy one."

"I think Taohua has been keeping the little girl quiet for my sake. But why does she have so much homework to do? After all, it is Children's Day."

"It's just my guess—I might be wrong. But it looked as if she was burying herself in workbooks."

"That little girl is only ten, still in elementary school, but she acts like an adult. Children of her age should be naughty and cheeky, playing around... mischief shouldn't be regarded as a flaw at that age. I still cannot understand why some people believe that assigning infinite homework to children is the best thing for them." She got up and moved toward the door. Watching me scoop the notebook and papers she'd been using to prepare for lessons off her bed, she asked, "Could you put them on the desk in the study for me?"

"I'll do that," I said, piling up the papers on top of the notebook in my arms. "I don't really know Meihua — this is only the second time I've seen her. The first time was during my wedding dinner. But Mother, I feel the same way — she seems loaded down with something I'm not clear about. Her mother even feels more like a child than her."

She sighed. "Let's see what we can do to buck up the little girl."

When I returned to the living room from the study, my mother-in-law was sitting on the settee, her legs stretched out next to Meihua, who was still squatting on her heels at the coffee table. "Come, come, show Granny what you are busy with," she coaxed, leaning forward and looking over Meihua's shoulder while stroking her ponytail.

Without raising her head, Meihua jiggled a little. "I'm doing math exercises," she muttered.

"But it is Children's Day. Come, tell Granny, what else do you get today other than math exercises?"

"I have Chinese exercises, too," Meihua droned like a mosquito, her pencil not pausing as it moved across the paper.

For once, for a moment, words seemed to fail my mother-in-law. In the silence, I could hear noises from the kitchen, where Taohua was slaving over the stove, interspersed with her intermittent warbling. As I walked to the dining area to fetch dishes and forks for the cakes, my mother-in-law finally said, "What about presents? Have you got any?"

THE ENVELOPES

"These exercises *are* the presents," Meihua said, raising her voice in agitation.

"The homework from your school? What a unique present!" My mother-in-law sounded surprised. "Are you happy with it?"

"No..." Meihua's voice trailed away again.

Seeing me approaching with the tray of cakes, my mother-in-law clapped her hands. "Well, how lovely! We have something better than the exercises. Granny thinks we can discard the homework for now and just enjoy the holiday."

Instead of looking up at me, Meihua left off writing, plonked both hands on her workbooks as if shielding her treasured possessions, and cried out, "No! I can't throw away these exercises. They aren't presents from school. They're from my Ma and Daddy. They cost a lot of money."

That knocked us two for six. My mother-in-law's face mirrored the consternation that must've been on my own, but she quickly put her arms around Meihua's shoulders. "Forgive me," she said. "Of course, we are not throwing them away. Let's just push them aside to make a little space for the cakes. Is that all right with you?"

Meihua inclined her head and stacked up the books and papers. Putting down the tray on the table, I asked, "Do you like cake, Meihua?"

"Yes." she said, finally turning her eyes toward the tray. "I can have it only on my birthday. Only a tiny one."

"Well, you can tuck into these as much as you want. Aren't these cakes pretty?"

With her gaze on the cakes but without excitement on her face, Meihua rose to her feet and came around to my side of the table. She knelt down on the floor, picked up a dish of strawberry mousse, and began to consume it at leisure with the fork, now facing my mother-in-law.

HASU AUGUST

"Is it delicious?" my mother-in-law asked, arms propped on her legs as she angled herself closer to Meihua. The girl nodded and gave a purr of satisfaction but didn't speak.

I rose to put the electric kettle on for tea, still listening.

"Well, old Granny is not very with it today," said my mother-in-law. "Could you help me to get my head round your present?"

"How can I help you?" Meihua asked, in a small but serious voice.

"You said the exercises cost a lot of money. Do you mean your ma and daddy bought you theses math and Chinese exercises?"

"My ma and daddy paid for me going to the remedial classes after school," Meihua said in a clear voice. "And there they gave the exercises out."

"Why do you go to the remedial classes? You don't think you are learning enough in school?"

Meihua shook her head slowly, licking the cream off her lips, as I set the teapot and a glass of water on the coffee table.

"Do your ma and daddy make you take the remedial classes?" my mother-in-law asked gently.

For a few seconds Meihua bit the fork in silence, her eyes downcast. Then she said quietly, "Teachers in school don't like to teach me."

I again zipped back and forth across the room to fetch two teacups, then finally settled down in an armchair at the coffee table's far end and poured my mother-in-law a cup of tea. She took it and went on, "Do you know why they don't like teaching you?"

This time Meihua shook her head quickly, before scooping the last piece of mousse into her mouth.

"Then how do you know they do not like to teach you?"

"I didn't get what teachers taught at classes. I went to ask them questions after classes, but they never gave me answers.

THE ENVELOPES

Instead, they always said, 'Why don't you come to my remedial class? Many other students have come, and they become smart.' I think they don't like to teach me because I don't go to their remedial classes."

My mother-in-law blew off the steam from her cup and took a sip of her tea. "So you told your ma and daddy you wanted to join those classes?"

"No, I didn't. But I flunked exams." Meihua scooped up her glass with both hands and slurped her water.

My mother-in-law waited for her to finish. "Is it because you could not catch on to what the teachers taught in school?"

"Um." Meihua dipped her head. With her eyes straying over to the cake tray and then to me, she answered, "My daddy was called to school. The teachers told him I should go to their remedial classes. My ma and daddy paid, and they said that would be the present for Children's Day this year."

"Meihua," I chipped in, inching the tray closer to her, "go ahead, have more cake. Take whatever you like." She giggled and chose a slice of gateau.

"Are you glad to be in the remedial classes?" My mother-in-law was straining to smile, but her face betrayed her growing apprehension.

Meihua stared at my mother-in-law, her immature face clouded over with a strangely adult ambivalence. Swallowing the mouthful of cake she'd just eaten, she said, "We have remedial classes after school, and on Saturdays and Sundays too. I never have time to play, but I have to study hard. Teachers like to teach me in those classes. They answer all my questions and give me all these exercises. I make good grades at exams, and my ma and daddy are happy—"

"What are you saying I'm happy with?" Taohua broke in, popping up in her apron and surprising everyone. "Aya, silly, you alone are eating so much?"

"I—I—I'm having the, the second piece, Ma." Tongue-tied, Meihua looked over her own shoulder at Taohua.

I patted Meihua's arm. "Oh, you're scaring the girl off."

"Aya, I don't mean to make her quake. I'm sorry." Taohua beamed at Meihua and me, yet clapped a hand over her own mouth as if to muffle her voice.

Meihua tittered, turned back to her dish, and began to polish off the remains of the gateau.

My mother-in-law gestured for Taohua to sit down beside her. "Now let your daughter enjoy herself," she said to her softly. "I have something to ask you about. You may think it is not my business, but I want to know how much it cost you to get Meihua into the remedial classes."

"It cost me a half year's wages."

"That *is* a packet for you, Taohua," my mother-in-law cried. "You also send money back to your village for your younger daughter's living expenses, right?"

"Don't worry, Madam Sai. We can scrape out a living here with my man's income."

Though I was keeping an eye on Meihua, I couldn't help listening as my mother-in-law probed, "Have you ever thought about why your daughter must be in extra classes?"

"Her teachers said she didn't come up to the mark in exams, and she had to spend more time learning. They recommended that either we help her in her studies at home or send her to their remedial classes. They said the classes had helped other children pass the exams. My man has to live on the construction site—he comes back home only three or four times a month. And I myself have a thick skull. We're unable to help her with her schoolwork. And we trust whatever her teachers say—she entered the remedial classes, and she's got good exam results.

THE ENVELOPES

Madam Sai, have we done something wrong?"

My mother-in-law sighed. "It is not your fault. But it is just unfair. Meihua is a clever child. She could have done well in school if only the teachers took their responsibilities more seriously."

"I... I don't quite get it, Madam Sai. I think the teachers in the remedial classes are helpful."

"Listen, Taohua, primary education is not supposed to cost a lot. I know you have paid extra just to have Meihua enroll in school here— the national policy is that you cannot register your whole family for permanent residence in our city. And now you have to pay for remedial classes too—that is an additional burden."

"We just want Meihua to go to school, Madam Sai. I don't want her going down the wrong path I took. But it's true there're too many regulations for us migrant workers. We don't make much money, but we have to pay more than city people for our daughter's education."

"Listen, Taohua, your daughter has the desire and innate ability to learn. But that should not be proved by remedial class. Think about it—she is doing well there, why cannot she do as well in school?"

Taohua seemed at a loss for words. "In the future," my mother-in-law went on, "please let Meihua come to us. We could guide her in her study."

"Thank you for your great kindness, Madam Sai. But I don't want to trouble you. You are all so busy, going out in the early morning and coming back late every day. You're not even always able to sit down for dinner together."

"Well, as long as you let us know we are needed, we will find time for Meihua. It is no inconvenience."

They fell into silence for several seconds. Finally Taohua

said, "I'll do what you say, Madam Sai. I won't send Meihua to remedial classes again after the end of this term."

Just then the doorbell rang. Taohua jumped up from the settee and hared off to open the door, saying, "It must be Mr Lee. Aren't you waiting for him?"

"Hello, Taohua," boomed Felix Lee's voice from the entryway, and a moment later he was with us, his oversize sunny presence filling the room. Even as he greeted us, his eyes drifted to Meihua, who was now helping me to clean up the empty dishes and her water glass. Crossing the room in a few big strides, he stooped down to introduce himself to the girl. She took one look at him, threw back her head, and broke out in a fit of uproarious laughter, the first I'd ever heard from her, and wholly unexpected. It was as infectious as her mother's singing, and an air of gaiety suddenly permeated the room.

Felix looked a little bewildered, but he simply grinned at Meihua and bided his time until she stopped roaring. Then he asked in an encouraging tone, "Why are you laughing?"

Still chuckling, Meihua compressed her lips as if trying to hold back a secret she was dying to tell.

"She goes ape whenever she sees interesting new things," said Taohua, who was standing a little apart from us. "She's never seen a foreigner in person, much less one who speaks Chinese."

"How come your eyes are green?" Meihua suddenly piped up, staring at Felix, two hands behind her back. "They look like our cat's eyes."

"Be polite, Meihua!" Taohua said sternly, moving toward the kitchen.

The girl glanced apprehensively toward her mother, but Felix pulled her attention back, asking, "That's your name—Meihua?"

She bobbed her head.

"Such beautiful names! Mum's peach blossom, and you're

plum blossom."

"My younger sister's name is Lianhua," Meihua added eagerly.

"Wow, your sister is water lily," Felix marveled. "Your daddy is a lucky man, with all those beautiful flowers around him."

Meihua giggled. "Where are you from, Fe—Felix?" Having succeeded in pronouncing the name, which was quite a mouthful to her, she began gamboling around Felix. Despite the face she found so alien, it was clear she wasn't immune to the universal cheer he seemed to always bring.

"I'm from the United Kingdom."

"Where is that? Does everyone have green eyes there? Oh, but cats have eyes in other colors too…"

Felix began a patient explanation to the little girl. "Though we're not cats, we…"

Meihua was now bouncing off the walls, as if to burn up all the sugar she'd just taken in from the cakes. Resting on the settee, my mother-in-law looked on with a tranquil smile as they both danced for joy while talking animatedly.

After a short while, Taohua, her apron off, returned to the living room. Watching her daughter, she said gruffly, "Meihua is a little batty today."

"On the contrary, I think she is her natural self now, just as she should be," my mother-in-law retorted, winking at Taohua. "She is just a slip of a girl. Those two are getting on like a house on fire."

"But what good is it doing her to mess about like this?" Taohua began to pack up the stack of Meihua's exercises that were on the coffee table. "She should be studying. We've spent so much money on her schooling. Madam Sai, grub's up and kept warm in the kitchen. We've got to go now."

"Thank you for staying on this afternoon," my mother-in-law said to Taohua, and then turned to her daughter. "Meihua, Granny hopes you had fun here. Come here to play another time. Now your ma is taking you to have dinner with your daddy. Ready to go to enjoy your evening?"

After Taohua and Meihua went off, my mother-in-law and Felix remained in the study, batting around their project, until my father-in-law and Deping came home. Then Felix was invited to join us for dinner, as he often did—my mother-in-law regularly asked him over, even for ordinary family meals.

Once we were sitting around the table and had started to eat, my father-in-law began ribbing my mother-in-law. First, looking grave, he asked me, "Little Jve, do you think Mama is getting well?"

"Oh, yes, I think so."

"What mojo have you done on Mama?"

"I've done no mojo. I think the key is that Mother keeps her spirits up."

"Really?" His eyes fastened on his wife. "Mama, your sour face is barely in concert with your high spirits."

"Felix, here is your chance to see how Papa teases me," my mother-in-law said to Felix, who looked flummoxed. Then she sighed. "Papa, you are right that I am chafing at something. Meihua was here this afternoon..." She recounted what Meihua had told her about the unnecessary remedial classes that were draining her parents' resources, adding, "These practices are not unusual. Some of the teachers in our school are doing the same thing as Meihua's."

"So that's it," Felix said reflectively. "It explains why I've seen them more engaged in coaching a small posse of students than teaching their regular classes. But that they're doing it just for their own benefit... even after almost three years here, I find that hard to believe. We teachers earn salaries, just like other professionals. Aren't teachers already paid for nourishing their students' talents? And surely satisfying their passion for showing the way forward to minds hungry for learning should be a reward in itself."

"You might think so." Deping snorted derisively. "Unfortunately, there are many teachers who believe they're not paid enough for the standards of living they aspire to. Perhaps they even think themselves the victims of our nation's rapid economic development. I've heard some grumble that others are paid more and more, while their own salaries stagnate."

My father-in-law cleared his throat, and everyone looked at him. "Well, this is quite a coincidence. On the way home just now, when my driver Fu and I were shooting the breeze in the car, he asked me to help him find a way to dodge his eight-year-old son's teacher, who was planning to visit him tonight. I found the request puzzling, remembering how Deping's geography teacher in high school would often visit us at home — he took his students' interest in geography so much to heart, he couldn't stand to leave their questions unanswered, even on his own time. I told Fu he should appreciate that his child's teacher was so committed to her students, day and night. He just laughed, saying that things are no longer like they used to be. Then he grew bitter. By an unwritten rule, he said, a teacher's visit to a student's home is never free. A red packet enclosing money is expected. His son's teacher has visited his home twice this year, and Fu says he'll go broke if the teacher comes again — and there's still half of the year to go. I stated outright that he didn't have to pay. He said he has no option; since the other students' parents offer red packets to the teacher, he has to also, to make sure his son is treated well in school. He feels as if he's being robbed, by either his own son or the teacher."

Deping shook his head. "I would say their exchange is not robbery, since Fu chooses to pay."

"It is ridiculous!" my mother-in-law burst out. "I cannot understand how our education system has come to this."

Startled by the anger in her voice, Felix froze, his chopsticks suspended on their way to a serving dish.

"Calm down, Mama." Putting down his bowl on the table, my father-in-law stretched out his hand and rubbed her back. "Stay cheerful. Little Jve just said that is the key for your health."

Felix slowly retracted his chopsticks, still empty.

"Mother, you've put the wind up on Felix," Deping remarked playfully.

"I'm fine. I'm fine," Felix said hastily, turning to her. "It's just... I never saw Madam Sai fly off the handle before."

"Have some of this, Mother," I said, passing her a bowl of clear soup. "It will cool your temper."

"I beg your pardon, everyone," said my mother-in-law, looking a bit abashed. "I am acting like a coddled child throwing a tantrum." She drank a spoonful of her soup and let out a breath. "But it makes my heart bleed to live through such changes. Twenty years back, there were only two types of teachers — good ones who could realize students' potential and moderate ones who only cared about how to get students to pass their exams. Both types got by on a meager income, and none of them thought of trying to rake in more money somewhere else—"

"Wait a minute, Mother," Deping cut in. "One's memory of the past tends to be sweeter than the reality. Back then, getting more money was out of the question for everyone, but some teachers still managed to use *guanxi* to their advantage." He turned to Felix. "You know the meaning of the Chinese word *guanxi*?"

"Doesn't *guanxi* mean the relationships between people or

THE ENVELOPES

things?"

"Literally, yes. But it implicates much more. It's about the rapport you have with someone in power; someone who has control over things desired by others. Say there are some public toilets that one must pay a fee to use. An attendant sits at the doorway to collect this fee. If it happens that you have no cash at all, and you can't wait a second to relieve yourself, the attendant — you might think a toilet attendant is a power pygmy, but trust me, that would be a mistake — won't give a shit. You have to hold back, even to your death. Even for a toilet attendant, might is right. But if you're a friend of the attendant's, you're welcome to pee for free."

Diverted, Felix shook his head in disbelief.

"That is the wicked talking of my boy." My mother-in-law chortled. "I know that *guanxi* has been long in existence — though its history remains a mystery to me — and that its power has extended to matters of money. Still, it was different twenty years ago. Now some teachers still hold themselves to a professional code of ethics, but many do not. Some criticize the education system while taking advantage of loopholes in it, some just muddle along, and some — though fewer and fewer — still have not given up, and are still struggling to find better ways to enlighten children."

"Right, twenty years back," Deping chimed in, "a red packet was only a term for the money given to a child at the beginning of the new year, a sign of good luck. It would never occur to parents to use it as a means of pleasing teachers to get them do their job. But these days red packets are running riot in our society."

"Even hospitals — the places where lives are saved — are not immune to the red-packet epidemic," I couldn't help adding.

"But if I may comment..." Felix began slowly, then paused. "In the past twenty years, China has amazed the world with her economic development. Hasn't the living standard of the people significantly improved?"

"To my mind," Deping said, "in terms of hardware facilities and technology, yes, we've developed overwhelmingly — but in thinking and values, we've hardly advanced. The former actualizes an economic miracle in the short run, but the latter otherwise will sustain the former and, in turn, the economic growth. Sustainability is vital for a truly strong nation. I would say that the generation educated twenty years ago, driven by the material comforts that they could quickly obtain, became the backbone of our nation's economic development. Nonetheless, they'd tasted the sweetness of money. People desire more and more cash, riches now pursued by fair means or foul. Meanwhile, *guanxi* is not vanishing. Instead, it's expanded. Now it can even be bought."

"Son," said my father-in-law, "what you just said bears out that it rests with you to develop teachers who possess both competence and ethos. Do you think City Normal is currently producing elite educators who won't be vulnerable to the temptations of the red packet?"

"I don't think so, Father, I'm afraid. First of all, a university itself is already not immune to general social mores. Problematic incidents of the kind that you and Mother just described are now prevalent. From kindergartens to universities, none are unaffected. As I see it, despite the university's inefficient management approach and ineffective evaluation system, some lecturers and professors still have a zeal for fostering students' abilities and setting their minds in the right direction. But even if they work hard during their four years, once students say farewell to campus life, they will be reeducated by the society and find it very hard to live up to their own ideals. Unfortunately, most of them are likely to give up."

THE ENVELOPES

"A vicious circle is forming," my mother-in-law said, brooding. "Upon graduation from City Normal, students are assigned to elementary and high schools. Then they may discover some veteran teachers are riding the wave of economic development, abusing their teaching capacity in unprecedented ways such as forcing children into remedial classes to make much more than their normal income. The worse thing is there are much more than a few of those teachers. Then comes the scariest part: the graduates, as well as children in schools, are easily lost in the course of building up their values—monkey see, monkey do. That is grievous—misguided children and warped values. It makes me question the long-term prospects for our nation."

"Can't a school stipulate that it is forbidden to take extra fees from children?" Felix asked, blinking innocently.

"I believe some schools have issued such a stipulation," my mother-in-law disclosed. "But these rules cannot always rein in the shady behavior of some teachers, and often head teachers just turn a blind eye."

"And beyond that," Deping said, "you never know whether the head teachers themselves are clean or not. It precisely demonstrates the time-honored custom in China that a law can't be enforced where everyone is an offender."

"It sounds an abstruse custom to me," Felix remarked quietly, looking slightly addled.

"Well, we don't need to delve into the custom. The real crisis, again, is inside here," Deping said, tapping his head. "It's sad that people have been brainwashed by the power of the state apparatus. And it's even sadder that human behaviors are now programmed by the might of Mammon..."

"Son, your off-the-cuff comments are taking us a bit far," my father-in-law broke in out of the blue.

"If human brains could be formulated by animations that

show the beautiful prevailing over the ugly, I would have nothing to complain about," Deping bantered, casting an arch glance at me. I turned away to hide a smile I couldn't repress.

Felix sighed. "Suffice to say, the status quo of education here seems like a mare's nest to me. It obviously goes far beyond what my eyes have seen."

"A mare's nest not only to you, Felix," my father-in-law said, his voice calm. "This is a huge state with a vast population. The issue isn't just with educators — it involves people from all walks of life. We're only the pieces on a chessboard, unable to see the gestalt of it. Only the players that move the pieces might be able to. If you know anything about playing chess, either Chinese or Western, you must know the possible moves at chess are practically endless. And it's not uncommon that players foul up, and don't realize they've made a mistake until many moves later. By the time corrections are attempted, it can be too late, or those corrections themselves may incur other mistakes, only making the situation worse..."

"Papa, my boy might have taken us a bit far," my mother-in-law said, "but you are making the whole thing quite difficult to follow. Who are the players? What was the first wrong move made in the reality of our country? Could you specify?"

"I wish I could, Mama."

"I'm finding that analogy kind of interesting," Felix mused. "Developing the economy might've been the driving mechanism behind the chess game of education here, but it's the fact that many people have gotten so hooked on money that has really bogged things down. If city schools are marred by the lust for loot, I wonder whether the countryside, with much less economic growth, as far as I know, is still the unpolluted land."

Deping, his tongue loosened by Felix's doubt, said, "'Undeveloped' is perhaps a more suitable word for the

THE ENVELOPES

countryside because it faces another plight. Schools have disappeared from many villages."

"It is true," my mother-in-law broke in. "During Taohua's childhood, it was not difficult for her to go to elementary school. Now only one school remains in her neck of the woods, and it is shared by several villages that stand far apart, with no connection by roads for vehicles. If the school-age children in Taohua's village wish to study, they have to go to the only school on shank's mare, about a two-hour's walk each way. Taohua and Wenwu can afford only one child's education here, but their younger daughter, as well as her peers in the village, is going to be seven soon. There is a want of schools now in those villages with many children left behind."

"How could it happen?" Felix asked, goggling at my mother-in-law. "Isn't it the government who should take care of the compulsory education for all children?"

"That's the sixty-four-thousand-dollar question," Deping rejoined. "What is the root of a shortage of funds and teacher resources? There are no roofs or desks or chairs to accommodate classes. Even the aspirant graduates from Normal University cringe at the hardship foreseen."

"But my aspiration to help children like Meihua, as well as her sister Lianhua, is not dying away." Felix leaned forward, his face intense. "Working with Madam Sai so far, I feel I've been so protected, unexposed to adversity. My life goal is far from fulfilled. Meihua's curiosity has just inspired me. I'm serious about it. If I'm given a chance, I'd love to go to the country to help those children, although I will likely be operating on a wing and a prayer."

"Hats off to you, Felix," said Deping. "But there's a snag. Are you aware of the privations of living in a remote village in China, even if a school could be sponsored there?"

"Yes," Felix said earnestly. "In fact, I've hiked to several villages and experienced life there during school holidays, ever since I came to China. And I'm not alone. I have a German friend, and we have the same aspiration."

"Bravo!" my mother-in-law exclaimed. "Felix, we have worked together on a couple of projects for our school, but never had an exchange of views about this. If time could be rewound by even just ten years, I would join you."

"Mama, ten years plus being fit as a fiddle. Neither is dispensable," my father-in-law said, looking alarmed. "Otherwise, it would end up with others looking after you instead of your helping them."

"You sound as if I am already a geriatric, Papa. Well, I may be reaching the twilight of my career, but I am not yet ready to be put out to grass."

"I know you aren't paying lip service, Mama. I only mean that you must stay hale and hearty."

"Thanks for reminding me of that, Papa. I am as serious as Felix that I still can do something, though. For instance, I could raise funds and search for teachers who might volunteer to pitch in with the work during school holidays."

"Assuredly, Mama." My father-in-law turned to look at her. "And I believe Deping agrees with me that you've always been a live wire, giving your best to children for generations."

"That extra zing in Madam Sai never fails to bolster my morale, too," said Felix, and Deping nodded firmly.

———∽∽∽———

As the night wore on, stillness, like a sluggish dominator, finally took hold of the world. Nevertheless, the buzz of conversation between my parents-in-law in their bedroom passed through the walls to tickle our eardrums. Deping and I were already in bed, lying there in silence as if listening to them, though we couldn't distinguish their words.

"Good to see Mother back on her feet," I said.

"They must be discussing how to set the world to rights again now," Deping said, with a restrained laugh, "though they aren't always of the same opinion. And Felix's fervent desire to teach in the country has rekindled Mother's hope, I gather."

"Rekindled Mother's hope?" I was baffled.

"It's a long story—let me try to boil it down to a few words. Shortly after we took Taohua on as a housemaid over three years ago, we learned she was faced with the dilemma of whether to let Meihua stay in her village and walk to the only elementary school kilometers away every day or have her educated here. Taohua and her husband eventually decided to keep Meihua with them in the city for schooling, but leave two-year-old Lianhua with her grandparents in the village. But Mother realized that, five years later, Taohua would be in a bind again, with no resources for getting Lianhua a proper education. It was heartbreaking. I remember Old Man and Mother talked into the deep night then, too. You know Mother never waits. She said she couldn't change the world, but she wanted to solve this specific problem. Two years or so ago, she set the ball rolling by seeking a sponsor for building a school in Taohua's village from entrepreneurs who were her former students. She also tried to find graduates from my university who would be willing to go down to the country—"

"Hold on," I interrupted, despite myself. "I've been with you for over two years, but I still know nothing about the things Mother works on."

"No one other than Old Man, Mother, and I know about this undertaking of Mother's. I was involved too, as we thought I could help to find teaching resources for her plan. And apparently we didn't think it was time yet to tell Taohua about it."

"Then how is the project coming along?"

Deping sighed. "Unfortunately, the whole thing was soon dead in the water for all the odds."

"Oh, no," I said, somehow feeling guilty about having let my mother-in-law use so much of her time and energy coaching me in English.

"To find essential resources was much harder than we thought, and then there was Mother's physical degeneration." After a pause, he went on, "The hope that flamed in her was too soon extinguished by ice-cold reality. But I can sense that, somewhere in her heart, hope is still glowing through the ashes."

"And now," I said excitedly, "the dream of Felix and his friend is probably turning the spark of her hope into burning flames again."

"I gather so."

"In other words, one of the two resources needed for establishing a school in Taohua's village will be in place."

"I hope so."

"Deping, I've been admiring Mother for many things." Turning onto my side, I laid my hand on his chest. "And I'm impressed by the depth and subtlety of your insight into the thinking and values of our society in relation to the future of our country. I'd never thought about it in that way. Where do you get these concepts?"

"It's thanks to the language tool that Mother taught me how to use," he said, his hand overlapping the back of mine. I could feel his even heartbeat faintly in our hands. "I read whatever books and documents in this world that are relevant and available. In a way, Mother gave me a pair of wings and freed my mind—"

"—so your mind could fly beyond what many people see. But what Mother has given you cannot be just a pair of wings,"

THE ENVELOPES

I probed, following my intuition. "Your insight implies that you aren't always looking at life and work through rose-tinted spectacles."

For a while, he was silent, as if cogitating on the meaning of his parents to his life. Then he said softly, "I would say you hit the mark. Mother and Old Man have kept faith in what they believe in. There were times when incidents took the wind out of my sails, and I faltered in my effort to make great teachers. But I looked up to my parents. Even though people endlessly attempt to grease his palm, Old Man keeps to his principles. People who pursue the high entrance-examination rates always try to have Mother dance to their tune, but she perseveres with to cultivate children's interests and skills... I'm supposed to be a chip off the old block. So, when I felt it hard to develop my students into teachers like Mother, why couldn't I look down on setbacks and move on?"

Somehow, Deping's quiet talking calmed me, though a minute before I'd still been keyed up and tense, and I felt myself falling into sleep.

6

When the summer holidays ended and Meihua turned eleven, my mother-in-law, Deping, and I started to take turns coaching Meihua in her studies, whenever she had questions or wanted to learn more than what she was taught in school. Occasionally even my father-in-law spent a little time supervising her math work. Felix also stepped forward to gratify her inquisitiveness about English and the otherness of his culture of origin. For another thing, while she was approaching retirement, my mother-in-law, together with Felix, got down to brass tacks in her experiment with building an elementary school in Taohua's village, which was said to contain around fifty households. At the same time, my new career as a personnel professional, which I'd started around two years previously, seemed to be blossoming. I'd just been promoted to human-resources manager, and I expected that my life with Deping's family would move on smoothly. I believed that both Meihua and Lianhua would have a sheltered upbringing, and that Deping and I would be blessed with our own children, who would grow up happily. I was even further convinced when I discovered in the autumn — about five months after our honeymoon — that I was pregnant. At that time, longing for the fruit of our marriage, I was sensitive to changes in my body. Naturally, my confirmed pregnancy sent Deping into raptures, and he wanted to shout it from the rooftops. In early

THE ENVELOPES

October 2005, while my father-in-law happened to be away on a business trip, Deping revealed this good tidings at the dinner table.

My mother-in-law looked radiant in wonderment. Putting her palms together, she exclaimed, "You make me feel like I have just hit a jackpot! I am going to phone Papa right away to tell him the news. My girl, may our grandchild have a pair of dimples and smiling lips just like yours."

Taohua congratulated us, wishing us twins. Then she crooned a lullaby all day, until she finished work and went home.

That night, it seemed that felicity descended on all of us from heaven. Yet it was as if, when an angel came down to earth to make friends with us, it provoked the devil's envy.

Early the next morning, when the apartment should've been seething with activity as the three of us got ready for work, Deping and I realized that my parents-in-law's bedroom was strangely silent. When we went to check on my mother-in-law, we found that she had fallen into her eternal sleep. Madam Jingwen Sai, my mother-in-law was fifty-nine.

Six and half years later, I can still recall her last smile, when we found her still and cold, reposing in her bed. The smile hovered strangely on her colorless lips against the sagging flesh of her face; a mysterious, serene, contented smile such as I'd never seen on any of the dead I'd encountered during my years as a nurse. She must've been in a happy dream, even as she suffered from sudden heart failure. As I looked down at her, my eyes were dry, though my heart was wrenched by shock and sadness. Her smile felt like the evidence that she and I had fulfilled a promise—the promise of the new life to be born, which filled me with hope.

My mother-in-law Madam Jingwen Sai's memorial service was held in the sports hall of her school. As my father-in-law anticipated, umpteen city officials came to express their condolences. Less expected, however, were the current and former students who crammed into the hall, many of them in tears.

Taohua's family attended the service too. I first saw Meihua, looking as if she didn't understand death, positioned between her parents, in the line opposite me. Her eyes wandered back and forth, following the movements of the crowd. A while later, when I noticed her again, she'd slipped along the line to Felix's side, where she stood quietly, her hand clasped in his, her eyes still roving about the hall. From time to time she craned her neck to look up at his face. *What will now become of the bond forged between them by my mother-in-law?* I thought bitterly, gazing at that silent, unconventional pair.

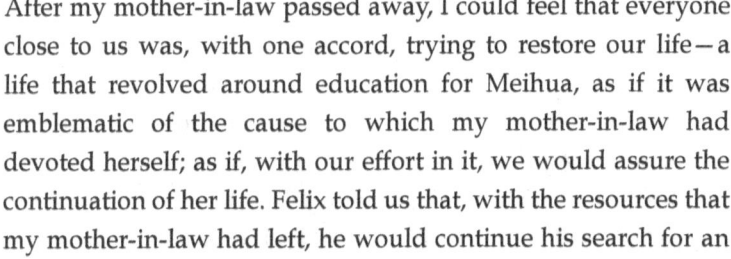

After my mother-in-law passed away, I could feel that everyone close to us was, with one accord, trying to restore our life—a life that revolved around education for Meihua, as if it was emblematic of the cause to which my mother-in-law had devoted herself; as if, with our effort in it, we would assure the continuation of her life. Felix told us that, with the resources that my mother-in-law had left, he would continue his search for an opportunity to teach in the countryside.

For my part, I told myself that life must go on, whether angels were watching over us or devils preying on us. The fact was that, while Deping strove toward his ideals and his parents stuck to their principles, I'd been no more than a bystander. Round the dinner table on that night several months ago, I could hardly participate in our family's debate about the nation's daunting barriers to education, but only listen. My life was more or less the same as it had been before I married Deping, a life holding neither enormous grief nor tremendous joy, both of which I deemed only

THE ENVELOPES

inventions in the tempestuous plots of anime. Even Madam Sai's death didn't feel like a real loss. We—my father-in-law, Deping, and I—had long mentally prepared for her untimely departure from this life, I told myself. Similarly, I deemed myself only an onlooker when I first met Waits and Daisy, despite my hunch about how they might change the lives of some of BrightLife China's employees.

Nevertheless, when I felt helpless and had to throw myself upon my father-in-law and Deping's mercy, I suddenly realized how my life was bound up with theirs and how high the price they'd pay for not compromising. That was how I then perceived the event that left within me the woe that Daisy sensed on her first day with BrightLife.

———∽∽———

The first trimester of my pregnancy was hell. I was frequently racked with serious morning sickness, and only when the waves of nausea and vomiting subsided, could I go to work.

Taohua sighed when she saw me, my face contorted in agony. "Aya, you city girls are as fragile as china dolls."

"That's not fair," I said, gasping. "Some women are lucky enough to escape morning sickness, and it seems you were one of those."

"When I conceived Meihua," she recalled, passing me a glass of water, "I became big and clumsy. My man had gone to work in a city. I stayed in our village and worked in the fields until the day right before I gave birth. At dusk, I told my grandma my tum hurt. She said I had labor pains. I sat on the ridge of the field and cried to her, 'I can't bear the pain. Do whatever you can—I no longer want the baby.' My grandma laughed like a drain, as if she were ignoring my pain."

"Did you really say that?" The water didn't help my churning stomach. I put the glass aside.

"Yes, I was daft. I was twenty, and I hadn't had much education." She chuckled, wedging a pillow between my waist and the back of the settee.

"Then they sent you to a hospital?" I asked casually, trying to find a comfortable sitting position.

"No. Meihua arrived at our village in my own bed the next morning." She started to dust the living room.

"I never heard of anyone in our generation, or even my mother's, delivering a child at home."

"You city girls go to hospital too often for checking this and that. I never went once during my pregnancies." She knelt to clear off the coffee table. 'By the time I had Lianhua, we'd lived in this city. I didn't have any pain at all, and, on the early morning of that day, I felt she was coming. My man was terrified, desperate to send me to a hospital. A kind neighbor of ours had a van and was willing to drive us. And my man asked me to hold on until we reached the hospital."

"He did? What an ignoramus!"

"Yes, although my man read more books than I did. How could I hold it in? I wish! In a twinkling, I gave birth to Lianhua on the way to the hospital. We never got there—we just went back home. Later a woman in the neighborhood who used to be a midwife came by and cut the umbilical cord for me."

"Good grief! Lianhua was brought to the world in a van?"

"Aya, Miss, I never expected to hear your voice as loud as mine." She giggled. "I never stepped into a hospital to have my kids."

"I'm stunned," I said, then quipped, "I feel much better now—I'm heartened by your daring deeds."

———∽∞∽———

THE ENVELOPES

For all that, my pregnancy progressed well. My body was becoming bulkier and bulkier. Though I went to the women's hospital where I used to work for routine checks, Taohua's singular story encouraged me to keep myself quite strong for my normal activities, including taking my turn to help Meihua in her studies.

One day in late April 2006, after Meihua finished her homework under my tutelage in our apartment, she came to sit beside me. Gawking at my bulging belly, she asked, "Auntie Bai, when will the baby come out?"

"Very soon," I answered. "Do you like babies?"

"Yes, I do," she said crisply, her forefinger pointing at my belly and then playfully circling in the air. "Is the baby a girl or boy?"

"I don't know yet. Which do you like better?"

"I don't know anything about boys. I like baby girls." She hopped out of the seat. Bouncing up and down on the floor, she punctuated her speech with gestures. "I liked playing with my sister Lianhua. My ma strapped little Lianhua onto my back. We were always together."

"When Lianhua was small, you were a little girl, too. You carried her on your back?"

She nodded, and turned to see her mother coming up to us from the kitchen.

Taohua had heard my remark, and her face was incredulous. "Meihua was about six then," she said. "Of course, she was able to carry her sister. At the same age, I carried my younger brother on my back while I helped my ma pull up weeds from the fields."

I shook my head, speechless. From what Taohua had recently been telling me about her family's life, they seemed like inhabitants of another planet. The world I lived in, as a girl, had been brimming over with anime heroines, dolls, and pretty clothes. They might've been mostly second-hand, but they were given to me on a silver platter.

Meihua stopped jumping around. She sidled up close to me and asked timidly, "Auntie Bai, may I touch your belly?"

"Sure. I think the baby likes to be touched." I smiled. "It might give you a happy kick."

Meihua laid her fingers on my belly through my loose-fitting dress and then gingerly, as if she was afraid to frighten the little life in the making, moved her hand about. After a short while, she said, "Auntie Bai, the baby isn't kicking at all." She reluctantly withdrew her hand, looking disappointed.

Her comment made me feel suddenly cold. I ran my hands over my belly, murmuring, "Er... It's odd. It's been inactive these two days."

Meihua was about to stretch out her hand once more when Taohua barked, "Your itching hand! Don't touch Auntie's belly again!"

"Shush," I pacified Taohua. "It has nothing to do with Meihua."

———∞———

By the time my father-in-law and Deping came back from work, I'd decided to look into the problem, if there was one, alone. Though I still felt slightly uneasy, I told myself that it was likely just a glitch.

The next day, without telling Deping, I went for an ultrasound scan at the women's hospital, The doctors I'd known three years previously were either unavailable or no longer there, so I had to speak to one I didn't know. The doctor looked young but confident. When I told her about the subtle change I'd felt in my seven-month-old unborn child, she didn't even touch my belly. "The ultrasound shows the little thing is perfect," she

THE ENVELOPES

interrupted. "You have nothing to worry about. Just take it easy."

If she'd been an armed mugger, I could've fought her. For a moment, I somehow wished she were. But she was a doctor, equipped with medical knowledge, experience, and self-assurance. My intuition and my rusty nursing skills were simply not enough to enable me to defy her.

I did try to loosen up, but a ripple of agitation lingered; the fetus still felt strangely inert. Not eager to consult yet another doctor who might again trust the scanning machine more than human feeling, I confided my worry to Deping. On the spur of the moment, I asked him whether he thought his father might arrange for us to see a famous obstetrician in the best hospital of our city, or that 'bureaucrats' hospital' — people from all parts of the country thronged to see highly skilled doctors there; without the clout of the *guanxi* network my father-in-law's position guaranteed, I would have to wait at least a month for an appointment. Deping pondered for a moment, and then took my hand. We went to the study where my father-in-law usually worked and read at night.

My father-in-law listened as we told him our concern for our unborn baby's health. "As the expectant grandfather," he said, "I understand how you feel." But he looked troubled.

"Father, please help us," I implored, overwhelmed by a compulsion.

My father-in-law sat deep in contemplation in his swivel chair for a while. Finally he spoke calmly, without looking at us. "I'm trying to hear Mama say what she would do if she were still around."

Silenced, we sat waiting. After a moment, he turned back to us. "Mama spent her whole life giving love, care, and attention to children," he said. "Throughout, she stayed strong in her convictions. She never asked me to lend her my power, even though without it, sometimes she was unable to achieve her goals. She said it wouldn't be fair to others—that I wasn't at liberty to abuse my power by fulfilling my wife's wishes. To be honest with you, I've often wondered how Mama managed to keep away from *guanxi* and the red packet all those years, even when she saw others—"

"Father—" Deping held up his hand to stop him. "I regret asking you for this thing. I hope you can forgive me."

"We're human beings with emotions." My father-in-law gave Deping a gentle but decisive look. "In fact, son, I don't know which of us deserves the other's forgiveness. Let's try to understand each other." Then he turned to me. "Little Jve, go to see that doctor again, and tell her about your gut feeling. It's not uncommon for a doctor to have a blind spot."

I was so contrite that I couldn't even make a sound. Deping took my hand again, and we left the study.

Deping tried to make me feel better, saying I'd done nothing wrong, that my concern was natural. But nothing he said helped; I felt myself crass and selfish. I had no right to whine and sulk.

You city girls are as fragile as china dolls. Taohua's words rang mockingly in my ears.

I resolved not to go back to the hospital. Probably the doctor was right, I told myself. I just needed to inhale deeply, relax, and wait for the blessed event.

———∞———

Before the expected date, I felt uterine contractions, followed by labor pains. That night my waters broke, and I was sent to the women's hospital. After an examination, I was wheeled directly into the operation theater for a caesarean.

They gave me an epidural, but I remained conscious. Though I heard all kinds of other noises, I waited and waited to hear the

THE ENVELOPES

first strong wail. Finally I detected a weak grunting. *That cannot be my baby's cry!* I thought.

The next thing I heard was not a cry, but a murmur in my ear. "You have a baby boy, but we need to transfer him to the intensive care unit now."

Feeling as if I were trapped in a nightmare, I strained every nerve to part my lips, but couldn't make a sound. Then darkness fell over me.

I came round to find myself lying in a maternity ward, with only Deping at my bedside. "Where's our baby son?" I asked, but he just held my hand and told me that we must be patient, and await good news. Looking up at his face, I saw the strain in the smile he tried to give me, and the shadow of fear in his eyes. Still unable to say anything, I closed my eyes. *May my mother-in-law in heaven guard our son through this baptism of fire*, I prayed.

Twenty-four hours went by before our child's lungs failed, and he stopped breathing. It was May 25, 2006.

I requested a quiet moment alone with my boy, who had lived on earth for only one day. Wrapped in a blanket, he lay beside me on my maternity bed. His eyes would open wide and look curiously at this world; the fine wisps of his hair would become thick, glossy locks; his lips would curve into the most beautiful smile; his dimples would enchant his beloved girl... I conceived all the fine things of his growing-up. But his tiny body lay lifeless. I cried streams of tears, for myself and my late mother-in-law, for the irrevocable loss that she would mercifully never know. The promise of the new life to be born—made on the day she met her end, eight months before—had been broken; the hope that had filled my heart that day had turned out to be a flash in the pan. On that spring day grief took root in my heart, a grief that could never be effaced.

———∞———

Later, in private, a nurse who used to be my colleague told me that she'd seen Deping weeping in the corridor while I was alone with my dead infant, wailing in the ward. And Taohua said that my father-in-law had prowled the empty flat from the moment I was admitted to the hospital until Deping returned home with his heartbreaking news, and to take him to the morgue. "It was the longest time I saw Mr Dai Senior stay at home," Taohua added.

I did suspect that sorrow had struck my father-in-law and Deping as sharply as it did me. But neither of them allowed their pain and fatigue to show. Instead they methodically dealt with the aftermath of the incident. While I wallowed in my own grief like a walking ghost, they quietly stowed the layette away, skirted around the subject of children, and, with actions rather than words, demonstrated how to move on with life in a temperate manner.

Then, as if the loss of my newborn wasn't enough, a month later the company that had employed me decided that my depression made me unable to work well, and I lost my job. My father-in-law and Deping supported me, suggesting that I make a virtue of necessity and take time to recuperate. But I felt I was staggering through my life with all purpose lost. I didn't want to do anything but curl up in my bed and stare at the ceiling, my mind paralyzed, as if time had frozen for me at the moment my baby boy's breath ceased.

Taohua submissively ministered to me for some time. But one day she ran out of patience with my lying around, and insisted that I get out of the bed and eat at the dining table with her. I obeyed her only because I had no strength to tolerate her

THE ENVELOPES

ear-splitting voice as she ranted on about spoon-fed city girls. Slouching at the table, I ate mechanically. It felt as if I were chewing wax.

"I have no appetite for these tasteless dishes," I grumbled, wondering when Taohua's cooking had become so bland.

"Tasteless?" Taohua frowned as she quickly sampled each dish. "No, there's no difference in my food. I've used the same recipes and cooked them the same way. Maybe it's your taste buds that have changed."

I looked down at my plate without responding, and we ate in silence for a while. Finally Taohua opened her mouth again. "Miss, I can't keep it to myself—I have to speak up. Please don't tell me off. I know that it's a horrible experience, to have your child die at birth. I know I was lucky. But in the country, a baby's death isn't rare. A woman in the village near mine lost two babies before she had the third one, finally healthy. Okay, maybe our country people's lives are cheaper than—"

"I get your point, Taohua," I said brusquely, cutting her short. "But I need more time."

"Then good." She smiled at me. "Miss, I know you're tough."

We relapsed into silence, concentrating on our food. I made an effort to eat as much rice and vegetables as I could, washed down with soup.

After a while Taohua, ever the chatterbox, could no longer restrain herself. "Miss," she said with great caution, "I'm a bit curious about... about what happened to the baby."

"Beats me, Taohua." I avoided her eyes, but I wasn't irritated.

"Did you sneak a red packet to the doctor?" she breathed, as if she was afraid that a third person might be in the room, listening.

"Why should I have?" I asked, somehow nonplussed. I'd never heard the words "red packet" come out of Taohua's lips.

"What do you mean, Taohua? You know what a red packet is?"

"Of course. With money inside." She clucked. "If you don't give a red packet to the midwife in our village, you won't get much help delivering a baby. But during my time, it wasn't like that. In those days, people always lent a hand to one another. Who knows when red packets traveled from city to countryside — but nowadays, without money, you get stuck. I'm wondering... perhaps they didn't save your baby because they got no red packets from you."

I shot her a stern glance. "Oh, don't talk like that, Taohua."

"I'm sorry," she said hastily. "I knew you wouldn't offer a red packet. Mr Dai Senior never took those envelopes. I know everyone in this family is upright."

"Please drop the red-packet topic," I said, raising my voice a little.

"Okay," she said, but after taking a mouthful of soup, she went on. "I think it was only the decision of the King of Hades, who determines that one lives for centuries and the other only hours. If the King of Hades wants one to die today, one can't live till tomorrow. Being unhappy doesn't do yourself good. Having it in for the King of Hades does no good to anyone, for we can't stop his decision..."

Her words touched a raw nerve. *What if I'd had the opportunity to consult a more experienced and efficient doctor when my intuition told me that there was something abnormal about my pregnancy? My son might've had a chance to live,* I voicelessly protested, hearing Taohua's theory about death.

"How can we know what the King of Hades' decision was?" I heard myself asking.

"Ah?" Taohua looked confused.

"Forget it," I muttered. Pushing away my plate, I rose from the dining chair and shuffled back to my bedroom.

7

In late July 2006, thanks to Taohua's well-meaning stridency, I eventually forsook lounging in bed and started to potter around the apartment. That seemed to lift the spirits of my father-in-law and Deping, and I began to discern a little mirth in their dinner-table conversation. Several days later, Deping left to attend an international academic exchange in the United States. He'd been preparing day and night for quite some time—in hindsight, I believe it was his way to release his pent-up feelings about our late son.

Almost simultaneously, Taohua asked for three days' leave to escort Meihua back to the village for the summer holidays. My father-in-law suggested that I accompany them—for some relaxation in the countryside, he said, though the subtext was clear; he hoped the trip would distract me from my misery. I accepted, conjuring up the inviting pastoral scenes in Hayao Miyazaki's anime creations: a patchwork carpet of rice paddies, stretching toward the horizon as if they could merge into the blue sky; grassy slopes spattered with colorful wildflowers, tilting skyward as if to lead one up to kiss the passing, puffy clouds; wisps of cooking smoke spiraling from the chimneys of cottages nestled in the woods, where fairies had just stealthily done their magic to decorate the dining tables.

HASU AUGUST

It was early in the morning of a hot summer day when Taohua, Meihua, and I set off. At the city terminal we boarded an air-conditioned coach, which rocked along the roads around six hours before arriving at the closest town to Taohua's village. The town's main road, flanked by low-rise buildings mostly constructed of prefabricated slabs of concrete, would've been called an alley in my city. Along it, various shops plied for trade. Taohua took us to one of these, a dumpling stall, for a late lunch.

Perched on a rickety stool, I looked at the ground below me, scattered with crumpled tissues, broken chopsticks, dirty liquid, phlegm, and food scraps a dog was licking up, and asked if we might eat at a cleaner stall.

Taohua smirked, glancing at the shop owner, and lowered her voice. "Same everywhere, Miss. You'd better get used to the countryside." Then she said more loudly that we should eat our fill, as we had a long journey ahead.

I picked at my dumplings while Taohua and Meihua wolfed theirs down. At last they were satisfied, and we took up our backpacks and hit the road.

The town was small, with only a few narrow side streets branching off the main road. Farther along, unexpectedly, a couple of new ten-story blocks of flats came into view, but most of the units seemed unoccupied. We passed an inconspicuous grilled entrance, which Taohua told us led to the town's primary school, as announced by the once-bold characters, now faded, on a pocked wooden board at one side. I stopped and squinted through the gate, a little surprised at the place's forlorn look. A ramshackle two-story building faced a small, bare playground, parched in the midday sun. Nobody was in view, probably due to the summer holidays.

Hearing Taohua calling me, I turned my head and found

THE ENVELOPES

that she and Meihua were waiting for me on the street corner. I hurried to catch up, and we rounded the wall of the school and walked onto a cement-paved path winding up to a hill.

"Where are we going?" I asked, confused. Meihua was already trotting up the hill ahead of us.

"To the village," Taohua said.

I hesitated. "We have to climb over this hill?"

Advancing slowly, Taohua added, "Yes, Miss, and the mountain after the hill."

"Isn't there a road where we can take a bus or something else to your village?" I asked, a little unnerved. "Or are we taking a short cut?"

"Miss"—Taohua stopped and pointed ahead—"this is the only way to our village. The road stops at the town. From there, people have beaten paths to the villages scattered through the mountains. There're twelve or so of them, as far as twenty kilometers away." She started walking again, a little faster.

I hurried to keep up, since I had no other choice. "How many people live in all those villages?"

"Over one thousand, when I left for the city."

"That many villagers hoof it all the way to town?" I felt tired just thinking about it. "Why aren't there proper roads connecting all the villages and the town?"

"You're asking me? But I've got nobody to ask." Taohua made a comically pouty face, and then laughed. "It's just the way it is. You've never been to the countryside, have you?"

I said nothing, steeling myself to endure her teasing.

"I'm sorry," she said, backing off. "I know you're not a pampered city girl."

"Well, I just didn't expect this." I stopped for a moment, a little out of breath. "I did go on a hike on the outskirts of our city, but that was a long time ago."

HASU AUGUST

Bringing up the rear, I labored up the hill, the idyllic images of country life I'd conjured up slowly fading. Eventually the paved path gave way to a dirt trail. Just as I was beginning to feel at the end of my endurance, a scene enchanting enough to rival my anime fantasies opened up below us, and we paused to drink it in. Sweeping around from the other side of the town, a river curved below us, its swift water glinting in the sunlight. Behind it, a green mountainside rose steeply, bright emerald against the blue sky.

"Years back, the river so full of fish that you could often see them jumping out of the water—even onto the bank," Taohua said. "But now there're hardly any left. Nobody knows exactly why, but it happened after the building boom started in the town."

She chattered on in this fashion with inexhaustible energy, walking slowly to keep pace with me, as we set out on again along a well-beaten path, winding on before us through low shrubbery with scattered white gardenias and some colorful flowers. The strong scent of the gardenias, the sharp green smell of herbs and grass, even a whiff of something rotten, all blending together to fill my nostrils—pleasant or not, it was so different from the smells in the city I'd been so used to... Soon the scenery had lost its enchantment for me, as I bent my head and slogged along. The sun was hot and glaring with no trees overhead. The trail turned and twisted as we very slowly climbed, ascending and then descending, over and over. It seemed as if it would go on forever.

After we'd trekked for what seemed like hours, I began to see the trail streaked and dotted by wobbling shadows. A breeze had sprung up, cooling me down from head to toe. "See," Taohua said brightly, "we've already reached the mountainside."

I stopped in the shade of a tall, dense tree to rest, panting for

THE ENVELOPES

breath. Ahead, the trees — shame on me, I could hardly name any, though my coming from the 'city forest' of skyscrapers shouldn't be an excuse — grew taller and thicker. Meihua, like a jolly fawn, scampered into the woods, quickly nearly disappearing from view.

"Slow down!" Taohua shouted at her back. "It's dangerous! Come back here!"

Meihua returned in a sulk, dragging her heels as Taohua started telling her about some close shaves she'd had with snakes crossing the trail. A chill crept through my backbone, and I quickened my pace.

"Now I can see how there was no way to get you to a hospital when you were expecting, Meihua," I broke in hastily, hoping to ward off any more stories about scary creatures. "This path isn't even wide enough for two full-grown people to walk side by side."

"Well, the path used to be much wider than it is now, because it was more used. The fewer people walk on it, the narrower it becomes."

"It's true we haven't run across a single other soul this whole time. The one-child policy must've really cut down the population out here."

"Oh, it's nothing to do with the policy at all —" She broke off. "Meihua! What did I say? Slow down and stay with us!"

"What do you mean, nothing to do with the policy?" I asked, puzzled.

She laughed. "We country people don't care a jot about the policy. We still make babies as many as we want."

"Doesn't that mean that there're a lot of children now illegally living in the country?"

"Yes, there're some. But most families manage to get their kids legally registered in their villages, one way or another. If they didn't, their kids couldn't go to school."

"Then why are there so many fewer villagers?"

"Almost everyone between twenty and fifty years old has gone to make money in cities, like me. Only the old folks and some of their grandkids — people like my parents-in-law and my daughter Lianhua — are left. The old folks don't walk these paths every day — only the children who have to trek to the school in town."

"That's a long way for a child!" I cried, glancing at my wristwatch. "We've been walking over an hour."

"Look at Meihua. Kids seem to run a little faster than you." Taohua grinned at me. "It takes children less than two hours to get from our village to town — though it's true that the journey from some of the other villages is longer."

"Well, I'm not very fit," I admitted. "But a two-hour walk is still awfully long, and it's not safe. Did you do that when you were small?"

"There was a school in our village when I was young. But now there're less kids left, and they say it doesn't make sense to have a school in every village for just a few children. The school we passed in town serves all the villages around, as well as the town itself."

"No one fought against having their schools closed down?"

She shrugged. "Some people did cry foul, but it was no use — the village officials said there was no money to run the schools."

I gaped at her, still in disbelief. "In other words, Lianhua will have to walk all this way to school every day?"

She sighed. "Some families let their kids take up farming at home. Oh, I don't want to think about it now. I'll admit, Miss, I'm troubled... I don't know whether to insist that Lianhua goes to school in town or let her stay at home to help her grandparents." She rubbed her eyes, and said again, raising her voice, "I don't

THE ENVELOPES

want to think about it now."

I could only stare at the ground, at a loss for words. But Meihua halted, spinning on her heel to face us. "Ma," she begged, "Can't my sister live with us? You promised before. Ma, I want to be with her."

"Saying 'I want' doesn't help," Taohua said, sniffing. "We don't have enough money to keep her in the city. We spend everything on your schooling. Cut out that racket now, let's move along!"

Wordlessly, Meihua pursed her lips and stamped her feet. Shouldering her aside, Taohua began to stride ahead.

I stepped forward, holding my hand out toward Meihua. "Come on, your sister is waiting." She only turned away and loped off to overtake Taohua.

In silence we filed along the path. And for the first time that day, my ears were filled with the sounds of breezes whispering, trees rustling, birds chirping, water flowing, my clumping footfalls and the lighter ones of the two ahead of me—all fused into a kind of march, the music of returning home. And as I listened, I thought about Madam Sai and her unfulfilled dream, of building a school in Taohua's village.

After some time, the trail leveled out and broadened. Squares of fields straggling along the gentle slope on either side. Taohua paused, and looked back to hail me, "Miss, here we are."

Meihua was already pelting toward several tile-roofed adobe houses scattered on the hillside, against a backdrop of tall bamboo—well, that was the only plant I recognized. "Piggy! Piggy!" she called out as she ran, "Where are you? I'm home!"

I shoot a quizzical look at Taohua, and she clarified, "Piggy is the pet name for Lianhua."

"Why Piggy?" I said, secretly amused. "It's not a girlish name."

She cackled. "We nicknamed her Piggy because she cost us a fat pig we had raised for the Spring Festival."

"You sound as though you bought her from someone, instead of giving birth to her in the van."

"Of course she is my own baby. But the one-child policy says she shouldn't have been born. When she was one, we sent her from the city back to our village. To have her legally registered, we had to pay a fine. People from the village family planning office came here to collect the money, but we had none then. They saw our pig—a very good, big one—and took it away, in lieu of cash. It seemed like we swapped our pig for Lianhua. That's why we call her Piggy, in memory of the animal that was sacrificed for her."

I gaped at her. "Oh, that cannot be true."

She shook her head, motioning me to follow her. "You city girls know nothing about how things work in the country."

The houses were nothing like the cottages of my fantasy. They were built of plastered mud brick, not wood; in places the plaster had fallen away, exposing the brickwork and giving them a forlorn, fragile look. There was nobody in sight; even Meihua had disappeared.

Murmuring that her parents-in-law must be working in the fields, Taohua led me into the nearest house. A wood-fired earthen oven stood on one side of the kitchen, across from a square, wooden table flanked by several stools. There were two bedrooms, each furnished with a sizable bed and a wardrobe. The furniture all looked old enough to have come out of the ark, yet it was solid, with fine craftsmanship. The floors, made not of cement but a mixture of stone and earth, were rough and uneven. Nothing in my world had prepared me for such a primitive dwelling, though I could dimly recall seeing something like it in a movie about the hard life of the people, before the Chinese

THE ENVELOPES

Communist Party's reign.

The worst came when I asked where the restroom might be, and Taohua led me outside to an outdoor latrine, sheltered only by bamboo screens.

I was still reeling from the shock of this uncivilized sanitary facility, when Meihua appeared, bringing with her Lianhua. The six-year-old girl bore a striking resemblance to her mother. Her pellucid dark eyes shone with innocent curiosity. At intervals she wiped her perspiring forehead with the back of her hand, which she then quickly dried on her t-shirt, and she hid her mouth in her hands when she smiled, as if to hide her teeth. An urban soul, seeing these mannerisms, might think her a bit simple. Yet somehow to me she felt like a ray of sunshine, making the dreary house seem suddenly cheerful and welcoming.

I followed Lianhua out of the house, my nervous tension melting away as we scattered corn for the hens and roosters in her charge. We looked all around the house for the green-eyed cat that had gone missing, gathered leafy weeds to feed to her buck and doe rabbits, and stroked a litter of their fuzzy babies. Then we went out to the fields and picked vegetables for the dinner table. Such simple pleasures easily occupied the rest of the afternoon.

When night fell, though, and we were sitting around the table, eating the rice congee Taohua had prepared with the greens Lianhua and I had picked, I made another discouraging discovery: there was neither tap water nor a shower. Suddenly I felt acutely conscious of my sweaty and smelly self.

Taohua drew water in buckets from the well in the yard, and heated it on the stove until it was lukewarm. Then, using opaque plastic sheets, thin bamboo stalks, dried-mud bricks pierced with holes, and a few other odds and sods, she expertly erected a temporary "bathroom" near the well, with a stool placed inside.

HASU AUGUST

Unenthusiastic about this arrangement, I first tried to disguise my reluctance as courtesy, objecting that Taohua's parents-in-law should go first. But they laughed and said they'd bathed in the river at the foot of the mountain. While I was dawdling, Taohua read my mind. She enclosed herself in the "bathroom," demonstrating to me that no parts of her body except her calves and feet were exposed to watchful eyes... Then, for the first time in my life, I soaped and rinsed myself in the moonlight of a summer night.

Afterward I squashed into one bed with Taohua and Meihua, under a mosquito net. The quietness of the country night only seemed to make my hearing more acute. I could distinguish every tiny sound: mosquitoes droning above my head, outside the net; some small creature skittering across the room, and something larger stomping outside the door; a squeak in the distance... As indifferent as I was to the hustle and bustle of the city, I could hardly tolerate this mountain village's slightly sullied serenity, in the same way that, as a nurse, I could harden myself to the bliss or distress I saw in the maternity wards, but could not deaden the pain of losing my son.

I turned over gingerly, trying not to rouse those sleeping beside me. I didn't succeed.

"Miss, I know you can't sleep," Taohua whispered. "I'm sorry we're unable to offer you comfort."

"You don't have to feel sorry," I murmured.

"Here, we don't have all the things you're used to in the city. We have only unpolluted air and plain fresh food. We live off the land."

"I'm fine. I—I'm just not used to the bed," I said, a bit sheepishly. "Though the bed is not bad."

"My man handmade the bed frame. Actually, he crafted all the furniture in the house." There was pride in Taohua's voice.

THE ENVELOPES

"He is well known for his skill in the villages. I still call him 'Carpenter' at home..."

Taohua seemed to be in a talkative mood. Giving up on sleep, I decided I might as well play along. "How did you meet him, your Carpenter?" I asked.

"A matchmaker arranged the meeting. I'm from a neighboring village, about ten kilometers from here. In those days, many people admired his carpentry."

"And you were one of his admirers?"

"No—I didn't know him. My father brought me here to meet him and his parents."

"Then you fell in love with him at first sight?"

"No such thing. I had no idea what love was. But my father said Carpenter wanted to marry me, and that was it. Carpenter was bold. After I gave birth to Meihua, he took us to the city. He was determined that he'd give the kid a good education and make us a better life."

"And you began to take a shine to him then?"

"I tell you, Miss, I still have no idea what love is. That's the stuff of you city people. We only live our daily life together."

"No way. What keeps you together, if there is no love between you?"

"It was arranged that Carpenter and I would marry. Later, when we had kids, we formed a family bond. I just know we have to work hard together to make our living as a family... But we still can't afford schooling for both kids." She sighed, and when she spoke again her voice was troubled. "I have no idea what to do with Lianhua. She'll be seven next year..."

"There must be a way out," I consoled her.

"Life doesn't seem easy for anyone. You lost your baby... but sometimes I think I should never have given birth to Lianhua, if we're unable to make her a good life. It might've been better for everyone if she'd not been—"

I cut her off. "Don't say that, Taohua."

"I'm sorry. I shouldn't have mentioned your baby. And I really love Lianhua. She gives us so much fun. As her mother, I owe her love, care... everything. I'm desperate to have her live with us and go to school..."

"Shush," I said, alarmed. Meihua, who lay next to me, had begun to wriggle a bit.

We fell silent. Taohua rolled over on her side, and soon soft snores announced that she was asleep. But I couldn't sleep; the voice in my head would not let me rest. *If I'd had a chance to consult an excellent doctor, my son might have lived. But if my son were alive, I wouldn't be in this village, realizing how many things in my life I take for granted. No, I wish my son had lived, whatever price I had to pay. I wish he could've brought to my life all the things I've never experienced before...*

All the next morning, Taohua worked with her parents-in-law in the fields while Meihua grudgingly did her schoolwork at the square table. Taohua had drummed it into her that she must finish all the exercises on time, as her teachers had emphasized right before the summer holidays. Periodically I checked on Meihua's progress, as her mother had asked me. The rest of the time I followed Lianhua around, acting as her assistant as she did her chores, cleaning up the yard, the rabbit nest, and the chicken's coop, feeding and watering her animals.

We were both in the yard when I heard a soft *mew, mew*, too faint to tell where it was coming from. "Listen," I said to Lianhua, and we held our breath and sat still for a while. There was no sound but a dog barking in the distance. Then Lianhua told me that her green-eyed cat—the cat she'd been looking for when we first arrived—had been mysteriously vanishing for a while. The cat had grown round, with rolls of fat, and then disappeared. When it finally showed up again, it was much thinner.

"Maybe she felt lonely and went out to find her kind to play with," Lianhua said. "But she can't find enough food, so she comes back from time to time."

A little before noon, Lianhua's small flock of hens began squawking loudly, one after another. Seeing how this startled me, she giggled and tugged me to the coop, where she reached into the nest box.

"Here's what all the noise was about," she said, and put an egg in my hand. As I stood holding this smooth, round form, which still held the warmth of the hen, I was overcome with a sudden ineffable joy.

At noon, Taohua and her parents-in-law came back. They cooked a fresh-egg dish as a treat to me as their guest; otherwise, they usually sold the eggs in town on market day. After lunch everyone had a snooze, waiting until the midday heat wave eased off.

Probably because I'd hardly slept a wink the night before, I was sleeping like a log when the sound of someone crying and raving outside abruptly roused me. In a daze, I swung out of the bed. Reaching the doorway in several long steps, I was flabbergasted by the chaotic scene in the yard before me. Lianhua was laying about with a stick, trying to hit the cat, while Taohua clasped her from behind, and managed to keep the cat away. Two baby rabbits lay motionless by their feet. The cat skedaddled to a corner of the wall and crouched there, meowing, almost yowling. Lianhua dropped the stick, plopped down on the hot ground, and scooped up one of the rabbits in her hands. "Evil pussycat!" she wailed. "Evil pussycat killed my bunnies..." She sobbed miserably.

Taohua made threatening gestures toward the cat, which finally fled, though it hesitated, looking back longingly at the rabbits, for a moment.

I went up to Lianhua and took her into my arms, using my handkerchief to wipe away the tears and sweat from her face. Taohua squatted down to examine the baby rabbits. "It's strange," she mused. "Our cat's caught rats and sometimes birds... But I never saw it raid a rabbit's nest."

"Isn't that your pet cat, the green-eyed one?" I asked.

"Right. But really strange... After attacking the bunnies, it didn't run off... Piggy, did you see how the pussycat killed the bunnies?"

Lianhua shook her head. "I, I saw the pussycat caught a bunny by, by the scruff of its neck," she sobbed. "The, the other bunny on, on the ground."

"The cat's teeth didn't tear the bunnies' flesh, I think," Taohua said slowly, fingering the dead body of the other rabbit. "It looks like they were choked by the way the cat caught them."

I had no time to make sense of Taohua's words; at that moment Meihua began screaming, "Ma! Piggy! Ma, come here!" Scooping up the baby rabbit, Taohua sprang to her feet and ran toward a small separate building next to the house, which, Taohua had told me the day before, was a disused pigsty. Lianhua and I went in hard on her heels. Beside bales of hay and a mound of dry sticks, a bamboo ladder led up through an open trapdoor to a loft. Meihua was descending the ladder as we came in. Reaching the bottom, she moved aside to give way to her mother. "Ma, there is something up there."

Taohua set the dead rabbits down on the floor, snatched up a long, thick stick, and, holding it in her hand, nipped up into the attic and out of view. We could hear rustling and crackling sounds, as if she was rummaging through something. Then she said loudly, "Aya! You won't believe what I'm seeing here."

We all looked up at the opening, but couldn't see anything.

"I saw it," Meihua said in an exaggeratedly menacing tone. She paused dramatically, opening her eyes wide as they swept from the attic to Lianhua and me. "It looks... like a... Eek!"

Lianhua gulped. My skin crawled, and it felt as if my hair was standing on end.

Just then Taohua's face, dampened by perspiration, appeared in the opening overhead. "It's a snakeskin," she said calmly. "A snake must've sloughed it off here. It's intact."

"I want to see it! I want to see it!" Lianhua jumped up and down.

"I'm afraid it'll scare Auntie Bai to death," Taohua hedged, smiling at me.

"Well, I'm ready to take fright." I nerved myself to make a stand.

Taohua's face disappeared again. In a few seconds we saw a stick slowly move into the opening, a brown, curled snakeskin dangled from its end. Despite myself, I recoiled in horror, but both girls stepped forward eagerly. "Wow!" said Lianhua.

"It's a pretty snakeskin," said Meihua. "What are we going to do with it, Ma?"

Taohua was still out of sight. "You can go ask your grandma and grandpa later," came her disembodied voice. After a pause, she went on more somberly, "I've thought through why the cat killed the baby bunnies. I've found these... Look!" Taohua's solemn face emerged, and then her raised hand, a pinch of soft yellow fur held between her fingers. "There's a nest," she added, "with some more strands of cat fur in it. The cat must've carried straw in its mouth to build the nest up here, and then it kittened... I'm coming down now."

"That must be right—I thought I heard a kitten cry," Meihua said while Taohua was climbing down the ladder, "when I was doing my homework in the house this morning."

"Auntie Bai heard it, too," Lianhua put in. "Ma, you saw kittens up there?"

"No, not even one." Taohua placed the snakeskin on the floor and picked up the baby rabbit. Holding it in her cupped hands, she said sadly, "Piggy, baby bunnies aren't the only unlucky ones. I think the snake swallowed the litter of kittens in the attic when the mother cat wasn't there."

Looking appalled, both girls goggled silently at their mother.

"When she came back," Taohua went on, "the mother cat couldn't find her kittens. She must've been out of her mind with worry. She must've searched everywhere, and then decided the baby bunnies must be her kittens."

"But why did the pussycat kill my bunnies?" Lianhua broke in, her eyes shimmery with tears.

"The mother cat didn't mean to kill them. She thought they were her kittens and just wanted to take them back to her nest. That's why she picked up the baby bunny the same way she'd carry a kitten, by the scruff of the neck. "But bunnies are different from kittens, and the way the mother cat carried them unfortunately throttled them."

"But my bunnies died. It's still the pussycat's fault," Lianhua grumbled, staring at the limp rabbit still in her hands. "I hate the pussycat."

"Piggy, it's not the mother cat's fault. Don't hate the mother cat. She wanted to love the baby bunnies as her kittens. It's just an accident. The kittens and baby bunnies died because that was their fate. It was the decision of the King of Hades."

"What is fate?" Lianhua asked, her voice softer. "Who is the King of Hades?"

THE ENVELOPES

"It's something out of everyone's control. You'll get it when you grow bigger," Taohua said, sounding almost bored. She patted Lianhua on the head. "Piggy, get on with your work. Take care of your bunnies, and they will make more babies for you."

As I followed the others out, I looked back at Meihua. She was still standing there silently, staring in disgust at the snakeskin she'd been so happy about, lying at her feet on the floor.

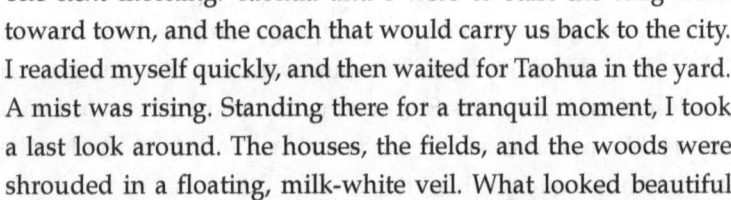

The next morning. Taohua and I were to start the long walk toward town, and the coach that would carry us back to the city. I readied myself quickly, and then waited for Taohua in the yard. A mist was rising. Standing there for a tranquil moment, I took a last look around. The houses, the fields, and the woods were shrouded in a floating, milk-white veil. What looked beautiful yesterday was not getting prettier. What seemed ugly was not becoming nastier. Only the border between the pleasant and the unpleasant was now blurred by the veil of mist... And I heard Lianhua blubbering in the room — probably because she was told that mother could not take her to the city.

Taohua came out of the house, followed by her daughters. Lianhua tried hard to hold back her tears, to no avail. Seeing her still sobbing, wiping her cheeks with the backs of her hands, I felt my own eyes grow moist. To pacify Lianhua, Taohua allowed the two girls to walk a short distance to see us off.

Taohua led the way, while I brought up the rear. The two girls, hand in hand, walked between us. After a short while, the mist began thickening. Taohua halted and enjoined Meihua to take her sister home, warning them against snakes.

Turning back, Meihua said abruptly, "The snake is evil."

"If you don't provoke it, it won't harm you," Taohua advised.

"The snake is evil," Meihua insisted, "because it ate the

kittens, and—"

"Enough!" Taohua cut her short, shooting her a dirty look. "We have no time to waste on your nonsense."

"Oh, come on. Why not have her let off steam?" I gave Taohua a nudge in the ribs. "She's probably smoldered for a whole night."

Taohua became quiet, keeping her temper. As Lianhua looked up at her elder sister, Meihua burst out, "If the kittens were not eaten, the baby bunnies wouldn't have died. It was the snake that killed both."

"Well," I said, somehow feeling obliged to comment, "the snake might've starved to death if it had nothing to eat. If that had happened, would the cat or the rabbit have been evil?" I sharply closed my lips. All three of them now fixed their eyes in befuddlement on me. Realizing that I had to clarify, I went on a little uncertainly, "I—I—I mean, the cause for someone's death is—is rather complicated. There might be no evil. It just happened. Like Taohua said before, it was an accident."

"Even if the snake was hungry," Meihua objected, "it shouldn't have slipped in and swallowed the *kittens*. Kittens are too small to fight back. Why didn't it try to eat the ma cat? The ma cat would pounce on and crush it, I promise. The snake is the evil hand that makes all these troubles. I won't forgive—"

"Stop blathering now, Meihua!" Taohua snapped. "Auntie Bai and I will be late for the coach." Jogging both girls' arms, she said to Meihua, "Go back now! Take care of your sister! And remember to finish all your schoolwork before I come back to fetch you!" Meihua nodded and gripped Lianhua's hand. They turned back toward the village. Soon they had melted away into the mist.

Taohua and I resumed our walk. The mist was turning into fog. The river down in the valley and the mountains beyond it

THE ENVELOPES

were disappearing in the haze. But the water sounded as if it were roiling, louder than it did two days ago. Taohua walked on quickly, as if unaware of me. As I hurried on to keep her in sight, my mind raced. Just now, it hadn't been Meihua but *me* who was so eloquently speaking to about the "accident". I could not forget that day, not so long ago, when she'd tried to argue me out of the abyss of grief. She'd said that my son had lived just one day by the decision of the King of Hades. Now I understood that, just as the children had imputed the death of their beloved little animals to either the cat or the snake, in my heart I'd harbored a grudge against my father-in-law, who'd declined to exert an influence that I assumed would give my baby a chance of survival. To my parents, who had occasionally visited me during my pregnancy, but later continually questioned the cause of my newborn's death, I'd flanneled and waffled. Nevertheless, I'd stored up resentment somewhere in me, resentment against my father-in-law and probably also against Deping. Neither had done anything wrong; they'd only held to their values. The cat's desperation to love her 'refound' kittens might be beyond Lianhua's comprehension, but I understood it all too well. Resentment had festered in me, preventing me from empathizing with my father-in-law. How sad he must've felt, losing his grandchild. How harshly he must've blamed himself, for his inability to do anything about the accident...

Raising my eyes to the path that zigzagged up and down before me in the thinning fog, I felt the terra firma under my feet. With a lighter and quicker stride, I fell in step beside Taohua. Looking a little surprised, she glanced at me and smiled. We silently walked on, the birds' chirping and the river's loud music in the background. A question came to my mind, and made me open my mouth. "Taohua, why haven't you sung at all since we came out on this trip?"

"The cramped and noisy city gets me down sometimes. I sing to make myself happy. But the sounds of nature here please me more—my singing can't rival them. I don't need it."

"Do you like it here more than the city?"

She paused. "Um… how shall I put it?" she said hesitantly. "Life here is boring. You know I'm a barely educated person. To me, life in the city isn't really interesting, either, but of course it's convenient. My man says that the city is exciting, and that there he has more choices, and that if our kids get a good education, they'll have more opportunities than he. They won't have to work in the fields their whole lives, just to fill their stomachs. But here I like the trees, the water, wild flowers in the spring, birds, the fresh air of the fields and mountains… It's a pity, now, the mountains no longer look like they used to. Many farmers have fled to the cities. Few are left to cut firewood for cooking, or keeping their families warm in the winter. The mountains are covered up with dead grass and wood, and then, in the spring, new plants seem to get no space to grow. Nowadays, you seldom see mountainsides covered with flowers… Aya, look!" She halted, pointing ahead. "The fog is almost gone, and we're reaching the town, Miss."

And indeed the fog had lifted. The buildings at the foot of the hill appeared, and the line between the concrete jungle of the town and the verdant landscape of river and hill was clearly visible now. Descending along the final stretch of dirt track that led to the cement path, I contemplated the empty school, forlorn among the empty new apartment buildings.

8

The trip to Taohua's village had not worked a miracle; it did not improve my spirits in leaps and bounds. But it was gradually undoing the crippling knots of emotion tangled around the death of my son. A few days after my return, for the first time I visited his grave. There I told him that he would forever live in my heart, and prayed that I could say goodbye to grief.

By the time Deping had returned from his summer academic exchange program, I'd begun to deliberate on my purpose in living on. I sorted out the things in my untidy bedroom, which I'd forbade Taohua from removing since I came back from the hospital after childbirth.

On the night that Deping and I retired to bed together for the first time after we'd lost our son, we renewed our habit of confabbing before falling asleep. After he told me a little about his three weeks in the United States, he asked, "How was your trip to the village?"

I shifted uncomfortably, unsure what to tell him. "I don't really know where to start," I admitted finally.

"Well...how about telling me about something that surpassed your expectations."

I thought for a moment. "Then you'll be disappointed," I said lamely.

"Nothing?"

"To say the least," I said crossly. "If I'd known I'd have to pee and shit in a latrine, and bathe in the open air, I'd rather have died than go there."

He chortled. "You were a little shaken up, huh? You really are a babe in arms."

"That's unfair," I said defensively. "I'm just one of many sad city people, struggling with adversity."

"Jade, no one in this world—man or woman, boy or girl—escapes some sadness. And I know not everyone can get over it. But you fought off a mugger. In my eyes, you've always been extraordinary. You have nerves of steel." He turned to throw his arm around my shoulder, his nose coming up to rub my cheek.

In the dim light, I squirmed slightly, twisting my head away. He pulled away and rolled onto his back, lying still. I harrumphed. "I could see the mugger, and I was clear about what I was fighting. But these past months, it's like I've been fogbound. It's made me feel helpless. I don't know how to fight the invisible. Maybe the trip did surpass my expectations in some way. It sort of turned the invisible visible…"

"A nice try for a tongue-twister, hey, hey," he said, and tactfully changed the subject. "Around two years ago my parents asked Taohua on some pretext to take them to her village. That was during the time my mother was planning to build a school, as I mentioned to you before. She stopped in town and visited the school there—she didn't have the physical strength to climb over hill and mountain to the village. Old Man, whose actual mission was to accompany Mother, went on her behalf, taking a field trip to survey the village, which then was home to over fifty families. Old Man described the conditions there as bad, but he said one thing did surpass his expectations…" His voice trailed away.

"And that was?"

THE ENVELOPES

"I thought you were already asleep."

I turned to look at him. "Oh, don't leave me in suspense."

"He said four-year-old Lianhua and her little friends made the run-down village feel as if it were teeming with life."

The words instantly evoked memories of my two days on the mountain. Yes, Lianhua! How could I have forgotten the way her fresh, unselfconscious nature delighted me! At six, she seemed like the only thing in the village that seemed to belong in Miyazaki's vision of country life.

My tongue suddenly loosened, I began to tell Deping all about the rambling town, the filthy streets, and the school building, so dilapidated in contrast to the brand-new blocks of flats. I told him about our exhausting hike along the river, the strangeness of Lianhua's nickname, the primitive living conditions, the drama of the cat, the rabbits, and the snake, and the dispute over which was the evil, Taohua's complaint about the abandoned mountains ... And when I'd told him all I could recall, suddenly it seemed as if my own telling had driven away the fog.

"Deping, I think I understand it now," I said. "Father wanted me to go with Taohua to her village to make me count my blessings... What do you say?"

In return, Deping gave me his rhythmic, reassuring snoring, and I suddenly realized I hadn't heard it by my pillow for quite some time. Then I recalled the end of my first date with Mr Dai Deping, whom I'd deemed so reticent. *Conversing with him was like playing a piano*, I'd thought then. *If I hit the right keys, he would return the melody.* But now it was as if our positions had reversed: I was like a piano that had fallen out of tune, but my husband held it steady and tapped on the keys, and the piano played an epic solo. And as I thought about my father-in-law and the trip he'd sent me on, I thought it sounded a final harmonious chord.

HASU AUGUST

In September 2006, three months after my baby's death, school began again. Taohua brought Meihua back from the village for her final year in elementary school. She told me she'd given her daughter a sound spanking, infuriated that she'd put off doing her schoolwork, instead spending her summer holidays playing with her sister and other village children. She complained that, unlike Lianhua, Meihua was a hard nut; when she was beaten, she never howled but just gritted her teeth. "Every time I cane her, I see tears swimming in her eyes, but they never roll down." Taohua sighed. "I never know what's spinning in her little head. She's just as tough as her father. Anyway, at least she sat up half the night doing her schoolwork, in the end."

It occurred to me that, since my son's death, we'd no longer been coaching Meihua at home. I apologized to Taohua for failing to keep our promise, and then asked whether we could begin again. She smiled and skated over my offer, saying her husband would get around to helping Meihua. Knowing that both my father-in-law and Deping were swamped with work, and that I needed to pull myself back together, I didn't insist. In any case, I hadn't had much contact with Felix in the past months.

My mind still swinging like a pendulum between desire and despair, I began to skim the help-wanted pages. Deping encouraged me tactfully, leading me into conversations in which he at first acknowledged the impact of our loss, but then veered into envisioning the years ahead, and our limitless opportunities. Sometimes, when no one else was around, he just cuddled me for a silent moment. In his arms, with my ear against his chest, I heard his robust heartbeat and wondered how it could be that sorrow had never discouraged him, but the question seemed too awkward to ask.

As far as Taohua was concerned, it was children, not love,

that held her and her man together, but in my childless marriage, I did believe in our love. Yet to my mother's harsh words before my wedding — *Then for what reason do you love him?* — I still had no answer. Love made possible the vow I took in the subway train after our marriage registration, to share life's joy and misery with Deping. Love was the hinge on which our shared life turned, including our sex life. But it does not ensure that all the questions should be asked and answered between the husband and wife.

Though by degrees I was emotionally recovering, I found that something inexplicable had happened to me. Whenever sexual feelings flared between Deping and me, I could feel myself split into two, as if my body were separating from my soul. My soul seemed to hang above my body, needling it, *Hey, you — what are you doing, looking for some diversion again?* My body, mortified at its failure to bear a healthy child, refused to cooperate with my soul in its craving for love and tenderness. During intercourse I would keep my eyes wide open, as if I were keeping tabs on the movement of my other self. I was uncertain whether Deping was aware of this eccentricity, especially during those times when my body vigorously interacted with his but my soul had just flown into the air. He never showed the slightest sign of disappointment or suspicion. The sense that I was somehow going behind his back made me feel uneasy, but I told myself that time would lend a healing hand.

In the end it was not the passing of time but a visit to City Normal that changed things. Deping's school recommenced in September. One day soon after that, at dinner, he brought up the subject of his heavy class assignments in the new semester. My father-in-law remarked in a jocular way, "Well, it would be a criminal waste of resources for someone like you, so full of beans, to sit idle. Little Jve, have you ever seen him lecture?"

I shook my head.

"But I'm left not much time to work on research papers," Deping said. "As I'm sure you know, under the current management, my chance at a professorship depends largely on the number of papers I can publish in quality journals."

"I wasn't aware that becoming a professor was that important to you," my father-in-law said calmly.

"It's not *that* important," Deping said. "But it's one of my goals. Without achieving it, I don't feel my career is complete."

"You're not even thirty-five, son. If you can't have your cake and eat it too, do the most valuable thing for society first—and from my standpoint, that's lecturing to the coming generation. Our country is long on theory but short on practice."

"Well said." Deping laughed. "So I have no other choice but to reach for the moon, becoming a super professor teaching in a classroom every day, ho, ho…"

"Go to it, son. You've never let me down."

Several days later, Deping had a solid day of classes. He rushed off to the university early, leaving his mobile phone and a stack of notebooks behind in the study. Before my father-in-law left for his own office, he asked me to take these things to Deping, who might need them for his class.

I took a taxi to the university and hared off to Deping's department, but I was too late; the administrator told me that his class had already started. I beseeched her to pass the lecturing materials to Deping. She looked at me, perplexed. "Professor Dai never brings materials to his class, though sometimes he uses a PC and projector to illustrate. But who are you?" Feeling deflated, I replied that I was Deping's wife. She smiled at me and added, "Everyone here admires his brain. He stores and retrieves data and information like a computer. Students all love his classes."

THE ENVELOPES

Returning her smile, I was about to leave when my mother-in-law's words flashed through my mind. "He is a very different person when standing on the dais and lecturing to an audience," she'd said.

I hesitated a moment. "Can I ask you a favor?" I asked the administrator.

———∽∽———

As I slipped quietly into the lecture theater, the audience exploded with a peal of laughter that startled me. The whole theater was heaving with people, but I managed to find a seat in the last row. At the front, on the dais, my husband was holding forth on the subject of the differences between Chinese and Western pedagogy.

There was, I soon realized, a world of difference between what was happening in this theater and the dreary classes I'd endured through all my days in schooling. Deping paced back and forth as he spoke. When he asked for the students' ideas, dozens raised their hands, and he pointed to one after another, allowing each a chance to speak. He stepped forward, listening to the students' propositions and then responding. He shifted right and left, mediating in a debate between two speakers. He even spun on his heels all the way around, hurrahing an idea or opinion... Sometimes his sonorous voice alone filled the theater. Sometimes it rang with gales of laughter, or resonated with discussions at various decibels... As he stood on the dais, radiating passion and wisdom, I saw my husband as a conductor, directing an orchestra of diverse voices, in music that lilted and swung.

Immersed in this concert of ideas, I replayed on the screen of my brain our first date, our wedding, our honeymoon, our loss of his mother and our baby... *He has fortified himself against sorrow* with his dedication to a cause, I thought. *His great heart extended far beyond our little family. That was why he could see the sun on rainy days, and feel a zephyr in the stuffiest room. Could this be the answer to my mother I'd failed to find? Could this be why I loved Deping at the deepest level of my psyche?*

When the class was dismissed, I remained in my seat, waiting as the audience drifted away. After a short exchange on the dais with several students, Deping ascended along the tiers, smiling at me as if he'd anticipated my appearance.

"What brings you here today?" he said, sitting down beside me.

"You don't look surprised."

"I was when I spotted you during the class."

"But you kept as cool-headed as your dad usually does. Oh, he asked me to send you these." I passed him the mobile phone and notebooks.

He grinned at me. "You didn't have to come here for this," he bantered. "I think you missed me, and couldn't wait to see me at home."

"You flatter yourself," I said, chuckling "Father was afraid that your lecturing would be severely handicapped without these things."

"But Old Man knows I don't bring my phone or papers to class," he said, looking a little puzzled. "Uh-oh. He's a little long in the tooth... Is he getting forgetful?"

But I knew it wasn't that. For a second time, I realized, my father-in-law had given me a push, made me stop shutting myself up at home to mourn while others were moving on with courage and faith. "Oh, no, I think Father is very thoughtful," I said. "Deping, I'm glad I came. Now I understand what Father meant about you being 'full of beans'. Your class was an eye-opener for me." I rose to my feet and edged toward the theater's

THE ENVELOPES

exit.

He walked along with me. "I have another three classes today," he reminded me.

I gave him a fond look. "Conductor Dai, I know you'll just coast to the last one of the day."

"Another new title for me? But why? Give me a clue." He blinked at me, a curious smile on his lips.

"There is no why." My face deadpan, I held out my hand. "I salute your energy. Where do you get it?"

Taking my hand as he pushing the door open, he chuckled. "I think I got it from Mother. The dais and the students just excite me..." He paused, his smile widening. "The dais, the students... I get it. That's why you were calling me conductor."

From that day on, I made a point of slipping into Deping's lecture theater from time to time, to listen to the piquant 'music' that freed his students' minds.

I had not been left to sink or swim, I finally understood. My father-in-law, my husband, and Taohua had all been, in their individual ways, helping me through. By early October of 2006, my self-reliance was burgeoning. Eager to make up for the time I'd wasted, I invested all my efforts in hunting for a job in which I could recommence my career in personnel. On another front, I was agreeably surprised to find my erotic pleasure restored during sexual intercourse with my husband. My soul and my body were patching things up, beginning to stay together in harmony.

In November I romped through an interview with Fred Cheung, then head of BrightLife China, and walked into the position of human resources manager. I was surely drawn by the company's name, which played on my own longing, though

HASU AUGUST

I was unfamiliar with the industry; BrightLife made safety products that protected employees from various risks at work. I had to work hard to sharpen up my rusty skills, but dealing with people was my forte, so I soon settled in. I soon noticed that all the managers who directly reported to Fred were women. It was hard not to notice that — Daisy Sweet would feel it was unusual, too, on her first day with BrightLife seven months later. But it took me a little while to become aware that my predecessor had been male, and that in hiring me, Fred had finally built his all-female team.

Despite my usual compulsion to dig out the truth — the compulsion that, years ago, had driven me to uncover the secret of my birth — I accepted this all-female team as a matter of personal preference. Still, I found one of the activities that Fred organized annually a bit peculiar. At the beginning of every year, he had a couple of hired coaches convey all the employees of BrightLife China — regardless of their religious beliefs — to a famous temple in the suburbs of the city, where they were expected to pray to the Buddha for the company's prosperity. Having been told that an eminent Buddhist monk in that temple had inscribed the enormous 愛 — the Chinese character for love — that hung behind Fred's office chair, I thought he must be a pious American Buddhist — as well as, by his own admission, keen on the music of South America.

When 2007 rolled around, I had to join the ranks of the worshipping crowd heading for the temple. Facing the enormous Buddha, in addition to fulfilling the requested yearly routine, I prayed that my family might have a life free of suffering.

———∞∞———

After the Spring Festival in February of 2007, Meihua entered her final semester of elementary school. Taohua and I had seen little of each other since I started working at BrightLife. In the morning, I was usually already on my way to the office when she arrived, and when I returned, she'd already gone, having left dinner ready on the table. The one time we did meet, she complained about Meihua, who was becoming more and more defiant, especially after the winter school holidays, during which she'd gone back to the village, and about her husband Wenwu, who, she said, cared for nothing but money. I tried to smooth her ruffled feathers, and in the end, she seemed to soften a little, acknowledging that Wenwu had to work hard to take care of the whole family.

On April 5, Deping and I returned home from work to an apartment that had not been cleaned, with no dinner waiting. I'd never known Taohua to fail to let us know if she couldn't come, and when I tried to call her mobile phone, it was not on. That fact somehow boded ill, and I became anxious. To ease my mind, Deping went off to Taohua's place while I stayed home to whip up supper, since my father-in-law would be coming back soon.

It grew late, and still I heard nothing from Deping. Finally, at my father-in-law's suggestion, we ate dinner while we waited for him. We hardly spoke during the meal; my nerves were jangling, and my heart was praying to the Buddha for everyone to be all right. My father-in-law also looked as if his thoughts were in a faraway place.

Finally we heard the door opening, and Deping walked in, looking as if he was in a trance. He hardly seemed to hear my greeting. I'd never seen him look so somber, not even when his mother died or when we lost our son.

Finally he pulled himself together and, hesitantly at first, told us the whole story. That morning, as she usually did, Meihua had gone up to the roof of the block where she and her parents lived to do her stretching exercises. When Taohua called out

HASU AUGUST

from the kitchen window that it was time to have breakfast and get ready for school, she'd lost her footing, perhaps because she was hurrying too much. She had fallen four stories to her death.

That night Deping soothed me into bed, but then he went to the study and stayed up late, talking quietly with his father.

———∞∞———

We told Felix what had happened, and together the three of us helped Taohua and Wenwu to arrange Meihua's funeral. Whenever we saw him, Wenwu looked numb, silently huddled in a corner as he watched the activities around him. Somehow it made me think of the cat, on that day in the village, crouched at a short distance, staring at the dead baby rabbits and the crying little girl. Deping and Felix tried to console him, but at home Deping and my father-in-law hardly spoke for days. I felt helpless, with nothing to do but yet again wait for time to heal all of our broken hearts.

Around two weeks after the funeral, Taohua returned. After she'd cleaned the apartment and cooked us dinner, she stayed to talk to us. I happened to be the first one to come home after work. With a wan smile, she told me that she had decided to quit the city and go back to the village.

Though I empathized, I was loath to see her go. Despite myself, I asked, "Will Wenwu leave with you?"

"No, he'll continue to work on the construction site."

I snatched at a glimmer of hope. "Will you be back some day?"

"I don't think so. I won't bring Lianhua to the city."

"But she'll get a better education here, once she's at schooling age. Will you send her to the school in the town?"

"I don't know. Miss, maybe I was wrong."

"Wrong? About what?"

THE ENVELOPES

She didn't answer for a moment, but instead took off her apron and fiddled with it. I sensed that something was troubling her beyond the fact of her daughter's death.

"Miss," she said finally, "I—I didn't get much education. I wanted my kids to have a better chance than I did. But now... now Meihua is dead. ... Maybe I was wrong to put so much pressure on her to study. Maybe I'm paying for it now—"

"It was an accident," I cut in. "Remember what you said before about my baby? Perhaps it was her fate."

"I don't know ..." She sighed, shaking her head wearily. "I don't know."

"What do you mean, Taohua?"

"I've been thinking... Our flat is tiny. There's no room to swing a cat. We found a space on the roof for Meihua to play, and she seemed to like it. Whenever she played her disappearing act, we always found her there. We weren't worried when she was up there. It was a safe place, unless... unless... she walked too close to the edge." Taohua's voice trailed away, and her brows wrinkled.

"I don't understand, Taohua."

She rose, instead of answering, and went to the entrance hall to fetch her bag. Sitting down again, she put the bag on her lap and rummaged through it, finally pulling out an exercise book. She flipped through the book and stopped at one page, staring down at it.

Finally she raised her head and looked at me. Her eyes were red. "Miss, when I was tidying away Meihua's things several days ago, I discovered this exercise book. She wrote in it the essays she was assigned at school, and then her teacher wrote remarks below each of the essays. I can't read all the characters, but I went through her essays and read as much as I could. The last one was dated three days before she fell down. It read ... It read like..." Her voice broke, and she put her head in her hands.

"May I read the essay?" I asked, gently rubbing her arm.

She nodded and handed me the book, open to a page headed with the bold title, "My Dream."

"My dream is to become a pile of shit that smells to high heaven," I read below. The sentence felt like a physical blow. I took a deep breath, composed myself, and read on.

> ... *Then I will stink my math teacher to death because he doesn't teach me about the problems I can't solve, and I fail exams. The uncle Dais liked answering my questions, but they work hard and have no time to teach me anymore.*
>
> *I will stink my Chinese teacher to death because she says my essays are bad and punishes me by making me copy out the text sentence by sentence for 100 times. Granny Dai praised my essays, but she is dead.*
>
> *I will stink my head teacher to death because he always gives long useless speeches but never stops teachers taking money from my ma and daddy for remedial classes.*
>
> *I will stink my classmates to death because they make fun of me and call me mountain tortoise. Felix says I am a lovely girl, and my younger sister likes playing with me, but I must study hard so I have no time to see them.*
>
> *I will stink the hospital people to death because they didn't save Auntie Bai's baby.*
>
> *I will stink the snake and all the evils alike to death because the snake caused the death of a litter of poor kittens and baby bunnies, and broke their mothers' hearts...*
>
> *And I will stink myself to death because I have stunk others to death. I touched Auntie Bai's tummy, and inside, her baby got sick. And because of me, my parents have no money for my younger sister to go to school.*

THE ENVELOPES

I will come to no good end... I just want to become a pile of shit that smells to high heaven."

In angry red ink characters below the essay I read, "You have a good imagination but very serious mental problems. Ask your parents to come to school to see me!!!"

My heart thumped painfully in my ears; my skin seemed to crawl. I could not put down the book. As if from far away, I heard Taohua saying diffidently, "There're several words I can't read. And I haven't told my man about this. But I know what the essay means."

"Did Meihua tell you that her teacher had asked to meet you?" I asked.

Shaking her head, she began to sniffle. "Silly girl, she... kept things to herself. She must've been afraid...I scolded her... She never cried in front of us. Silly girl... she was only twelve..."

Tears welled up in my eyes, and words failed me. All I could do was offer my shoulder for Taohua to cry on for a while. And for a moment, a memory flooded my head, so vivid it was as if I was back in the village, feeling Meihua's sleeping body moving beside me as Taohua whispered. I could hear Taohua's words. *Sometimes I think I should never have given birth to Lianhua, if we're unable to make her a good life. It might've been better for everyone if she'd not been* – Had Meihua been awake? Had she overheard her mother's words?

The front door opened, and we could hear shuffling noises from the entrance hall. Taohua quickly picked up the apron beside her, rose to her feet, and bolted into the bathroom to wash her tear-streaked face.

A moment later my father-in-law stepped into the room. "I saw Taohua's bicycle downstairs," he said. "I'm glad she's here – I've been wanting to talk with her."

HASU AUGUST

My father-in-law and Taohua were still shut up together in the study when Deping got home. Before he had a chance to open his mouth, I grabbed him and, laying a finger to my lips, pulled him into our bedroom. There, it poured out of me, without a break, everything I'd just learned from Taohua. He listened to me, from beginning to end, evincing no surprise.

"It read like a suicide note," I said at last. "What do you think?"

He paused for a moment, reflective. "Jade, I already suspected it that day, when I was there." He let out a breath and went on. "They took me to the roof and told me what had happened, but not much about how. I saw that the roof was level and dry, and that there was even a guardrail running around it. I wondered what Meihua was doing so close to the edge that she could've fallen despite the rail. But I couldn't think of any sign that she was suffering from a mental strain."

I thought for a moment. "That night, when you went to talk with Father after I went to bed, you told him about your suspicion, didn't you?"

"Yes." After a pause, he said, "It's a thing that Mother was always afraid of when she was alive. Several years ago, she stopped a high-school boy from killing himself just in the nick of time. Father must've been thinking, 'What if Mother were still around...?' This kind of tragedy just now happened under my eyes. It makes me doubt my cause... It makes everything I'm doing seem meaningless. No matter how hard I try there're some things I'm helpless to change in this society. Too few teachers are left who put their whole hearts into true education... and without teachers who really care, children will always become victims."

I remembered how quiet Deping and his father had been

lately. "This is what has been haunting both of you since Meihua's death, isn't it?"

"It's sad to see the gap between reality and my ideals."

"But Deping, don't blame yourself."

"I feel hurt yet helpless." He gave me a cynical smile. "It just makes me doubt the value of what I am doing."

"But can that be the justification for throwing in the sponge?"

"No, Jade, you're right." He brushed my cheek with his hand. "No, I have no reason to give up trying to make a difference at City Normal. Especially if there's a chance I could forestall another tragedy."

We both paused, hearing sounds outside the bedroom; Taohua and my father-in-law were coming out of the study. We went out to the entrance hall, where Taohua was packing up her things.

"Taohua," said Deping, "Jade told me you're leaving the city."

"She'll discuss it with Wenwu," my father-in-law jumped in before she could respond. "Taohua, Wenwu deserves to know everything. And tell him I'm available to talk with him, anytime."

She nodded, making a noncommittal noise. "I'll tell him all the things we've talked about. Thank you, Mr Dai Senior." The door closed behind her with a click.

My father-in-law stood gazing at the door. "Let's have dinner," he said finally, turning back to us.

"Did Taohua tell you about Meihua's essay?" Deping asked.

"Yes," he said evenly. I thought that was all he would say, but as we were sitting down at the dining table, he sighed. "I dreamed about Mama these several days."

"You must be missing her terribly," said Deping.

My father-in-law glanced at Deping. "Buck up, son. Keep on doing what you know you should. Mama just told me we've all got to do whatever we can."

HASU AUGUST

Taohua and Wenwu eventually made their decision; she would keep working for us, while he went back to their village to look after Lianhua, who was nearly seven now. She'd be starting school in four months. I never knew what my father-in-law had said to Taohua, but whatever it was, it seemed to be the main thing that changed her mind. I wasn't sure it mattered; I was just happy that she'd stay. My father-in-law, on his own initiative, made his bedroom into a dual-purpose room for reading and sleeping, and we converted the study into a bedroom for Taohua. We saw no need for her to rent an apartment, since she no longer had family living with her in the city.

As my father-in-law had hoped, Deping continued to throw himself into lecturing and researching in the field of pedagogy. I, for my part, tried to do the same with my job at BrightLife China, but Meihua's death had knocked the stuffing out of me. *Even if my baby son had lived,* I thought, *it would have been hard to believe in his future after this. Could I have survived the death of a child I had raised for over twelve years? Was there any justification for bringing a child into such a cruel world?*

These questions seemed too delicate to ask my husband. Perhaps that was why now, yet again, my soul once again seemed to split from my body whenever Deping and I made love.

Part Two

9

The volume of the television feels just right. It's loud enough to take the edge off being alone in the hotel room, yet soft enough to let me think. And it doesn't drown out the ring of my mobile phone. Deping rang me after midnight. I didn't notice that night was drawing on until he said he'd hesitated to wake me up at this hour. He'd called with bad news: Father had just been rushed to the hospital, and his final days were likely not far off. I had an impulse to tell Deping about my pregnancy, but my revived memories nipped the urge in the bud. In those memories, I'd just got to the moment of losing Meihua and, not long after that, of Daisy Sweet seeing the grief in my eyes on her first day with BrightLife. The death of my son and Meihua has been gnawing at me for years, but I've been unable to do anything beyond getting through my work at BrightLife every day. I'm still uncertain why my soul and my body remarried on that passionate night with my husband, weeks previously, at the end of my day of red lights. I have yet to reach a decision on what to do about the new life inside me. Nevertheless, my subconscious might've been yearning for a change, ever since Daisy embroiled me in her cause for BrightLife China. Meanwhile I had gradually realized what had been running in the depth of my family life, which seemed like still waters after the two tragedies.

THE ENVELOPES

———∞———

Daisy's short private talk with me at the welcome dinner, as well as her forthrightness, endeared her to me. On that first day I sensed that groundbreaking things would take place, but I couldn't imagine what or how, nor did I think I'd be involved. Then, probably, the housewarming party that she threw for all four of us female managers and Cathy, one month after she moved to our city, would begin bearing out her words, "By and large, truth finds me in time."

On the afternoon of that sunny Saturday, when I went to Daisy's rented house, Cathy was already there, helping Daisy arrange flowers, put together snacks, and cook the spaghetti with clams we were having for dinner. Located on a secluded street, the house was small, with French windows looking onto a tiny garden. Dominated by a blond wood table and chairs upholstered in pale shades, the living room was light and elegant. An upright piano stood unobtrusively in a corner. An easel set near the window held an unfinished charcoal drawing of roses, from the looks of it the same red and pink ones that covered the white trellis in the garden. The elegance of Daisy's home fascinated me as much as how she dressed. Her sense of style had consistency.

Rose, the sales manager, and Pearl, the marketing head, who seemed to stick together most of the time, were next to arrive. Edith, the supply chain manager, who was something of a loner, followed soon afterward. They exchanged pleasantries, admired the roses in the garden, then started to play cards, two against two.

Daisy and I were making salad in the kitchen when we heard Rose's voice rise sharply in anger.

"What's happening at the poker table?" Daisy whispered. "Sounds like Rose is on the warpath."

I shrugged. "She has a strong personality and a short temper."

"You've gotten the rough end of her tongue a few times, haven't you?" Daisy said as she tossed the greens in a big bowl.

I reached for the oil and vinegar. "Oh, sure. I don't think there are many people in the company she hasn't unloaded on once or twice."

Pearl was talking now, in a high-pitched, mocking tone. Daisy and I exchanged uneasy looks, bracing ourselves, but it was Cathy who spoke next, breaking the tension. "My, you're quite a team, you two," she said, her voice light and bantering. "Edith and I love to hear you matching wits."

Rose laughed, and after a moment Pearl joined in. Harmony seemed to have been restored.

"But Pearl is hardly a sympathetic listener for Rose," Daisy murmured, as if she were talking to herself. "Well, Cathy is so easygoing, and Edith so quiet."

We exchanged a conspiratorial smile, but I said nothing. Looking back down at the salad, I brushed a lock of hair back from my face, pushing it over my ear. Glancing over at me, Daisy said, "I thought I saw a scar on your forehead the other day — you hide it under your bangs, don't you? What happened?"

I told her about the incident with the mugger. She looked. "Gee, you have a bit of a temper too..." she said thoughtfully. "But seems like you picked your battle wisely." She turned back to put the finishing touches to the salad, and I went out to tell the others that the dinner was ready.

Dusk was falling by the time we'd set the table and brought in the meal. When the salad bowl was being passed around the table, Edith muttered, "I have difficulty eating Western food. I'm not used to it."

"Really?" Daisy smiled tightly. "I asked every one of you what you like and don't like before I decided on the menu, remember?

I don't recall you mentioning that then."

"You're the boss. I didn't dare say no." Edith smiled as she said this, but it was hard to tell if she was joking.

"Oh, poor Edith." Daisy laughed. "But actually, I'm not your boss. Fred is. Especially when off work, I'm just a person like you."

"Oh, poor Daisy," Cathy mimicked, "don't be fooled by Edith. We all know she's a finicky eater. She's just pulling your leg. She's not half as obedient to her boss as she claims."

"But we can't be like you, Cathy," Pearl defended Edith. "You studied aboard and were exposed to Western ideas. You may dare to challenge your boss."

"Fred is not a boss who can be challenged," Cathy retorted with a giggle.

"That may be true," Pearl agreed. "Otherwise, he wouldn't go around saying that women are usually obedient while it's hard to control men. And he walks the walk. Look at us — his management team is all made up of women."

"Wait a second," Daisy broke in. "It's sex discrimination to base a hiring decision on gender. In the States, a company could get sued for that."

"But we're in China. There's nothing about that in labor law here," I said. "Why should he care?"

"He's an American, isn't he?"

All four sniggered. "In terms of the language he speaks, absolutely, yes," said Pearl.

Looking at Daisy's wry expression, I wondered what the sniggering was about. "Fred told us at a company dinner that his family took him from China to the States when he was around ten. In his youth, Fred said, he was rather rebellious. He spent quite some time in South America, and fell in love with the local music there."

Daisy nodded thoughtfully. "Interesting…"

Edith prodded at her spaghetti with her fork, her expression sour. "Well, he may have a taste for South American music, but he behaves like a Chinese boss. He even asks all his employees to go to temple and pray to the Buddha once a year. I prefer to pray to my own God, thank you. Anyway, I don't go."

"It doesn't bother me," said Rose. "I believe in Buddhism. Besides, he organizes the activity for the good of our company."

"Fred really does that?" Daisy asked, slightly shaking her head. "Is it because he's Buddhist himself?"

"I think so," I said slowly. "I remember how proud he looked when he told me that the Chinese character for 'love' on the wall in his office embodied the magnificent bosom of Buddha, full of mercy."

This time Pearl, Edith, and Cathy chuckled. I shot Cathy a questioning look.

"Well," she said, "to my knowledge, that 'love' character in his office—"

"He can't even write it in Chinese," Pearl cut in.

"That's true," Cathy said. "Anyway, it's more of a *feng shui* thing."

"What does *feng shui* mean?" Daisy enquired.

Unexpectedly, it was Rose who answered. "To people who believe in it, it's an ancient art and science developed over thousands of years in China. The idea, put simply, is that the arrangement of the things around you generates either good or bad energy, which affects you in many ways."

Pearl added, "I've heard that *feng shui* is more closely linked to Taoism than to Buddhism, so actually it originates in China. But to people who don't believe in *feng shui*, it's just a superstition."

Cathy forked some pasta into her mouth. "Obviously Fred takes it as gospel," she said, after she'd swallowed it. "He asked me to find him a *feng shui* master who could balance the energies in his office, and assure him good fortune. It was Master Zhong who suggested that Fred commission that calligraphic love character from a monk in that temple. He also rearranged all the furniture."

"Has it been working for Fred?" Daisy asked, a trace of doubt in her voice.

"I think nobody except him knows," I said dryly. "After all, he's the one who believes in *feng shui*."

"Anyway," said Pearl, "Fred's swanky *feng shui*-protected office really puts yours and Waits' workspace to shame. I'm curious — when you accepted the job offer, did you think you'd be put in that small room next to Fred's office? It used to be a storage room. And I bet that Waits never imagined that the position of vice president for Asia-Pacific would earn him only a table in the meeting room, right outside Fred's office and yours."

"Well," Daisy said, grinning, "Waits and I would rather take it as a sign that we'll work hard and sacrifice so that BrightLife can thrive."

Most of her audience nodded approvingly, but Rose turned to Pearl, "To be fair, Pearl, we all know — well, all of us but Daisy and Jade, since they're still new — that it wasn't easy for Fred to fill the position of the general manager. His current status is the result of his blood, sweat and tears, working hard as an underdog. In the past two years —"

"Cut it out, Rose," Daisy said sharply. "I believe that moving forward is more constructive than looking back."

For a moment we all concentrated on our food. The clash of forks and spoons sounded unnaturally loud and harsh in the silent room.

Finally, I cleared my throat. "So, Daisy," I asked casually, setting my implements down, "what has impressed you the most so far in this city?"

"Let me see," Daisy mused. "The way pedestrians are always running across the road against the light."

"Isn't that normal?" Cathy interrupted, her eyes flashing. "I saw people jaywalking in London too, though it wasn't common."

"Well, that's the point. People do it in the States, too, but it's the exception, not the rule. What amazes me in China is that pedestrians are supposed to know crossing the road against the light is dangerous not only to themselves but also to those in moving vehicles. But there is always someone jaywalking, and as soon as one person does it, everyone else follows suit. They must believe that the risk is minimal, just because someone else just made it safely to the other side. I've even seen kids dragged across by their parents, looking panicked but still stumbling along. Only a tiny minority stays put until the light turns green. In other countries I've seen a few jaywalkers, but here I see a *mass* of them."

"But there are people posted at each of the main crossroads to prevent it," Pearl cut in. "Haven't you seen them — two people in uniforms with bright green stripes? 'Secondary traffic police,' they're called. Their job is to get pedestrians to comply with traffic rules."

"Sure, I've seen them," Daisy said. "If they manage to prevent the first jaywalker, everyone stays. But once anyone gets past them, it all breaks down: jaywalkers keep going, the secondary police officers keep shouting fruitlessly at them, and drivers have to brake to avoid them, swearing all the while. Unfortunately, that happens a lot."

"My, Daisy, you've been watching like a hawk," Cathy exclaimed. "I've never really noticed all those details."

"I always stand there wondering what those pedestrians

THE ENVELOPES

think they're gaining that's worth jeopardizing their lives as well as others'. They'll only get where they're heading a few seconds sooner?"

"Seem to me you're overthinking it," Rose chipped in. "Maybe it's just a bad habit."

"No, poor Rose," Cathy intoned, imitating Daisy's tone. "It's a horrible habit that could kill them in a split second."

"Seriously"—Pearl's smile faded—"the mother of a schoolmate of mine was killed in a traffic accident at a crossroad. Ignoring the rules does hurt people… But they do say the secondary traffic police have helped cut down jaywalking and reduce accidents."

"Anyhow," Rose said, giving Daisy a smug look, "sooner or later you'll get used to it. Some day you may find yourself among the jaywalkers."

"Really?" Daisy's eyebrows rose. "How do you figure that?"

For an instant, we were all silent. Then Edith announced languidly, "I have finally finished my whole plate of foreign noodles. Actually, the clams were delicious."

"Congratulations, Edith!" Daisy clapped her hands with exaggeration. "I appreciate that you struggled through it."

"Damn!" Rose suddenly cried, springing to her feet. "I forgot my other appointment. What a nice gathering! It made me completely forget time. I must dash now. Thanks for the dinner." She snatched her handbag from a chair and rushed toward the door.

After seeing off Rose, Daisy served us a fine, fragrant port wine as dessert, and we all shifted to the living area, with its warm subdued lighting. There Daisy, at our request, picked out a melody on the piano, against the soft background music playing on the stereo. Cathy reclined on the chaise sofa, resting her head against the cotton upholstery. Daisy and I sank into the pearl-white settee. In front of the French windows, drink in hand, Pearl danced with slow and sinuous movements. Edith stood beside her, gazing at their reflections in the darkened window glass and applauding Pearl now and then.

I watched this all, feeling slightly detached. As a matter of fact, Daisy's complaints about pedestrians and traffic lights had sent me into a brown study. I was picturing things in my life that seemed somehow associated with the scene she'd sketched out. I thought about all the people taking or giving red packets full of money to gain at every turn, while my parents-in-law cleaved to their values and principles. I wondered whether they were ever tempted to go with the flow, follow the others across that road…

"Daisy, this is a nice house you're renting," Edith said, disrupting this chain of thought.

"I've been to Fred's townhouse," said Cathy. "It's like a palace. He's rich, and it must've cost a fortune. But even if I had all that money, I'd still rather curl up in a pretty, cozy home like this."

"We're two of a kind, Cathy," Daisy remarked. "But it's just too far away from our office here."

"It's more appropriate to say that our office is too remote from the town area," Pearl pointed out. "It's actually in the middle of nowhere."

"That's true," I said. "BrightLife China's location is inconvenient for almost all of our employees."

Edith turned to Daisy. "I have to admit I was disappointed to hear you tell us in our last managers' meeting that the company can't afford to move to a better location, for the time being."

Daisy shrugged. "I know it wasn't nice of me to have ended the love affair you'd all been having with an illusion. But, as I said then, the true state of the company's finances leaves no leeway to do what Fred wants."

Cathy snorted. "What made Fred do that? He promised us

the moon, and like saps we believed him."

"I suspect," said Pearl, "that Fred himself didn't know about our financial problems. He asked Daisy whether the company's situation was that bad."

"It's possible," Daisy concurred. "Perhaps Lucy—wasn't that the old finance manager's name?—didn't disclose the big cash hole to Fred. But I can't see why she didn't."

"Lucy seemed scared," I put in. "Around two months before her resignation, she came to ask me what she could do. She said she'd been forced to do certain things, though she wouldn't specify them. She was afraid she'd become a scapegoat."

Pearl looked thoughtful. "If there was anyone at BrightLife who could've frightened her, it could only have been Fred, her boss."

Daisy smiled at me. "What advice did you give her, Jade?"

"Oh, I tried to convince her to put her foot down on the things she wasn't comfortable with. I didn't know she'd decided to leave the company instead, until she sent in her letter of resignation."

"I have refused to do some of the things Fred asked," Edith said, "but he just bypassed me and asked one of my underlings instead, and then that underling even bossed me around. But I don't want to be carrying the can when the day of reckoning comes. I'd rather not join the jaywalkers either."

"Ha!" Pearl laughed. "Were you paying attention after all, Edith? I thought you were struggling with your food."

"Right, Edith." Daisy swung around to face her. "Why didn't you tell me the menu I'd proposed wasn't to your taste?"

"That's a mere trifle. I didn't want to complicate things for you." Edith's mouth twitched, and she took a sip of wine.

"Hmm... a mere trifle," Cathy said reflectively. "It strikes me that the tasks Fred has allotted to me—finding him a *feng shui* master, hunting down rare South American music, looking for fine restaurants where he can entertain customers — are also mere trifles, for the most part..." Her voice trailed off for a moment. "But here's the question. To what end do we work? I've been thinking about that for quite some time."

"For many people, it's a lifelong question." Pearl drained her glass.

"So this doesn't seem the time to look for answers," Edith said, getting up. "But it *is* time to go home."

The party was over.

After Cathy, Edith, and Pearl went off together, I volunteered to help Daisy clean up. For a while she bustled around, clearing the table and tidying up the living room, while I washed the dishes at the kitchen sink.

I was still preoccupied, pondering the question that had been so lately raised, dismissed, and abandoned. *To what end do we work?*

Perhaps we work only to make a living, I thought, *and our occupation is a matter of luck. This might be true of Cathy, Edith, Rose, Lucy, myself, and the majority of employees in BrightLife, as well as Taohua. Perhaps some — like my parents-in-law, Deping, and Felix — worked to realize a dream or an ideal, and their career paths were well planned. Perhaps yet others, well provided for and without ambition, worked simply for fun, a distraction, something to fill the time. Pearl had told me it was better to measure her wits at the office than twiddle her thumbs, waiting for her rich businessman husband to come home. As for Daisy, Waits, and Fred, I couldn't fathom their motivations. The lure of ill-gotten money, like a red light facing us, could be a kind of test. We all could react differently, just as the pedestrians at a crossroad did... What could Lucy have balked at? Could Fred have enticed her to jump a red light?*

THE ENVELOPES

"Jade, your eyes look troubled. Is something on your mind?" Daisy's voice jolted me out of these musings. She was standing beside me, tilting her head to survey my face.

"Oh... I was thinking of our conversation about pedestrians at a traffic light."

"What's bothering you?" she asked casually as she started to dry the dishes with a cloth.

"Nothing," I said, unsure how to explain. "Sometimes I just get into navel-gazing."

"Do you think I'll follow the crowd and become a jaywalker some day?"

I smiled. "No way. On your first day with BrightLife, I was already sure about you. I know you'll wait for the green light, no matter how many others jaywalk."

"I appreciate that."

"But, Daisy, what if it's more difficult than that—say, if the controlling system has gone haywire, and the light will never turn green? Would you wait forever?"

"Let me see. It's cowardice to blame the system for a decision to ditch my values. I'd first try to find a way to have the system fixed. If it went completely down the tubes, I'd find another place to cross the road. In our working life, there will always be great temptations, but I can't let them destroy the values I believe in. By choosing to turn away from them, I give myself peace of mind." She hesitated. "Lucy might have a skeleton in her closet. She isn't my type, but she's become a part of history."

"Yes, I've already kicked off the recruiting process for her replacement," I said, and updated her.

"I don't want anyone like Lucy. I expect someone who will fight for fairness, like you, Jade."

"I'll keep that in mind."

She sighed. "I'm seeing lousy numbers for our company,

issues with operations. The status quo is just like your red light with a faulty control, and it's holding our company back. There're so many things we have to do before all the red lights turn green. We'd better gird up our loins."

"I'm not sure whether it'll be all hands on deck. But I think you and Waits can count on many employees who would be happy to become a part of our success story."

"I have no doubt about it."

As I turned on the tap to rinse the cutlery, she looked over her shoulder toward me. "Jade," she said, "how about you? Red light in your life?"

For a few seconds, I was still. Then, resuming my work at hand, I responded, "You astounded me with your sharp eyes when I first met you, a month ago. You saw something in me that I thought I'd hidden from everyone."

"Yes, I saw grief. And it's still in your eyes. Maybe you're just trying to forget whatever has happened, not trying to fix it. You still look like a damsel in distress."

"I'm no damsel any longer. I'm married." With a bitter smile, I recognized that once again I was digressing, as was my wont when trying to escape an unpalatable truth. I passed the clean chinaware to her and, wiping my hands with a towel, turned around to lean my back against the sink.

"And with one child, I suppose, to comply with the famous birth control policy in China?"

"Unfortunately, no…"

I hesitated, but Daisy had touched the tender spot. I could no longer help myself. As I poured out the bare bones of the tragedies of my baby son and Meihua, I held back my tears, but I could not repress my sorrow.

She dropped her work and embraced me. "Come here. I am sorry for saying you're not trying to fix it," she said in a voice

THE ENVELOPES

that melted my heart. "I take it back."

Her hug felt like that of my late mother-in-law, and it calmed me. When she released me from her clasp, I took a deep breath. "I'm doing much better than months ago," I said. "What happened in our life has to be put behind us. Taohua's family and mine are determined to make a go of it."

10

In the month following Daisy's housewarming party, my father-in-law and I developed a new daily routine, leaving the apartment in the morning and only returning at night. It was July, and summer holidays had begun, so Deping was freed from his heavy lecture schedule, but he buried himself in his research papers, shuttling between home and City Normal at irregular intervals. As for Taohua, she took care that our everyday lives ran smoothly. Our flat, which had become a home away from home for her, was again filled with her singing. After she was done with her domestic chores, she spent her time knitting. That had been her hobby, she told me, ever since her teens.

At BrightLife, the days passed uneventfully, or so it seemed. But rumors reached my ears that the finance department staff was now under pressure; Daisy was urging them to work closely with sales on collecting overdue payments from customers, as if the survival of the company might hinge on that. And then came an incident that triggered a turn of events.

Waits and Fred were out of town on a business trip that day. I'd gone through a stack of applications for the position of finance manager and short-listed a couple of candidates, one of whom was coming for a first-round interview in the afternoon. As I walked through the corridors, looking for Daisy so we could review the candidate's résumé together, I was struck by

THE ENVELOPES

the silence. It felt as quiet now as it had before Waits and Daisy joined us. Usually, these days, I could hear various sounds coming from the small meeting room just outside Fred's office where Waits temporarily worked, since there was no other space available for him then.

As I entered the meeting room, Daisy emerged from her office next to Fred's—previously a storage room—with a cup in hand. Fred had sent Cathy out on an errand, so her office cubicle at one side of the room was empty.

"We have the place to ourselves this morning, it looks like," Daisy commented. "Why don't we talk here, while I make myself some coffee?"

I nodded, looking appreciatively at Daisy's emerald taffeta dress, which had a beautiful sheen. As usual, I took great pleasure in the individuality of her fashion sense. An unusual choice of color in our staid office, the green made the most of her rosy cheeks. Pinned at her waistline was a butterfly-shaped brooch that took my breath away, its glass wings a shimmering mosaic of reddish purple and powder blue, subtly edged and veined, in silver. It looked as if it might at any moment come to life and flutter away at the drop of a hat.

I opened my mouth to voice my admiration, but Daisy spoke first, keeping her voice low. "Jade, first, I need to check up on something. I'm quite disturbed by the size of the traveling and entertainment expenses claimed in the office books."

"Which department is responsible?" I asked.

"The general manager's office, it looks like."

I frowned. "Fred and Cathy are the only two employees there."

"Well, I looked through each entry and its corresponding source documents for the GM's office. It seems like Fred's racked up a lot of unreasonable expenses, things like expensive suits from a department store. I can hardly imagine what sort of business necessity there is for buying clothes on BrightLife's tab."

"It doesn't make sense."

"But then it gets a little murkier. I can't find any record for salary being paid to him, though every other employee is on the payroll. I understand that in BrightLife China, the finance department handles paychecks and monthly personal income tax withholding. But it's your department that manages payroll, if I'm not mistaken."

"Yes, I update payroll every month and send it to finance. But when I first got here and took over the payroll, I didn't see Fred on it. I once asked Lucy about it. According to her, he has a special arrangement with BrightLife. Instead of ordinary salary payments, his compensation takes the form of the company defraying his expenses."

She groaned. "That's obvious tax evasion. With a salary, he'd owe personal income tax, while expense claims are tax-deductible by the company."

"But Lucy told me headquarters knows about this deal."

"No," she said firmly, shaking her head. "I've checked with corporate headquarters in Boston, and they said they know nothing about it. Hmmph... All right, let's move on to the candidate you mentioned over the phone."

But at that moment all hell seemed to break loose. Someone in the building was yelling at the top of their voice. Daisy froze, momentarily at a loss.

"It's from the sales department down the end of the corridor," I said after listening for a moment. "I think that bellowing is Rose."

We hurried out of the meeting room and along the corridor. The scene that greeted us in the sales office brought us to an abrupt halt in the doorway. Rose, in a towering rage, was hurling vulgar words at Bruce, the salesman. "Shit! Why the hell didn't you follow my instructions? You'll damn well do as you're told!" As we watched, horrified, she cocked her arm back and flung the coffee mug she was holding at his head.

Bruce, around five yards away from her, swiftly dodged. The mug whizzed past him to ricochet off a cabinet and shatter on the hard tile floor. We could see the dent it left in the wooden cabinet. Bruce, his face white, was stammering "I'm — I'm sorry. Sorry, I'll do — do it now." He hastened to his desk, plonked down at it, and scrabbled through some papers.

I strode across the room to Rose's side. "Come on, Rose," I expostulated under my breath, "you've got to control your temper. This is an office, not a saloon."

"Okay, okay," she brayed, her hands up but her eyes down. "Just give me a little time to get over it." She switched off her laptop, stuck it in her briefcase, and flounced out of the room with it, brushing past Daisy, who was still standing at the door.

A clerk with a broom cautiously edged into the room and began sweeping up the broken shards of mug on the floor. I walked back to Daisy.

She narrowed her eyes. "So is Rose taking French leave now?"

"Probably... who knows? Maybe she's got a meeting with a client."

"Well, if so, I hope she manages to cool down a little first. What's got her dander up now?"

I could only shrug and shake my head.

"Gee, that was awful, seeing Bruce cowering like that," Daisy said as we walked back to the meeting room. "I used to have a boss with a bad temper, always foaming at the mouth. But I've never seen such a knock-down, drag-out brawl in an office before."

"Me neither." I recalled. "Though several times I've seen her arguments with someone develop into a slanging match."

I thought that when the dust settled, Bruce would absorb the blow and move on, just as he and some of his colleagues had done previously. But by midafternoon of the same day he'd handed me his resignation letter. I tried to persuade him not to give way to impulse, but to no avail.

"I'm not quitting because of what happened this morning," he said. "This isn't the first time Rose has gone hysterical with me. If I hadn't been able to handle that, I would've left long ago. But I don't feel like I have any value in this company anymore. I'm finished. I quit."

"What do you mean, you don't see your value?" I smiled at him. "Without salespeople, our company wouldn't bring the revenue we need to survive."

"That's high-sounding, Manager Bai. The reality, though, is that I've lost my value. I've been ordered to give my sales territory to a distributor who has entered into an exclusive partnership contract with the company. Hell, I've spent two years building up a customer base there, and now—"

I held up a hand. "Bruce, hold on, please." I sensed something ugly that I couldn't precisely define, and I felt his frustration. I hesitated, and then said, "Could you come with me to Director Sweet's office?"

We all crammed into Daisy's poky office, the only place we could find any privacy. After listening to what Bruce had to say, Daisy came straight to the point. "What's the name of the distributor that you're expected to direct your customers to?"

"Shing Sheng Co," Bruce said.

"Hmm." Daisy looked thoughtful. "I was actually already

THE ENVELOPES

concerned about this distributor. The books are showing that they owe us tons of money. They have invoices months overdue."

"See, Director Sweet, our partnership with Shing Sheng doesn't work," Bruce flashed back. "If we'd been selling products directly to my customers, we would've be getting their payments on time."

"Maybe," said Daisy. "But looking the numbers, Shing Sheng's orders have been mushrooming recently. It's become one of our biggest customers, in terms of revenue."

"That's due to the exclusive partnership contract we signed with them half a year ago," said Bruce. "Since then, it's been a breeze for them to purchase from us, and then turn around and resell to my customers. Especially since I've been told to dump my customers and work with Shing Sheng only."

"So you're supposed to help us collect payments from Shing Sheng. Is that right?"

"I don't deny that," Bruce admitted. "And I've been chasing after them. But they keep coming up with excuses. Now they're saying we're violating the contract."

"In what way?"

"Director Sweet, have you read the contract?"

"Not yet. Actually, I tried to track it down in the finance department, because I wanted to check out the payment clause. But I had no luck."

"You'd better ask my boss about the contract," Bruce said bitterly. "Shing Sheng's been griping about the fact that I'm still making sales to my customers—that's why Rose blew a fuse this morning. She was angry at me for not doing as she wanted and refusing to make sales myself. It's putting us in breach of contract, she said. But hell, what am I supposed to do? My customers keep coming back to me because they don't like doing business with Shing Sheng. Should I turn them down, when they want to buy direct from us instead? Our competitors would love to see that happen. Everyone thinks I've got a cushy job!" He leaned forward, his face reddening. "Hell, I've been kicked upstairs, that's what's happened. I'm forbidden to do my job and serve my customers. What value am I adding to BrightLife China? I spend my time just mooching around in the market. Should I just go work for Shing Sheng?"

Sitting back again, he folded his arms, looking straight at Daisy. "What's more, the contract is lopsided. The so-called exclusivity is only imposed on us. BrightLife is forced to sell its products in my sales territory only to Shing Sheng, as the so-called sole distributor, but there is no clause binding Shing Sheng to sell only BrightLife's products. You know what their warehouse looks like now? Hell, it's full of other brands, including two lines of products they manufacture themselves."

"Bruce," Daisy cut in, "are you saying that you're literally out on your ear?"

For an instant, he hesitated, staring at Daisy. "Director Sweet," he said slowly, "you've been with us less than two months. You might not be aware yet of the changes in our sales strategy I've been seeing. I just don't get them. I feel I'm trampled on."

"Well, Bruce," said Daisy, holding his eyes, "I believe that you and the customers you've developed have great value to our company. And I hope you and our other employees can at least give Waits and me a chance to work with you all to make BrightLife China better."

Bruce just looked at her, saying nothing.

"Have you tendered your resignation to Rose?" I asked him quietly,

He nodded. "She's not in the office. I've emailed it to her."

"If I were in your shoes," Daisy said, "I'd talk with her about your concerns that we may lose our customers and our market.

THE ENVELOPES

Waving a red flag to the management embodies your value, too."

Bruce let out a long breath. Finally he said, "I'll think about it."

"Oh, one more thing," Daisy said as he was getting up to leave. "On a side note, what's the term of the partnership contract?"

"Five years," he said.

———∽∽———

When the door had closed behind Bruce, Daisy and I looked at each other in dismay. "I'm no expert on sales operations," I said finally, unable to help myself. "But I can tell that the contract Bruce just described is putting us at a distinct disadvantage. Why would BrightLife China enter such an arrangement with any distributor?"

Daisy folded her hands under her chin, looking grave. "Jade, if what Bruce told us is true, I'm pretty sure BrightLife China has a tough row to hoe." She exhaled sharply through her nose. "What a day!"

"Yeah, and we still have this prospective finance manager to interview," I reminded her. "She should be here any minute."

———∽∽———

Wings Zhan came exactly on time. The last candidate on my short list for the first round of interviews, she turned out to be the most impressive, though she was only twenty-seven. Her neat one-page résumé was appealing, indicating a four-year stint studying and working in France. Yet the first half of our interview was lackluster. Still preoccupied with what Bruce had told us, both Daisy and I asked hackneyed questions, and Wings' answers sounded rather preformatted, too. Twice Daisy even gracefully raised her hand to disguise a yawn. But the second half of the interview took a twist. Without a scintilla of attitude,

Wings lifted us out of our ennui with a vibrant demonstration of her skills and working experiences in both China and France. Her tenacity, her intelligence, and her positive attitude amazed both of us. Despite a minor disagreement between Daisy and me — Daisy appreciated her aggressiveness, while I interpreted it as a sense of superiority stemming from the fact that she was among the cream of white-collar professionals — we both fell under her spell. And I was secretly dazzled by one thing I'd never thought about in a job interview before: the moment I shook Wings' hand, a waft of delicious scent drifted into my nostrils. *Perhaps her stay in France had made her a perfume addict,* I thought, rather amused. The small meeting room was heady with her fragrance through the entire interview.

I quickly set up Wings' second meeting with Waits and Fred. Waits raved about her fluent French, though privately I wondered how relevant it was to her job. And Fred rejoiced at another female manager joining his team. Somehow it had happened this time by chance rather by premeditation; she'd earned the position through her merit, not her gender. Wings accepted our job offer and agreed to be on board in one month. That was good news for all.

While I was taking care of the formalities for Wings' employment, I didn't hear anything more from Daisy about the arrangement between BrightLife China and Shing Sheng Co. Nevertheless, there were a few signs that she was teasing out the details of the strange partnership. One of these came up about a week after Bruce's incident.

That morning I was up to my eyeballs in tackling urgent personnel issues, and had to skip lunch. When I finally had time for a break in the midafternoon, I sat at a table in the empty canteen,

THE ENVELOPES

nibbling at the packed lunch Taohua had insisted on getting up early to prepare ever since she moved into our apartment. Gradually I became aware of raised voices coming through the wall that separated the canteen from the big conference room, though I could hardly discern any words. The commotion died away, but several minutes later it rose again. I recognized Rose's voice, among other unfamiliar ones, and wondered what kind of meeting was going on.

A few minutes later, Pearl crept into the canteen, holding a mug. Spotting me, she exhaled deeply, as if she was just recovering from a bad case of the shivers.

"Oh, you don't need to tiptoe like that," I joked. "There's enough noise coming from the next room to drown out the sound of your footsteps."

"I had to sneak out of the meeting there. It's a melee." She sighed again, walking in a more normal fashion to the water dispenser. "I can't take it any longer. Could you hear them?"

"Only sounds... What meeting are you having there?"

She filled her mug with water. "You know our distributor, Shing Sheng?"

"Yes, a little."

She set her mug on the table and settled into the chair across from me. "The owner and his team are now in the conference room. Daisy asked for the meeting. Honestly! Shing Sheng owes us millions of yuan. Ha! It's not surprising we don't have any money to move the office to a better location."

"That's why Daisy wants to meet them, I think."

"It goes far beyond that. Daisy must've finally got a good look at the partnership contract. She handed it out in the meeting. Good grief! Some partnership contract. It's only three pages long! I can't believe it."

"You mean you didn't know about the contract before?"

"Just now in the conference room was the first chance I've had to read the whole thing." She furrowed her eyebrows. "Fred and Rose had broken down the draft into several sections, and asked me to look over only the marketing part. I guess Lucy got the finance part. Fred discussed the marketing clause with me, telling me it was a minor section, and not yet written in stone. Then Fred and the sales department finalized the whole contract. Once it had been signed, Fred told me to implement what I'd wrapped up for the marketing part, but he never gave a copy of the complete signed contract to me. Nor to Lucy, I guess."

"Rose never talked with you about the contract?"

"No. She only needed my support on the marketing part, which is straightforward." She curled her lips.

"Oh, I thought you two were thick as thieves."

"Thick as thieves, my foot! We have some pastimes in common—shopping, going to movies, you know, that kind of thing. But Rose is discreet, shall we say, about how her team makes sales."

We could hear another fierce burst of polemics in the conference room, through the supposedly soundproof wall.

Pearl snorted. "Here it goes again."

"Well, I've heard a little about the contract," I said. "But I can hardly imagine what about it is causing such a stir over there."

"Daisy demanded immediate payments from Shing Sheng. But they bit back, reproving us for violating the contract by making direct sales to customers. Then Rose started gnashing her teeth. She tore into them for not achieving the target set in the contract for their purchases from us, and defended our direct sales. You know how it is—an everlasting chicken-and-egg problem, each side pointing fingers at the other. I think it will end badly for us, though."

THE ENVELOPES

"Why?"

"Because the payment clause in the contract is only three words long: 'To be determined.' That's it."

"Good grief!" I couldn't help crying. "Probably that's one of the things Lucy talked about being forced to do. Daisy must be pissed off."

"Daisy was cool in the meeting, though. She never raised her voice. She warned Shing Sheng's team we wouldn't ship any goods to them until they paid us. They exploded with anger, she responded with a thin smile, and I came out of the room. But really! How could Fred have signed such a stupid contract?"

"Are Waits and Fred in there too?" I asked.

Pearl took a drink from her mug. "Waits only was there for a while. The representatives of Shing Sheng don't speak English—he must think it's a waste of his time to sit through a whole meeting all in Chinese. I guess he works closely with Daisy to keep his finger on the pulse. Fred's in there—he usually has no problem understanding Chinese. But they're speaking so fast now, he can't get a word in edgeways."

"Oh, so that's why I've been hearing mostly just Rose and the Shing Sheng people. I don't think I heard you at all."

"Marketing plays only a passive role in our partnership with Shing Sheng. So does Edith's supply chain department. If we can't solve the sales issue, Edith and I won't have much to do for them. Edith wasn't even invited to the meeting, perhaps because there's no clause at all in the contract concerning goods supply to Shing Sheng—"

"Oh, speak of the devil, here she is."

Edith had just come in, carrying her teacup. "My ears are burning," she drawled in her lazy tone, rubbing her earlobe while she stomped to the dispenser. "What are you saying about me?"

Pearl giggled. "I was saying you were lucky not to be in the meeting next room."

"Lucky?" Edith sniffed, joining us at the table. "This morning, I was called in by Daisy—she wanted me to find a lot of documents related to purchases from a supplier that doesn't even appear on my list. I spent my whole morning hunting them out. It's a headache, hardly luck."

"You have any idea why Daisy asked for those documents?" I asked.

Edith looked grim. "Apparently our sister company in Switzerland, our affiliated supplier, is chasing her for payments."

"Honestly! This company has had it," Pearl piped up. "We're being hounded by our creditors, and our major debtor won't give us our money back. We're up against the wall."

"Shush," I said, alarmed. "Please, don't ever start a rumor."

Pearl grimaced at me. Then, remembering that she was supposed to be in the meeting, she murmured, "They seem to have quieted down. I'd better sneak back in," and left.

Having finished the contents of my lunch box, I was about to go back to my office. But Edith looked preoccupied, and she seemed to have no intention of leaving the canteen. Instead of getting up, I asked her kindly, "Is there something weighing on your mind?"

"Scarcely weighty, but a bit weird." She sipped at her teacup and then, putting it down, turned her gaze on me. "I've been thinking hard. Maybe you can help me see the light."

"I can give it a try, if you don't mind telling me about the weird thing. But give me the short version, and try to skip the jargon."

"I'll do my best," she said, and took a deep breath. "Our sister company in Switzerland contacted Daisy to collect payments for two invoices they'd issued to us. But Daisy couldn't find any record in the account books of money that we owed them. She first had me check two purchase orders we'd placed in the past months with the Swiss company, corresponding to the two invoices they sent to her. That was as easy as pie, since the order tracking numbers were printed on the invoices. I brought her the purchase orders I'd found, and also confirmed that I'd been working with Switzerland all the time, and had approved every purchase order personally before my staff released it to them."

"Finding those documents couldn't have been the headache you mentioned when you came in."

"No, not those. But later…"

"Hold on, Edith. This is already sounding strange. You just said Daisy couldn't find our owing money to BrightLife Switzerland in the account books. That means that the finance department has no record of invoices, though you've made the purchases. But why? Have we received the goods? And if we have, do you have any paper showing the receipts?"

"Jade, I always appreciate quick-witted people like you."

"It's just common sense, I think."

"Not everyone has common sense. Anyway, there's slightly more than common sense here. The goods we purchased were shipped directly from Switzerland to an address in Hong Kong, as per instructions from the sales department, namely Rose, whose signature is on the delivery notes—"

"In other words," I interrupted, "we didn't physically receive the goods, because a customer bought them from us and requested direct shipment from our supplier. Then you must've got the sales orders from the customer."

"Yes," Edith said. "New Tech was the customer. Since the goods were not our standard inventory items, I said I needed the sales orders from New Tech before I could place the purchase orders in Switzerland. I hate to see our warehouse bursting with goods that salespeople will sell only in their daydreams. Our warehouse is running out of space."

"That makes sense to me," I said hastily, trying to keep her on the subject. "So New Tech is a customer in Hong Kong, which is where they wanted the goods delivered?"

"No, it's not. It's registered in China. Actually, since BrightLife China is not licensed to export products, by law we can't take a sales order from a foreign customer. But according to Rose, New Tech has a subsidiary in Hong Kong, which is defined as foreign when it comes to business transactions."

"In other words, New Tech, the parent company in China, bought the goods for its operation in Hong Kong. But why didn't the subsidiary, not Rose, acknowledge receipts of goods?"

Edith grinned. "Jade, you're quick!"

"Oh, please, stop buttering me up. Just answer my question."

"It *ought* to have been signed by the subsidiary," she conceded with a shrug. "But Rose said it wasn't convenient for them to do the paperwork. I was okay with that, so long as there was someone responsible for the whereabouts of the goods."

"I see. It sounds like you've filed your documents properly. When Daisy demanded them, you ought to have been able to find them blindfolded. So why did you say it was such a headache?" I paused, thinking. "Oh, don't tell me that she asked you for the missing invoices from Switzerland!"

"Jade, I'm not flattering you. You're following me well. Daisy is absolutely clear-minded. In fact, she wanted me to inspect two *different* purchases, even though the items and quantities were identical to those ordered from Switzerland. BrightLife China made those purchases from a local company called K.J., which is *not* on my supplier list."

"Now I'm lost. If you didn't know about K.J., how did Daisy? Oh, no — is K.J. pressing her for payments too?"

THE ENVELOPES

"On the contrary. We paid K.J., when Lucy was with us. The accountant told Daisy she'd never received the two invoices from Switzerland, but she remembered payments authorized by her boss, Lucy, and Fred for invoices from K.J., showing *exactly the same* items and quantities. So that's why Daisy came to me, wanting to find the documents for K.J., but not having order tracking numbers."

"But K.J. isn't on your supplier list? In other words, could purchases have been made without your approval?"

"The long and the short of it is that they were." Edith's voice was getting hoarse. She drank to moisten her throat and put the cup down, sighing heavily. "Anyway, I bust a gut to dig out the purchase contracts—four altogether. The two most recent listed items and quantities identical to our purchases from Switzerland. And they eventually reminded me that Fred had once mentioned K.J. to me, and recommended we buy goods from them. I objected because our sister company already offered us good-quality products at a cheaper price. He never bothered me about it again."

"Then how could the purchases from K.J. have been made?"

"Do you remember Amanda—my underling, the purchasing supervisor? She was always trying, in the name of Fred, to tell me off. She'd signed the purchase contracts with K.J., and added the words 'on behalf of...' in brackets next to them."

"In other words, Amanda knew she'd overstepped her authority and facilitated transactions that might be inappropriate. Probably she was also clear about whose behalf she was signing on."

Edith nodded. "Not on mine, that's for sure." After a pause, she added, "One more weird thing. In the purchase contracts with K.J., the shipments were directed to a Hong Kong address that belongs to a New Tech subsidiary, to which BrightLife

Switzerland delivered the goods — actually, Daisy spotted it. But then I realized that these contracts corresponded exactly, in the type and quantity of goods sold, to the sales orders from New Tech that you and I just talked about—"

"Hold on," I said, feeling a little dizzy. "What a tangled web! Let me try to sum up all the information we have here. We, BrightLife China, made duplicate purchases from BrightLife Switzerland and K.J., and instructed both of them to directly ship the goods to New Tech's subsidiary in Hong Kong, which drew up *only one* sales order to us. We've paid K.J. for the purchase, but not even booked the invoices from Switzerland. Am I overlooking anything?"

Edith shook her head with a bitter smile.

I lowered my voice. "Now comes my question: New Tech only bought one from us, but we delivered two to its door via two suppliers. How does that work? Um... unless one of the deliveries didn't happen at all."

"I never thought about such a possibility. But it can't be true that our sister company faked the transactions." She blinked, chewing over my speculation.

"Good grief!" I exclaimed. "We've cleared our debts to K.J. How will Switzerland be paid? Probably, that's why Lucy put aside its invoices. Probably she was forced to authorize the payments to K.J. Probably that's why she was scared."

"My God! Oh, my God," Edith was gibbering. "What was the point of all this? Why was the whole shebang arranged?"

"Heaven knows," I said soberly. "But it can't by any stretch of the imagination have been for fun."

"My God, and now Daisy is onto them." Edith buried her face in her hands. "Good for Lucy that she's no longer with us. Luckily, I didn't do what Fred wanted me to do."

The truth was finding its way to Daisy, I thought. She'd always

THE ENVELOPES

been seeking any whiff of it, and now she must already be on the scent. Something was terribly wrong at BrightLife China.

11

The scorching heat of August wilted the city's residents, just as the warm sun made plants droop. Even my husband would rather remain at home than travel in the baking sunlight to City Normal University, which was still closed for the summer vacation. Taohua twice took one-week leaves to go back to her village, and then he could justify staying at home to help with domestic chores. Our family was less convivial in the evenings, as if everyone's vitality had evaporated in the summer heat.

At BrightLife China, some of the employees had gone on holiday, but there were more salespeople around the office, since they weren't out on the road as much. Daisy still seemed snowed under with work, yet she was always perfectly dressed, with a chic air that was a joy to behold. She and Waits had been shifting in and out of the big conference room, sometimes with Fred. When Waits jetted away to Europe for his summer break, he delegated Daisy to act in his stead. Even when she was run off her feet, she carried an air of calm, like a sleeping child's top, spinning and still at the same time. She seemed to spend a lot of time talking to Fred behind his closed office door, sometimes even having lunch with him, until he too left for summer holidays, in his case, back to the States.

Wings came on board in mid-August. In helping her get into the swing of things at BrightLife China, Daisy threw herself into a whirlwind of orientations. Her energy made me think of my late mother-in-law, that human dynamo, driven by her own inner force. It helped that some of our departmental managers worked in tandem with Daisy on anything other than routine jobs, giving her all the background information available to us.

Before long, Wings had impressed many people with her financial expertise and strong personality. Guided by Daisy, she was straining at the leash to improve the company's monetary situation. One day Edith, with mixed feelings of disappointment and hope, brought up again the two unpaid invoices for purchases from BrightLife Switzerland that we'd talked about in the canteen two months before. Due to the government's capital control regulations, we couldn't settle a bill with a foreign company that had not physically delivered goods to our warehouse. But Wings, Edith said, was working out a lawful way to clear our debts, so we could continue normal business with Switzerland. Edith was overwhelmed with gratitude for Wings' involvement. Others, however, were rather irritated by Wings' outspokenness, by her vocal dislike of ambiguous talk and for fishing in troubled waters, and by her tendency to defy the conventional approach. She tackled Rose about her slow-paying customers and the deep discounts she granted to distributors. And I wasn't entirely spared either; she challenged any personnel practices that might incur unnecessary spending. As an ordinary human being, I found it hard not to feel somehow offended, yet I had to admit that Wings was a much-needed injection of new blood into a company where her peers tended to be either submissive or reactive rather than proactive. I trusted Daisy's instincts, in this hiring decision among many others.

And still I took a delight in Wings' perfume. It seemed to constantly change with her moods, I noticed, serving as a constant reminder of the individuality she brought to BrightLife China.

At the beginning of September, Waits and Fred returned from their overseas holidays. They looked more wearied than reinvigorated, as if they might need more time off to recover from the jet lag. But our headquarters in Boston had set a tight timeframe for our annual budgeting and business planning, so Waits hurriedly kicked off the process. On the Thursday after his return, he sent an email to Fred, Daisy, Pearl, Edith, and me, asking us to put in some overtime on the coming Saturday, building up next year's business targets for BrightLife China.

In that email Waits wrote that, for everyone's convenience, he would find a place in town for us to meet and work, and advise us as soon as he'd finalized it. We all responded that we could come instead of Fred. In his reply to Waits, copied to each of us, he apologized in advance for his absence; he already had a "momentously important engagement," as he put it, on Saturday, and he couldn't change it. Waits expressed his regret that Fred wouldn't attend, but didn't insist. Late Friday afternoon he sent out another email to the rest of us, leaving Fred out this time. The plan had changed, he wrote; he'd decided to meet in the office, as he thought we might need to look up some company records that were only available on paper.

Saturday morning found the six of us seated around the table in the meeting room outside Fred and Daisy's offices. Waits set the tone for the budgeting and planning. After a general discussion, everyone got into gear to focus on his/her assigned task for an hour.

THE ENVELOPES

We were all up to our elbows in work when we heard the voices and footsteps in the corridor outside. Moments later the meeting room door swung open, and Fred appeared, followed by a tall, thin man with spectacles and an aquiline nose, a woman in a tight black dress that hugged her curvy body, and Cathy. They looked as startled to see us as we were to see them, though Fred attempted to disguise his discomfort with a strained smile.

It was Cathy who spoke first. "Oh! You're all working on the weekend?"

"Yeah, that's right," Waits drawled. "And you are too, from the looks of it."

Fred opened his mouth and closed it again. "You said you'd be meeting downtown," he said finally.

"I changed my mind at the last minute," Waits said, a touch of sarcasm in his voice. "Is this the 'momentous appointment' you mentioned in your email?"

"Um...yes, it is." Fred pulled himself together, seemingly having decided to brazen out Waits' skepticism. "I'm showing an important friend around the office."

Cathy walked across the meeting room and unlocked the door to Fred's office. Fred ushered the two strangers in. "Cathy, could you make us some tea?" he said, poking his head back out, and then closed the office door as Cathy went off to the canteen.

None of us said anything. Waits shot Daisy a quizzical look, and she shrugged. Pearl and Edith glanced at each other, exchanging surreptitious smiles. We went back to our work at hand, and after a while, Cathy came in with a tray of tea. She knocked on Fred's office door, went in, and a minute later came back out, the door clicking shut behind her. Padding through the meeting room toward the outside corridor, she whispered to us, "I'll go and wait for them in the car."

Twenty minutes or so later the three filed out of Fred's office, but instead of leaving, they stopped outside Daisy's office. The hawk-nosed man peered in through the open door for several minutes while he and Fred muttered to each other about something, as if we weren't there. Waits stared at their backs, looking outraged at their nerve, while Pearl nudged Edith, who managed to suppress a smile. Daisy kept her eyes on the screen of her laptop, her fingers tapping away on the keyboard, as if nothing unwonted were happening around her. Finally, as Fred tossed us a hasty, "See you," they said and quickly disappeared.

"Strange," Waits said snidely. "After all that about his Very Important Appointment, all he did was show his friends around. And here we are, with our noses to the grindstone. He didn't even introduce them."

"That was his wife," Edith said quietly.

"And the *feng shui* master, Zhong," added Pearl. "They've both visited the office before."

"Oh yeah?" Waits tilted one of his eyebrows and lifted one corner of his mouth, a habit of his when he was both surprised and annoyed. The effect was so comical, I had to fight the urge to laugh. It reminded me of the grumbling conductor in *La Grande Vadrouille*, an old French comedy I'd watched long ago. The conductor was a hero, helping soldiers escape arrest by Nazi Germans during World War II, but his various amusing facial expressions were what, as a teenager, I'd remembered most.

"Waits," asked Daisy, "do you know what *feng shui* means?"

"Yeah, yeah, I've been living in China long enough to know this stuff, though I'm nowhere near as knowledgeable about the culture as Fred." Waits turned to Pearl and Edith. "His wife believes in *feng shui* too?"

Pearl nodded. "His wife is a local. By all accounts, it's she who got him interested in *feng shui*. They've spent a fortune decorating their fancy townhouse on *feng shui* principles."

THE ENVELOPES

"So he and his wife brought the *feng shui* master to study his office setup. I suppose you could call it a momentous appointment from their point of view."

"I guess so," Pearl said dubiously.

"Oh, poor Cathy." Daisy sighed. "She must be wondering why she had to work overtime yet again for — what did she call it? — 'a mere trifle'."

That evoked a knowing laugh from the four of us who'd been there at the housewarming party, though Waits looked baffled.

"But why were they looking at *my* office?" Daisy asked, frowning. "If we hadn't purely by coincidence been here today, I'm pretty sure they would've gone in."

That had been puzzling me, too, but Pearl and Edith giggled. Daisy stared at them. "What's so funny?"

Pearl hesitated for a few seconds. Finally, she said, "People say he thinks you're the bane of his life. Ever since you came here and started splitting hairs, nothing has been going right for him. From a *feng shui* point of view, your room is right next to his. My guess is that he brought in Master Zhong to check whether your office might be influencing the energy of his, and then find a way to stamp out his bad luck."

"Oh, yeah?" Waits chuckled. "Daisy, you hear that? You're a threat to him."

"Oh, poor me." Daisy pretended to look innocently dismayed. "Fred loathes me, I know. But I don't mean trouble."

"Don't worry about it," said Waits. "We're all in the same boat, yeah." His eyes swept over us, and he rubbed his palms together briskly. "Now let's get on with our work."

But it took me a while to settle down again and concentrate. I could hardly comprehend what Waits meant by "We're all in the same boat." I wondered whether Fred's personal belief in *feng shui* had alienated Waits. One thing seemed certain — for

HASU AUGUST

whatever reason, Waits had it in for Fred.

———∽∽———

That Saturday I plugged away for hours on next year's human-resources planning. I left in the late afternoon, feeling dazed and exhausted. When finally I reached home, and the elevator doors opened on our floor, I stepped out and ran almost square into Felix, whom I'd last seen at Meihua's funeral.

"Hi Felix," I said, hailing him. "I have seen neither hide nor hair of you for ages."

He grinned. "Well, I'm still here in China. But Jade, I'm leaving the city. I hate to do a bunk, so I came to say goodbye. Your father-in-law told me both you and Deping were working today. I'm so glad to see you here before I pack my bags."

"What gives?" I asked casually.

"Nothing really special. As you know, I've been a bird of passage all my life. I like to find interesting places to go."

"Where are you heading?"

"I'm going to the countryside."

My interest sharpened. "To teach there?"

"Yes." He nodded firmly, but looking a bit shy.

"Congratulations! You've always had an aspiration to help needy children in the country." Excited by his news, I was becoming loquacious. "And you seem to have put down roots in China. Where exactly are you going?"

"I'd love to tell you more about it." Looking a bit distracted, he glanced at the lift's floor indicator on the wall. "But Jade, you look whacked. Let's stay in touch. I've got to run now." The lift stopped with a crisp *ding*, and the door opened. He dashed in. Then, waving and bestowing on me one last beam, he added, "Please remember me to Deping."

Later, at the dinner table, we talked with gratification of

THE ENVELOPES

Felix's great career move. No one seemed to be paying any heed to where he would go.

"That's marvelous," Deping said emotionally. "Mother must be smiling down at us from heaven."

My father-in-law, still chewing a mouthful of food, only offered a cryptic smile, uttering no words.

"I'm going to touch base with Felix and invite him to our university," Deping went on. "I'm positive his passion and experience will inspire my students."

"You never miss an opportunity to help your students, just like Mama," my father-in-law said approvingly. "However, son, Felix must survive first. It's not going to be easy for anyone. It would be wiser to wait until he's had some time to build up experience."

Deping nodded. "I'll second that."

"Hopefully," I commented, looking at Taohua, "more and more young people like Felix will want to teach in the country. Then children like Lianhua could have a better chance for schooling."

Taohua made a noncommittal noise, and kept eating her meal. *She'd been quiet that night while we were talking about Felix,* I thought, *as if disinclined to take part in the conversation.*

"Ah, yes, Taohua," I said, changing the subject, "Lianhua is old enough for school now. You were back home not long ago— how was she? Is she going to that school at the foot of the hill in town now?"

"She's fine," she said impassively. "My man is taking care of all that kind of thing—I don't bother my head with it. There's nothing I can do, anyway." She rose to her feet. "I'll go get the fruit."

As she disappeared into the kitchen, Deping signaled to me to hold my tongue. I might've just unwittingly hit a raw nerve in mentioning her daughter's schooling, I realized. Meihua's death was only a few months back. Probably she still blamed herself.

———∾∾———

The weather cooled down in September of 2007, but it heralded the hottest period of my career. The collision of Waits' budgeting group with Fred's *feng shui* team at the beginning of the month was followed in mid-September by the company's decision, announced in a management meeting, that BrightLife China would seek legal advice on terminating our exclusive partnership contract with Shing Sheng Co, which would otherwise be in effect for more than four years. Wings instantly reminded us at the meeting about the millions Shing Sheng owed to us.

Rose said sulkily that the company would pay off their debts, if we'd only give them more time.

"We're reserving the legal right to compel Shing Sheng to settle their debt to us," Waits explained. "But because of our exclusive contract with them, BrightLife risks losing its footing in the China market. If we don't terminate this contract, we're hanging ourselves on one tree, with our hands tied behind our backs." Holding both arms up, he made a hanging gesture. "The tree is prospering, but we're perishing. I can't—I won't—let that happen under my nose. No, no." He shook his head.

"Everything is hard in the beginning," Rose said stubbornly. "I admit we've had a bumpy ride with Shing Sheng. But I believe we need more time to make this partnership work. They can bring us customers we're unable to reach alone."

Fred, poker-faced, toyed in silence with his Montblanc pen.

Waits straightened his back. "Yeah? You mean what we've been doing with them is a long shot? But we've already lost a good number of the customers we already had, as well as the money Shing Sheng refuses to pay us, and now *they're* accusing *us* of

THE ENVELOPES

violating the agreement! Unfortunately, from the beginning, the contract never set up a true partnership. It was always lopsided. It doesn't serve our best interests—not by a long chalk—and never will."

"To date," Daisy added, "we've had several meetings with Shing Sheng, intending to hash out a consensual approach to partnership. But as I see it, we're flogging a dead horse trying to get them to work with us. What they want is for us to finance them."

"You're kidding me," Rose sneered. "They're richer than BrightLife China."

Daisy smiled at Rose. "Then why don't they pay us?"

Rose said with some asperity, raising her voice, "Because my salespeople are still selling..."

"Rose—" Fred suddenly cut her off, setting down his pen on the table and leaning back in his chair. "You can argue yourself blue in the face, but Waits' decision is carved in stone. We have no alternative."

Fred's grudging acceptance of Waits' decision could be easily read between the lines. We all fell silent for a few seconds while Waits jotted something in his notebook. Then he looked up and cleared his throat. "I thank Fred for making it crystal clear that the *company* has decided. And everyone, we need to work together if we're going to get the exclusive partnership contract with Shing Sheng terminated in court without a crippling cost. Shing Sheng can choose: they can either become our true partner or turn into our competitor. Otherwise, predictably, what we'll lose in the coming years is not merely millions of yuan but also market—as a ballpark figure—worth hundreds of millions."

Waits proceeded to designate Daisy to lead the action, working closely with Fred, the local lawyer, and the legal team in our Boston headquarters. Meanwhile, he emphasized, the sales team should be allowed to work freely on expanding the company's customer base, whether Shing Sheng liked it or not, and Rose should work with me on motivating our salespeople to generate maximum revenue.

It was at that management meeting that I first saw firsthand how sharply BrightLife China's old guard disagreed with its new leadership about its strategies of developing business. But I also suspected the fierce debate between Waits and Fred had been going on for some time, remembering the many occasions when they, and sometimes Daisy, had shut themselves up in either the conference room or Fred's office over the past months.

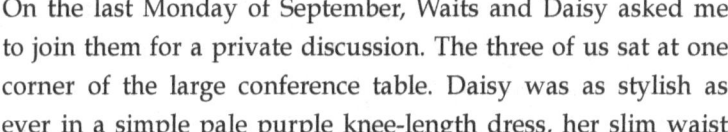

On the last Monday of September, Waits and Daisy asked me to join them for a private discussion. The three of us sat at one corner of the large conference table. Daisy was as stylish as ever in a simple pale purple knee-length dress, her slim waist encircled with a broad lavender chiffon belt tied in a bow. But the soothing effect of this outfit didn't last long.

Without preamble, Waits, his face grave, said, "Jade, I am requesting that you and Daisy assist me in getting a hard job done. I believe you understand that BrightLife China must abandon her old ways of doing business and embark on a new path. But before that can happen, Fred will have to be dismissed... at once, to be frank—"

Despite myself, I held up my hand. "If I may just interrupt?" I would normally have been more patient, but I needed to understand why the company and Fred could no longer coexist. "Is it because of that day he came in with the *feng shui* master while we were working overtime?"

"No... no," Waits said, waving his hands. His voice had become high-pitched and one of his eyebrows was twisted, as if he'd just heard a risible question. "No, I don't care a whit about his hobbies or what god he prays to, though his rudeness that day did serve as something of a catalyst, and helped make my decision more cut-and-dri—"

"But Waits," Daisy broke in, "I think Jade has just asked a valuable question, which raises a valid concern. If we don't effectively communicate just why BrightLife has given Fred the bum's rush, our employees may assume that it's due simply to a power struggle within management team."

"Yeah, yeah." Waits bobbed his head. "Proper communication is vital. That's why I think it's best now to give Jade a rundown of Fred's covert scheme of fraud. Get on with it, Daisy."

What Daisy sketched on the whiteboard in the conference room didn't take me entirely by surprise. But it did fill in the other half of the picture that Edith and I had sketched out together, based on those unmatched purchase and sales transactions. Apparently Daisy had gotten further with the numbers in the account books, unraveling the complicated flows of goods and money used for an embezzlement scheme. As I'd presumed during my talk with Edith in the canteen two and half months before, the purchase orders from K.J. were indeed forged, while the corresponding orders from BrightLife Switzerland were real. But neither of us had known then that though the items and quantities in both sets of purchase orders were the same, the *monetary worth* of the ones from K.J. was actually much more. The finance department paid K.J. for the higher-valued fake purchases, but never entered the real, lower-cost ones from Switzerland in the books. Our sales to New Tech Co, on the other hand, were authentic—but their payments had been directed to Fred's personal bank account in Hong Kong. Using that account, Fred had managed to transfer the amount we owed to Switzerland. Thus an accumulated one million yuans had gone astray, the difference between what

BrightLife China had paid to K.J. for the fake purchases and what BrightLife Switzerland had received.

I was thunderstruck. I'd seen how doctors in the hospital where I used to work accepted from patients red packets enclosing money. I'd learned from my parents-in-law how teachers unethically profited from students. I'd even witnessed a man trying to bribe my father-in-law. But I'd never envisaged such a fiendish scheme for personal gain. I was staggered that Fred could've carried out such a scheme without turning a hair, and I still had many questions.

"Good grief! It's..." I shook my head in disbelief. "I don't know what to say. But Daisy, it was my understanding that our Boston headquarters employed a world-renowned auditing firm to check the company's books every year. Before you arrived, in fact, they'd just come to examine our operations. Didn't they notice anything wrong?"

"Lucy fiddled the books very cleverly," said Daisy. "As long as Fred paid BrightLife Switzerland on time, and was careful to send his receipts from New Tech back to BrightLife China, all the outstanding accounts were cleared, and the price difference was pocketed seamlessly. He made these types of transactions so infrequently that the auditors could easily overlook them if their sampling size wasn't large enough. The auditing firm did detect the weak internal controls that were partially responsible for the fraud."

"In other words," I hazarded, "this time, Switzerland tried to recover what we owed to them because Fred hadn't settled their invoices through his Hong Kong bank account. Was that how the scheme was brought to light?"

"Yes," Daisy nodded. "The latest transactions related to the scheme occurred after this year's audit, and were half accomplished before Lucy left because BrightLife Switzerland hadn't been paid."

"I see." I recalled that in August, before he went on his summer holidays, I'd often seen Daisy talking with Fred. "Has Fred admitted his wrongdoings?"

"I tried to wring an outright confession from him. He was economical with the truth, but he pulled no punches. He claimed he'd been using his personal account for BrightLife's sake, because the particular Chinese thing called 'capital control' made it difficult for BrightLife China to pay its Swiss sister company, which never shipped the goods across the border into the Mainland. In the latest case, he said that since New Tech was behind in remittance to his account, he hadn't wired the due amount to Switzerland. However, he never breathed a word about the dummy purchase he'd booked and paid for. It's very likely that, because Lucy is no longer with the company, he doesn't suspect that we're already in the loop on the issue with K.J."

"And there was one last thing," Waits piped up. He'd been scribbling in his notebook so quietly that I'd almost forgotten he was there. "We have some doubt about what Fred said about the company in Hong Kong you mentioned just now. We don't believe it's really a branch of New Tech. In fact, we have evidence that it's affiliated with K.J. Co BrightLife Switzerland THAT drop-shipped the goods to that Hong Kong company, which in turn sent them to New Tech, which is located in a Chinese city near Hong Kong." He paused, looking fairly mysterious. "What's more, this scheme cannot be an isolated one. The betting is that our exclusive partnership contract with Shing Sheng is part of another of Fred's plots." Waits paused again, giving me time to absorb this appalling idea. Then, shifting gears, he went on, "But we're not detectives. It's not our job to prosecute Fred. What Boston headquarters expects of us is to develop BrightLife's business in China. Unfortunately, Fred's been feathering his own nest, and we don't foresee that he'll clean up his act. His misconduct and his sloppy management are making our mission impossible, and that's why he has to go. The timing is perfect—Daisy and I have been here only a few months, and if we can free BrightLife China from the burdens of the past, it will have an opportunity to make a new start."

He looked at me with an encouraging smile. "Jade, we need to work together carefully to terminate Fred's employment with BrightLife and restructure the company. Meanwhile, we must get down to building up BrightLife China's vision, mission, and values cohesively. With your personnel skills, we expect you to be deeply involved in these activities and make good contributions."

Waits' plan sounded grandiose compared to my everyday work, which until now had offered nothing as dramatic as combating fraud. It would be disingenuous to deny my excitement—though I drew a veil over it—at this challenging assignment. It would turn me from an onlooker into a figure of action, doing things that would put BrightLife on a new track, and make its employees' lives better.

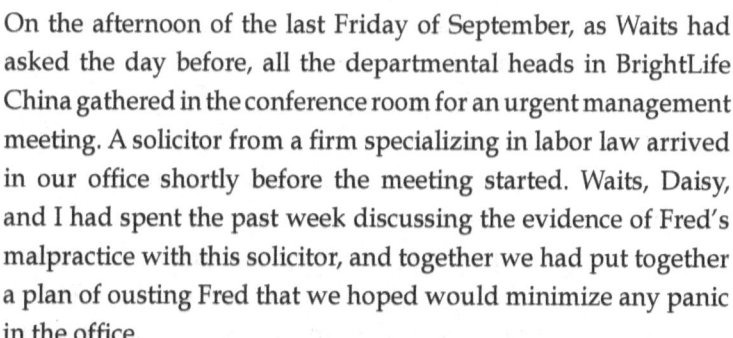

On the afternoon of the last Friday of September, as Waits had asked the day before, all the departmental heads in BrightLife China gathered in the conference room for an urgent management meeting. A solicitor from a firm specializing in labor law arrived in our office shortly before the meeting started. Waits, Daisy, and I had spent the past week discussing the evidence of Fred's malpractice with this solicitor, and together we had put together a plan of ousting Fred that we hoped would minimize any panic in the office.

THE ENVELOPES

While Waits went to call Fred over, I led the solicitor to the reception room. Simultaneously, Daisy informed the relevant people that the meeting would be deferred for half an hour, without giving away its real purpose: to tell everyone about Fred's dismissal, once we'd finished speaking with him in the reception room.

Fred exuded an air of relaxation as he followed Waits into the room, but the muscles in Waits' face looked taut. That contrast, plus the sheer drop from Fred's stature to Waits', made the scene feel so unreal. Hypocrisy could cloak itself in the guise of a saint—that was what the good-looking, calm, well-mannered Fred impressed conveyed to me then. And a sincere man could look like a devil—like Waits, with his tilted eyebrow and the lifted corner of his mouth. Sitting down, Waits announced BrightLife's decision to discharge Fred and concisely enumerated the rationale. Fred neither seemed petrified nor went ballistic, but he fulminated against the decision. What he'd done was normal in a company in China, he retorted, and he deserved a fair hearing. Waits emphasized to him, with the support from the solicitor, that his misconduct had damaged the interests of BrightLife and was therefore unpardonable.

Fred glared at him. "You'll see my lawyer soon."

"If you like to make it complicated, we're ready for it," Waits responded, forcing a smile. "But right now, you have to leave. Jade will accompany you to your office, so she can collect the assets that belong to the company."

The solicitor went off, Waits moved to the conference room, where Daisy and the rest of the management team must've been seated by then, and I followed Fred to his office.

As we reached the doorway, Cathy happened to be coming out. Seeing Fred, she reported, "It's done. And they're gone."

"Thank you," Fred replied apathetically. "It doesn't matter

anymore."

Cathy blinked in bafflement, stepping aside to let us in.

My jaw sagged as I caught sight of the changes in Fred's office. Pulling myself together, I went straight to the laptop on the desk, now sitting perpendicularly to its previous position. Picking it up, I said, "No hard feelings. I just have to take it back on behalf of the company."

For a while, Fred said nothing as he strode around his newly redesigned office, which probably looked unfamiliar to him too, rounding up his personal belongings. He seemed much less emotional than we'd thought he'd be. If he felt anger and frustration, he was keeping it well under wraps; instead, he looked weighed down with disappointment.

"I'll fetch a cardboard box for you," I offered after I'd stood there for a short while, watching his stuff pile up.

I stopped by the personnel department, leaving Fred's laptop on my desk, then looked for a box in storage. When I returned to his office and passed him the box, Fred said in a genteel manner, "It's certainly *kind* of you. But what's really behind a woman's kindness?"

"Pardon me?"

"Are you confused?" he said snidely, not looking at me but putting his things, one by one, into the box. "I bet you're not as confused as I am."

I was speechless. I had no idea what was on his mind.

"My father used to say, 'Women are like fragile china vases. It's a delight for a man to keep them pretty and appreciate them, but it's a disaster for a man to listen to them.' I never believed much of what that man said, including his remark about women. I took my wife's *kind* advice on board—but Buddha and *feng shui* don't help me at all, do they? I trusted you women, I made you all managers here, but now I've been betrayed. What's behind your *kindness* is only Schadenfreude, isn't it?"

I said nothing, feeling sad for him; he was a hopeless case.

"The deuce!" he said, as if to himself. "Turns out that man has been proved right. Look at me now! What a disaster." He threw the last things in the box, leaving a few stray items on the desk. "Cathy!"

Cathy didn't appear.

"Is there anything else I can help you with?" I asked.

He didn't answer, only glared at me. "It's not over yet. See you soon."

I smiled silently, feeling an involuntary shudder of disgust.

He returned a faint sneer before, clutching the box, he stormed out of the office, without casting a glance at the giant 愛 that still hung on the wall, whose power he'd trusted to ward off misfortune. It looked more conspicuous now, above the rearranged furniture, which had taken on a desolate look.

I'd started to tidy up the office when Cathy dashed in, agog to know what had happened.

"Jade, what's going on?" She goggled at me. "I just now bumped into Fred in the hall. He said he's leaving the company, and then, like that, he just stomped off."

"Be patient, Cathy. The official announcement will be coming out soon. What happened to this room? It didn't look this way this morning."

She sighed. "Do you remember that Saturday, about three weeks ago, when Fred showed up here with his wife and his *feng shui* master while you all were working overtime?"

"Oh, yes."

"Master Zhong decided that the decor of Fred's office had to be adjusted to keep at bay the destructive energy from Daisy's office. Fred called me suddenly last night and demanded that, whatever it took, I had to get Master Zhong and his assistant over here, *today* — exactly when all the managers would be in the meeting called by Waits. My, his *feng shui* action came a bit late..."

I smiled ruefully. It seemed that Fred had truly been hoisted by his own petard.

12

In the wake of Fred's dismissal, it was challenging to disseminate the information on the company's action. I tried to downplay the reason for Fred's departure, focusing instead on the plans for BrightLife China's future. Between us, Daisy and I oiled the wheels of Waits' communications to all the employees. Most of them didn't read English, and many had concerns that needed to be answered with care by someone with a Chinese cultural background. Though there was no obvious, immediate boost in morale, at least the general feeling at the company didn't seem either hostile or cynical. As a matter of fact, the majority of employees openly showed their respect for Waits and Daisy's good faith, and demonstrated an eagerness to help the company rally. It was at that psychologically crucial moment that I found myself playing a major role in finding candidates to replace Fred, as well as organizing seminars in which managers and other key employees could brainstorm, rebuilding the vision, mission, and values of BrightLife China. Meanwhile, under the leadership of Waits and Daisy, BrightLife shifted its focus to a strategic move that had a direct bearing on its business in the long run: negotiating an exit strategy with Shing Sheng, through which we could part company on good terms, while still insisting that it clear its debts—a king's ransom's worth—to BrightLife China.

Waits, Daisy, and Rose were our delegates in the negotiations, assisted by the AnLong law firm behind the scenes. Rose, though she'd been looking glum ever since Fred was turfed out, at least managed to curb her temper now most of the time. In any case, she seemed to be on medical leave much of the time, claiming that she suffered neurasthenia.

We went through rounds of negotiation, to little avail. Every management meeting began with the same news: our dialogue with Shing Sheng Co, once again, had reached an impasse. By the end of 2007, Waits had had enough. After all the measured steps that BrightLife had taken to resolve the issue, he declared, with the blessing of our headquarters in Boston, BrightLife China had instructed AnLong to file a lawsuit in our city's court—the jurisdiction stipulated in the contract—to recover the money owed to us by Shing Sheng Co and terminate our so-called partnership.

Finally BrightLife China was emancipated from the straitjacket of its contract with Shing Sheng, and the sales team was gingered up. At almost the same time, the three-month-long recruiting process ended, and Charles Kai would fill the vacancy left by Fred. All in all, BrightLife China was expected to develop her business at full pelt, despite the legal battle we had just begun in court against Shing Sheng Co.

———∞———

Fred never brought his defense lawyer to us. Nevertheless, until that chill morning in late February of 2008, we didn't realize that his simmering resentment had become a sword of Damocles hanging over BrightLife China's head. I still have vivid memories of the day on which the crisis caught BrightLife China unprepared.

On that rather quiet morning, Daisy and I were having a discussion in the meeting room outside her office and the one that used to be Fred's, but now was temporarily being shared by Charles and Waits, who'd been taking Charles on business trips for orientation since he joined BrightLife, a month or so previously.

We were interrupted by Wings, looking unusually frantic with worry. "We have an emergency, Daisy," she said as she stomped in.

I excused myself and went back to my department. Before long, Cathy—when Fred's era ended, she'd been reappointed as office administration supervisor, and now reported to me—rushed in and helplessly notified me that three strange men had just barged into the company and made a beeline for the finance department, the innocent receptionist showing them the way.

I rushed over there, arriving at the same time as Daisy and Wings. I walked over to stand beside Daisy, and we watched a stout man, arms akimbo and his back toward us, plant himself in the center of the room. The other two men with him had begun rooting through documents stored in a cabinet.

The accounting clerk murmured, in a timid voice, "Here are our bosses."

The stout man wheeled and came up to us. "Who's in charge?"

"I'm in charge," said Daisy, calmly and firmly. "And who are you?"

The man, who looked middle-aged, eyed Daisy from head to toe with a disdainful smile. Then he fished his business card out of his coat pocket and presented it to us. "Qi Mu, Judge, Court of Shiwu City," it read.

"Judge Mu," Daisy inquired politely, "may I know on what mission you are here?"

"The answer is staring you in the face. We're sealing up your company's records related to the account of Shing Sheng Co," the man said drily as he drew a sheet of A4 paper out of a big envelope that he'd just taken from his shoulder bag. "You see this? It's the court injunction."

"In this case, Judge Mu," Daisy responded, her voice still even, "I'd like you to first talk with Mr Liang from AnLong, our appointed law firm."

While Daisy was connecting with Mr Liang via her mobile phone and then briefing him on what was happening, the man motioned to his minions to pause. Then, snatching Daisy's phone from her, he introduced himself to Mr Liang and read aloud the content of the injunction. Daisy stood straight as a ramrod, gazing as the man, with raw boorishness, was only disclosing, over the phone with Mr Liang, that Shiwu Court's action had been triggered by the lawsuit and legitimate request filed by Shing Sheng Co.

Passing the phone back to Daisy, he ordered his men to resume. Wings went in to look over their shoulders, ensuring that they retained no working papers irrelevant to the case. Daisy eased out of the room, softly conversing with Mr Liang over the phone. I followed behind until we were out of earshot of the rest.

Daisy rang off and turned to me. "Gee, I never imagined encountering a judge who behaved like such a bully."

"You certainly kept your cool with him," I said admiringly, "not bowing and scraping with your face wreathed in groveling smiles, the way people in China so often do under such circumstances."

"I'm gonna level with you, Jade. I was quaking in my boots only a moment ago," she confessed. "But I thought about the story you told me, about that time you faced down a hooligan. That helped to steady me."

"Your conduct must've looked unorthodox to that 'judge'. But I don't understand, Daisy. Waits announced before that we'd sued Shing Sheng in *our city's* court. Why did a judge from Shiwu

THE ENVELOPES

suddenly plunge in?"

"It's mystifying that the shoe seems on the other foot now," she mused. "At this point, even Mr Liang doesn't know why Shing Sheng has been able to request an injunction from the court of a city that is not the jurisdiction stated in the contract. He said Judge Mu had promised to see him about it tomorrow in Shiwu Court. But, Jade, BrightLife China is on the rocks — that's what Wings came to tell me earlier when you and I were talking in the meeting room. I'm racking my brains for a solution. Once those guys leave us alone, Wings and I need to fill you in on the situation. Come on, let's get back there now."

When Daisy and I reentered the finance department, the two minions were packing the papers into two cardboard boxes. The stout man was talking to the other party on his mobile phone loudly, as if he believed we couldn't see or hear him. "… You should be satisfied. I've already had their bank accounts frozen. Yes, we're now suspending their books, too. I'm calling a halt to it before you go too far. Listen to me. That's all for today."

Wings came over to us, shaking her head. "Is he really the judge who issued the court injunction?"

Daisy whispered in English. "He sounds like he's only the errand boy, and someone else is calling the tune."

"They say," Wings commented, in English too, "a judge in China is a wolf in the uniform of justice—"

She broke off as the trio, having finished their work, walked past us, flicking the dust off their clothes. The stout man shot us an imperious look. "Your lawyer is coming to my court tomorrow. I'll hand him the summons in person then."

They stalked off, leaving behind two cardboard boxes in a corner of the room, sealed by crossing white paper bands on which the name of court and the current date were handwritten in black ink.

Daisy, Wings, and I looked at each other, at a loss for words. Then Daisy shrugged. "Gee, that's adding to the richness of my career life. Well, we have no time to waste. Come on, let's go and talk."

Sitting in the meeting room, I was transfixed with shock as Daisy and Wings detailed what had happened *before* the trio showed up. No wonder the stout man had just now boasted about freezing our bank accounts.

"Let me see if I've got it right," I said when they were done, trying to get to grips with the situation. "To my understanding, this morning, when the accountant was trying to make a routine payment through one of our bank accounts, her request was rejected by the bank, which then informed her that the account had been frozen a short while ago by an injunction from Shiwu Court. She at once reported the problem to Wings. Wings quickly checked with the other banks that we do business through, and found *all* of our bank accounts locked. The frozen amount granted by the injunction is twice as much as Shing Sheng owes us, and way above the sum of cash in all of our bank accounts. Therefore, every incoming remittance to those accounts will also be frozen until our total cash reaches the amount stated in the injunction. In other words, we will have no money available to make payments. How can our company operate daily? Good grief!"

"And the first tough nut to crack is that we might not be able to issue the paychecks that are due in a couple of days," Daisy warned. "We have to think about how to break that to all the employees, if the worst happens."

"How about we open a new bank account and direct our customers' remittances to it?" I said. "Then at least we'd have some money for the payroll."

"I don't think so," Wings opined. "It remains a riddle how, but the fact is, Shiwu Court has traced *all* our existing bank accounts. I foresee the injunction following hard on the heels of any other account we open."

"The writing on the wall," Daisy added, "is that Shing Sheng is desperate to force BrightLife China into a cul-de-sac. Still, opening a new bank account might not be a bad idea, depending on the properties of the account. The court injunction can freeze assets, but not liability."

"Now there's an idea," Wings said, brightening. "If we have an overdraft account, as long as we maintain it with a below-zero balance every single day, Shing Sheng will have no way to take it from us, and we can keep operations running. It won't be difficult to ensure a negative balance," she said drily, "seeing as we're currently short in cash anyhow. But… the problem is that we don't have the borrowing power to get that kind of credit."

"Corporate headquarters in Boston does," said Daisy. "Corporate can endorse BrightLife China's request for credit. I'll get together with Waits and confer with corporate tonight, when their morning starts. Wings, right now you and I have to go meet with the local branch of a foreign bank that has been working with BrightLife worldwide. Let's get down to the nitty gritty and make our idea work before time runs out for issuing paychecks. But Jade, please keep your powder dry for the worst. Let's roll."

———∽∼∽———

The next day, as Daisy and Wings fought, by hook or by crook, to make sure BrightLife China weathered the storm, I worked on setting up Plans A and B, as per Daisy's advice.

Waits had received the bad news the day before from Daisy and now was already back, leaving Charles alone to continue the business trip. Mr Liang, right after seeing the stout man in Shiwu Court, came to our company in the late afternoon. Then, the three shut themselves in the conference room, where Mr Liang must have expanded upon the lawsuit filed by Shing Sheng Co.

On the morning of the second day after BrightLife China's financial operation was interrupted, Waits called an emergency meeting of the management team, and unfolded the ins and outs of the matter: Shiwu Court had accepted the filing based on a piece of paper submitted by Shing Sheng Co, which served as an agreement to shift the jurisdiction to Shiwu City, signed by — Fred. This piece of paper, with only two printed sentences, had equal legal force to that of the three-page partnership contract. Unfortunately, because it was signed on a date much later than that when the contract became effective, it automatically superseded, in the eyes of the law, the corresponding clause in the contract. The court in our city would have to transfer the case to Shiwu Court, which was now presenting the piece of paper as evidence. Our lawsuit would be annulled, and we would become the defendant in Shiwu Court, unless it could be proven that either Fred's signature was forged, or the date on the paper was wrong.

Waits passed the copy of the agreement that Mr Liang had brought back from Shiwu Court round to all the people at the meeting. Everyone looked shocked, shaking their heads, bitterly smiling, or whispering to one another...

"Looking at the date below the signature on this agreement," Daisy remarked, "I realized it was the day when some of you, Fred, and I had the very first meeting with Shing Sheng, talking about the partnership contract and what they owed us."

"Ha, indeed," Pearl said, counting dates on her fingers, "that was the day when I read the entire contract for the first time. And I remember Fred looked more heated than you over Shing Sheng's arguments. He was in a bad mood, apparently caused by Shing Sheng. If he signed an agreement so favorable to them on that day, I'll eat my hat." Instantly, Pearl's words summoned up the memory of my conversation with her after she sneaked out of that clamorous meeting and came into the canteen where I was having my late lunch, around seven months previously.

"Rose," Waits asked, "what do you think?"

"I never knew that Fred had any intention to change any contract term," Rose replied, her voice unusually calm. "And I don't think he had time on that day to reach any agreement with Shing Sheng. They actually drove off once the meeting ended — they didn't even attend the dinner we'd arranged to entertain them."

"The only clear thing is," Waits said, "that the signatory was Fred himself. Our lawyer also brought back a copy of Fred's oral testimony, dictated by Shiwu Court, in which he vouched for the authenticity of the amended terms signed by him on that day. Yeah, yeah, I've been hearing your perspectives on it. Can I summarize that we have reasonable doubt about the signing date? He didn't sign on that day, but *after* he left BrightLife."

"My God," Edith drawled, "Fred is playing hell with our company, and perverting the course of justice while he's at it. He must hate our guts. Or he's getting money for it from Shing Sheng."

Everyone fell silent for an instant. It seemed that Edith had a talent for always making a casual blunt remark that struck home.

"For another thing," Wings said, "Shing Sheng, as the plaintiff, must've put a huge amount of idle cash into Shiwu Court as collateral. It's supposed to be the same amount as what is in the accounts they're trying to freeze. If they've really done that, they must be in a pickle themselves."

Rose grunted. "As I said before, Shing Sheng is rich."

"Yeah?" Waits cut in, incredulous. "Our lawyer, in the course of trying to have the court injunction revoked, expressed doubt about Shing Sheng's financial capacity to request the court's action—but the judge, as was his right, remained silent on the question. What we know is that Shing Sheng is a powerful entrepreneur in Shiwu City, which is much smaller than our city. It's not hard to imagine that Shing Sheng has some influence on the local government authorities there, and Shiwu Court is unlikely to be an exception. We just don't know how Shing Sheng is holding sway over Shiwu Court. And—bad news for us—the court is not going to take back the injunction."

"However, regardless of the deal between Shiwu Court and Shing Sheng, it's fortunate," Daisy declared, "that we've already found a way to minimize the impact of the court injunction and continue our operations."

Secretly, I heaved a long sigh of relief, knowing that the Plan B I'd prepared for the worst-case scenario was now of little use. Daisy's affirmation in the meeting called off the state of emergency for BrightLife China, though she and Wings were still hard at work on turning an idea that could restore our cash flow, outside the frozen accounts, into reality. Operations in the office were being restored to normal.

———∞∞———

That afternoon, after a business appointment outside the office, I went back home slightly earlier than usual. As I got off the lift on our floor, I saw a man in a suit, coat in hand, coming out of our apartment, nodding toward someone inside, with a quiet "Thank you. Thank you. Bye." He turned and, the door clicking closed behind him, walked toward the elevator, brushing past me. He was very much in a world of his own, not even glancing at me, his face, perfectly unknown to me, radiant with satisfaction.

I unlocked the door with the key and slipped into the entrance hall, announcing aloud "I'm home!" The inner screen, I noticed, had been left open.

Taohua appeared in haste, wiping her hands on the apron she wore. "Aya, Miss," she exclaimed, "You're back early today."

While I was taking off my down jacket, I caught sight of two fat brown paper envelopes sitting on the corner table. "What's that?" I asked. "Just now, I ran into a strange man outside our door."

"It's... yes, the man..." Taohua spoke haltingly, as if her thoughts for a few seconds were jumbled. "It was a man bringing some papers Mr Dai Senior told me he was expecting." She quickly picked up the envelopes and, holding them, started walking into the living room. "I should've put them in Mr Dai Senior's room," she said over her shoulder. "But the pot on the stove was almost burning. I'll be right back and pour you hot tea. It's so cold today." And she disappeared into my father-in-law's bedroom.

"I want a warm bath now," I said. "It's freezing, for nearly the end of February."

Slowly my body relaxed in the steaming bathtub, but my head was still on edge. Until two days ago, it had never occurred to me that I'd ever have to worry that the company might suddenly be unable to pay its employees. They say the marketplace is a cut-throat battlefield, but it seemed incredible that Shing Sheng Co would be so desperate to bring BrightLife China down, or that Fred would hold such bitter animosity toward the many people he blamed for his expulsion. Was Buddha the one that Fred beseeched to give him love or pelf? Had he believed his job would bring him certain power that the Buddha had promised to make him wealthy? In the dead of night, had he ever pleaded for the Buddha to serve his personal gain, by harming BrightLife's employees? There was a world of difference between Fred and my father-in-law, an authority who'd lived a pure life...

Afterward, snug at the dinner table with my family, I felt as if I'd just returned to a peaceful and cozy harbor after a journey on the rough sea. The void left by my mother-in-law's death was still not filled, but Taohua's devotion to our daily life had made the apartment a true home for us.

My father-in-law seemed to be in a good mood too. "It's been quite some time since we family last ate together," he remarked. "Little Jve, is it your busy job that has recently made you so often come home late and miss dinner?"

"Sort of, Father," I responded, after sipping the steaming, tasty soup. "Things in the office have been coming thick and fast. They've been really mind-blowing."

"Let us hear about them," my father-in-law encouraged, smiling at me.

Refreshed by the warm bath I'd taken just before the meal, I felt a wave of energy, and in one breath, I briefed the table on the wave after wave of turmoil that had rocked BrightLife China, as well as Fred's latest maneuver and Daisy's countermeasure.

"I would say the key is not about the whopper Fred told, but the *guanxi*," Deping mused. "I gather the relationship between Judge Mu and Shing Sheng Co might've gone beyond that between a court and a plaintiff."

That reminded me of a detail I'd nearly forgotten, on the day when the stout man and his minions swooped down on our office. "You're probably right. Actually, that day, we all heard the stout man — the judge — telling another party on the phone that he'd done the things on their wish list. It won't be a wild guess that 'the other party' was Shing Sheng, which seemed to have power over him."

"It doesn't surprise me." Deping chewed thoughtfully for a moment and then resumed, "If there's dirty money involved in their *guanxi*. And if perjury cannot be proven and the trial has to be in Shiwu Court, I'd predict the odds are not in your company's favor."

"So does the lawyer who works for our company," I said, recalling the intent that Waits had revealed to the special task force formed by himself, Daisy, Wings, me, plus the lawyer, right after his urgent communication with the entire management team. "Therefore, as proposed by the lawyer, our company is going to apply to the court in our city, before it has to transfer the case to Shiwu, to carry out a technical analysis to determine the actual date Fred signed the change in jurisdiction term. The problem is, no one can guarantee that the analytic techniques available now are sufficient, though they're already more advanced than they used to be. If the analysis can't tip the scales in our favor, we're doomed to failure in Shiwu Court. But—we're going to appeal the verdict to the provincial court, a higher one in the area Shiwu belongs to, and less likely to be in thrall to Shing Sheng."

"If the lawyer isn't certain about the result of the technical analysis," Deping asked, "why take the trouble to do it, instead of just having the trial in Shiwu Court and then appealing to ask the higher court to overturn the ruling?"

"Daisy asked that question too," I recollected. "The lawyer explained that, when the appraisal is going on, he'll first approach the provincial court and try to build up *guanxi* with it to ensure an unbiased trial for our appeal."

Deping nearly choked on a morsel of food. "Ho, ho! Build up *guanxi* to do justice?"

"Oh, Deping, don't get worked up," I teased, patting him on the back, as I was sitting beside him.

Clearing his throat, Deping went on, "And your company is accusing Shing Sheng of having Shiwu Court in its pocket. Talk about the pot calling the kettle black!"

"Well, Daisy reacted the same way as you. Yet the French

head of our company expressed his approval of the lawyer's plan. He claimed that his experiences in China have taught him the importance of *guanxi* to any success. Anyway, Daisy has clarified her position that the lawyer should not touch bribery with a barge pole."

Taohua left the table for the kitchen. "Little Jve," my father-in-law said, "there's a possibility that your company will lose the battle in the end, even though the truth looks quite obvious to everyone, including the courts."

"Unfortunately, that's true." I sighed. "But if Shing Sheng wins, there will be no justice in this country."

"If you think so," my father-in-law continued, putting down his food and gazing at me. "If your company's lawyer resorts to obtaining *guanxi* with the court via money, and in turn, getting justice for your company, don't you reckon that the end justifies the means?"

"I think justice that can be bought is not justice and will never prevail," I replied, feeling a tad surprised. After a pause, "Father, as a matter of fact, I thought nothing wrong with the lawyer's plan until Daisy warned him that we're seeking not an easy way but an ethical way to have justice done. Daisy called up my memories of Mother. Mother never exploited your power in her great passion for improving children's education, even when she had no other means to achieve. I take Daisy's side, and apparently Deping is on my wavelength." At that very moment, it suddenly struck me that I had truly accepted the fact: my father-in-law's rejection of my request to use his authority to arrange an appointment with a renowned doctor had not caused my baby son's death. Reflecting on this, I fell silent, looking at my father-in-law.

My father-in-law was silent too, but I had a strange feeling that he'd put my stance to the test, and now he was in a mixed

THE ENVELOPES

state of relief and meditativeness. Then, seeing Taohua returning with a platter in her hands, he said cheerily—at least, so it seemed—"Tangerines of February, and pineapples of coming March. Thanks to Taohua, we've never missed fresh seasonal fruits... I almost forgot. Taohua is going back to her village early tomorrow morning for a personal matter. We'll have to take care of our meals on our own."

"I'll be back the day after tomorrow," Taohua hurried to add, sitting down again opposite me.

"Why not stay there a little longer, since you don't go home often?" Deping suggested. "Don't worry about us."

"Aya, one day is enough," Taohua insisted. "I don't have much to do at home. I'd rather work here."

"All right, suit yourself." Deping smiled, and then murmured, "Felix just came to my mind. I'm wondering whether it's time to contact him, to see how he's doing with his teaching in the countryside..."

At that moment I happened to turn my head just in time to see Taohua turn, with a glint of panic in her eye, toward my father-in-law. *It was as if she'd just been asked a question she was unable to answer*, I thought, *and voicelessly begged for his aid*.

My father-in-law seemed to have not noticed Taohua. He paused a moment, savoring every mouthful of his fruit, and then said slowly, "If my memory serves me correctly, Felix went to the country last September. So it's been less than half a year. He might've just become accustomed to the harsh conditions now."

"I hear you," Deping said. "I hope he thrives in his chosen cause. And I just want very much to have him inspire my students."

"Son, more haste, less speed. You'd better be patient."

HASU AUGUST

The next morning, right after I got out of bed, I pulled the curtain aside and looked out from our window on the fifth floor. At first, as usual, I saw the black sedan on the street below. I should've thought nothing of it. It had been my routine ever since I married and moved into the apartment: at the same time every morning, my husband and I were awakened by our alarm clock. Then I opened the window to let fresh air into our room, while Deping straightaway made his morning toilet. Therefore, unless my father-in-law was away on business, I always saw the car downstairs, with unfailing regularity: Driver Fu standing beside it, smoking a cigarette while dutifully waiting for his regular passenger, who was having breakfast in our dining room and would soon say goodbye to us. It was as if a videotape was rewound and then played each morning, sometimes with a slight modification of Driver Fu's position, depending on the weather.

However, that day, the scene was different. When I pushed the window open, I espied my father-in-law *and* Taohua coming out of our block and walking to exchange greetings with Driver Fu. My father-in-law took the front passenger seat, and Taohua crawled into the rear of the car as if she was under the heavy weight of the bulging backpack she was clutching to her chest. As soon as she closed the door, the car started, speeding off in a twinkling of an eye.

With a gleam of doubt lurking in my mind, I went through my usual morning procedures and dispatched the hearty breakfast that had apparently been readied by Taohua before she left. Only when Deping and I were on our way to work, rushing through the community park, did I say, "Dear, didn't you once say that no one in our family had ever taken a ride in Father's car?"

"Yes. And it's true. Even when Mother got sick, we either hailed a taxi or called an ambulance to send her to a hospital and afterward bring her home. What's up?"

THE ENVELOPES

"Oh, just now I happened to see the car downstairs whisk away both Father and Taohua."

"Hum, that's a bit odd..." He was first a tad unresponsive, but quick to add, "Well, I gather Old Man is giving her a lift to the coach terminal on the way to his destination."

"Probably..."

"You sound skeptical, Jade." He turned to flutter his eyelashes at me while we kept walking, hand in hand.

I shrugged. "Oh, I'm just a bit curious."

For a second, that faint plea in Taohua's eyes as she looked at my father-in-law at the end of dinner the night before flashed through my mind. But touching upon it to Deping would only leave him in confusion, as I found it impossible to explain my feeling about the subtle hints of something that might be happening between my father-in-law and Taohua. Deping and I were parting to catch, respectively, the subway and the bus. It was just another working day in our lives.

13

While wrestling in court with Shing Sheng Co, BrightLife China, under the leadership of Waits and with the support of Boston headquarters, navigated the ensuing three years, making various and rapid changes. By late 2008 we'd relocated our facility for sales, marketing, and administration to a skyscraper in the heart of the city. It's not just rodomontade to say this was a major administrative project, one that I was proud of. I'd been put in charge of general office matters as well as personnel when Fred's era came to an end. Cathy and I worked like furies, and everyone applauded the results. And then, as many other multinational companies did, we built up a logistic center on the outskirts by late 2009, and then a plant in this small town where I'm now spending my night. Both facilities were intended to serve for distribution of assembled-in-China products through BrightLife's operations in the Asia-Pacific region.

 The active role I played in creating from scratch a large workforce for these new establishments enriched my experience in human-resources management. As Waits had hoped, Charles, Fred's replacement, restructured the entire sales organization to conform to redefined selling strategies—an effort that brought on the departure of Rose, whose frequent skiving on the pretext of poor health could be no longer tolerated. "Restructuring," as a piece of professional jargon, sounds pleasant enough, but it

THE ENVELOPES

was the hardest part of my job, trapping me between ice and fire. The cold-bloodedness of sacking people was a challenge to my instinctive compassion, but recruiting new employees warmed my heart, much as I remembered feeling on welcoming a little bundle from heaven, when I worked as a nurse. Charles occasionally reminded me of Rose when he lashed out at someone in the office, but he led his team well. With the support of the other departments, his strategy for aggressive sales growth soon had sales branches spreading far and wide. Given the company's rapid expansion, I—as did Edith, Pearl, Wings, the two new sales managers who replaced Rose, and the managers of our new industrial sites—had my hands full throughout these years. By the end of 2010, all our hard work was paying off. BrightLife China had outstripped the market, leaving our competitors scrambling to catch up. On top of all this, Waits and Daisy had been devoting time and energy to the BrightLife subsidiaries in three other countries within the Asia-Pacific region that were also their responsibility.

In my personal life—which, unsurprisingly, was squeezed into a very narrow time band—I secretly preened myself on two achievements. First, having identified inadequacies in my management concepts and skills, in mid-2009, I enrolled in a twenty-four-month MBA program, and persevered with my studies. And second, Deping and I bought a car, and, straining every nerve, I finally acquired my driving license. By late 2009, I'd started commuting by car, though Deping still preferred the subway; on a train, he could read a book, no matter whether he was standing or sitting. On balance, our family lived a comfortable and peaceful life, for which Taohua deserved most of the credit. Several times every year, she put in for a short leave to go back to her village, and my father-in-law always readily accepted her request. I could empathize with her missing, if not her husband, her daughter Lianhua. Every time, the morning after she'd made the request, I would watch—as I had since the very first time I spotted the two leaving together, in early 2008—my father-in-law and Taohua, clasping her backpack, climb into the black sedan.

I noticed that Taohua never rode with father-in-law in his sedan when she went to her village on her regular holidays, only when she made a last-minute request. Once, observing them leaving together, a scene that had long since ceased to surprise me, I casually mentioned this oddity to my husband.

Looking a bit disapproving, he said, "I'm sure that's because when Taohua has time to plan ahead, there's no rush. Or maybe she usually takes her regular trip on public holidays, when Father isn't using his driver anyway."

I went blank. Noticing my speechlessness, Deping grinned. "My nosy wife, I have grave doubts you're cut out to be an amateur sleuth. And you don't seem to have time to waste on that, either."

I had nothing to say in my defense, but my silence didn't necessarily mean that I was satisfied. It still seemed very strange to me. It didn't help that every time Taohua returned from these visits to her family, and I tried to ask how Lianhua's education was going, I hit a stone wall. Taohua would only say that her little girl was fine, in the care of her husband. In the end I decided to drop the subject. Perhaps the loss of Meihua was still a dull pain to Taohua, and making her feel guilty about Meihua's melancholy school days would be imprudent, even though Taohua had evidently recovered her vigor as time went by.

It is fairly ironic that, in those years, I thought of myself as someone who could hear the grass grow, alert to the faintest hint of change. Nevertheless, Daisy's attitude toward truth-seeking carried some clout with me, and I had to admit that

THE ENVELOPES

this inquisitiveness consumed time that I could scarcely afford to waste. Therefore, I chose to believe that the truth about my father-in-law's unusual conduct would, in dribs and drabs, find me just in time, as long as I kept my heart and mind wide open.

The haphazard way I'm chronicling all these events and changes, at my work as well as home, might be a little dizzying. And, in fact, my recollection of those events is keeping my brain cells buzzing now, though it is already the small hours of the morning. On the double bed in this hotel room, I've been lying, or rolling, or sitting, unable to sleep... The television is still on, but the channel has gone blank; nothing except a flat earth labeled with time zones, stationary on the screen, soft music playing in the background. Memories keep streaming out, unbidden, beyond my control. It's like those times when you're half asleep, and vaguely intend to stop a dream you're having, but your mind is literally too weak to do so. In the end, I can only let myself relax, as my mind lands on a day approaching Christmas of 2010, a day turned significant by two incidents.

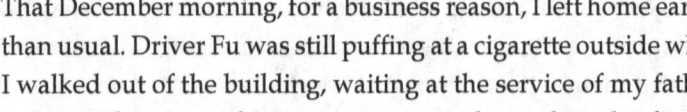

That December morning, for a business reason, I left home earlier than usual. Driver Fu was still puffing at a cigarette outside when I walked out of the building, waiting at the service of my father-in-law. When I met him on my way to the parking lot for my car, Driver Fu nodded a good-morning to me — we'd only had a couple of chance encounters before that day, when I was with either Deping or my father-in-law.

As I nodded back, I suddenly remembered that, last night, my father-in-law had told us that Taohua had asked leave to visit her village again. On impulse — in hindsight, probably even then on purpose—I said, "Oh, you're early. Will you be taking Taohua too, to drop her at the coach terminal? She's going home today."

For an instant he looked blank, but he quickly collected himself. "Yes, yes, Chief Dai has instructed me to send her all the way to her town."

I was astonished at what I'd just heard, but managed to remain outwardly calm. "Really? It must be very tiring to drive her there. It's a long way."

"Nay, it's nothing. Driving is what I do. I've already driven her several times." He smiled. "Chief Dai is very nice to your domestic helper. I've even never taken any of your family members."

"Taohua has been a huge help to our family, with extraordinary personal sacrifice," I said, in spite of myself.

"That's must be it," he murmured, taking a drag on his cigarette.

I walked away, picked up my car, and drove off. But my new discovery took up my head the whole way to my office. I brooded over whether my father-in-law had kept secret the fact that he'd been using a public resource for sheer private interest. Then I thought back to the moment the night before, when I offered Taohua a lift to the coach terminal in the morning: for a second time, I caught that glint of panic in her eye while she looked at my father-in-law, who promptly came to her rescue by suggesting that she go in his car, lest I be held up on the way to work. By this point, I could bet my life that my father-in-law had, *deliberately*, kept his car arrangement for Taohua secret. The next questions came relentlessly, inevitably. Why had my father-in-law, who'd kept his hands clean through almost his entire career, abandoned all his principles for Taohua, and for such petty gain? Why had he kept Deping and me in the dark? Harking back to that dark year of 2007, I remembered how it was an email from

THE ENVELOPES

BrightLife Switzerland, chasing payment, that led to Daisy unmasking Fred and exposing his embezzlement. I wondered: *what picture would unfold from Driver Fu's casual comment about my father-in-law's impressive kindness to Taohua? And even... Does my upright, esteemed father-in-law feel so lonely after his beloved wife's death that he has turned to Taohua?* I dreaded to think about it at all, but my mind could hardly sheer away from images I did not wish to dwell on...

But this fixation on my father-in-law and Taohua would be very short-lived. On that same day, in the office, Wings and I found ourselves "like birds shuddering at the sight of a bowstring" — just spend one second visualizing this Chinese idiom — after an afternoon raid by the local police. At least their conduct was much more civilized than that of the stout man from Shiwu Court, almost three years before. Two police officers identified themselves to the receptionist, and requested to see the head of the company. At the time, both Waits and Daisy had already left China on their individual Christmas vacations. And Charles was on the road, making sure that the sales team put on a spurt, so BrightLife China could finish the year with record-high annual revenues. In the absence of all three, the receptionist, who belonged to my department, spontaneously darted into my office to inform me of the unexpected visitors, who'd been guided into the reception room to wait.

I was appalled. Apparently, I had no alternative but to bite the bullet and meet them. However, in the first instance, they told me that they were here to go through our account books for the past five years. I exhaled deeply, realizing that Wings would be excellent company for whatever was coming up. I raced to fetch her, and then we both sat down with the officers. They explained nothing about what had driven them to our office, but ordered us to give them sheaves of documents that contained historical financial records of purchases and revenues. Wings inquired, in a tactful way, what they were looking for in the sea of numbers. After a brief hesitation, they admitted that it would be good if we could help track down all the business transactions that we'd made with two companies, namely K.J. Co and New Tech Co.

Wings and I exchanged a knowing glance: the old story was looming over us again, with a new face. The bird had flown; the office had been relocated; but the sword of Damocles still hung over BrightLife China.

With our on-and-off assistance, it took the officers almost the whole afternoon to scrutinize the records, make copies for themselves, and pack them into a suitcase. Wings and I tried to winkle their intention out of the officers, but they were very unforthcoming. Only at dusk, before they left with a full suitcase, did they hint that we'd better be prepared for investigations and summons coming soon from the Tax Bureau, as well as the ICB, the Industrial and Commercial Bureau.

Wings and I stayed in the office late, waiting for Waits and Daisy to wake up to their morning in the Western Hemisphere, and puzzling over what could've galvanized the police and the bureaus into digging up things that our company had constructively buried and moved away from. We speculated that Fred might've denounced BrightLife China to the authorities about his own very likely crime, but without turning himself in, just as he had most probably committed perjury, so that, to that day, our legal battle with Shing Sheng Co was still hanging in the balance. And we had a lingering fear for what would become of BrightLife China, facing the grilling by the authorities still to come.

We finally arranged a three-way conference call with Waits and Daisy, warning them that we had to give them a shock instead of Christmas present. Once Wings had finished elaborating on the police's action, a long, dead silence reigned over the phone—

THE ENVELOPES

quite as expected. I could even imagine Waits' customary look: the tilted eyebrow, the lifted corner of his mouth...

Finally Waits spoke at the other end of the line. "Ladies, do you have any idea who could've spilled the beans?"

Wings motioned to me to speak.

"We think," I said, "that of the people who know the whole history of the matter, the most likely culprit is Fred."

"It's hard to believe," Daisy reasoned, "that Fred would want to shoot himself in the foot. He never made a clean breast of his wrongdoings, but he knew he was not innocent. As I see it, the matter at hand is how we're going to deal with the threat facing the company, regardless of who has caused it."

"Yeah, yeah," Waits echoed. "We must zero in on the key issue."

"But we know nothing about what the authorities are after," cautioned Wings. "There's not a damn thing we can do except wait and watch."

"Even if we can only be reactive at this moment," said Daisy, "we need to talk about how BrightLife China should respond to the official calls from the authorities, which may come within days."

"That's true," said Waits. "Our Christmas holidays are ruined, but Daisy and I can't return to the office until the first week of January. On the other hand, Charles is shouldering the most important responsibility for the company, and we all must support him in hitting our sales target. Business growth is our top priority—it's what we're evaluated on by headquarters. I'm following up with him for it every day... So I'm now empowering you—yeah, Jade and Wings—to handle the investigations and meetings with the authorities. I expect you to be careful and play it by ear. And I ask you to keep Daisy and me in the picture, updating us every night."

HASU AUGUST

Now, teamed up with Wings, I was as busy as a bee, day and night. The company emergency had pushed the mystery of my father-in-law and Taohua right out of my mind. At once, Wings and I conferred with Mr Liang, our lawyer from the AnLong firm, about any hints the police officers might've given us. But Liang's meandering scenario analysis only overwhelmed us, and we still could not see the light.

Within a week of the police raid, a couple of officials from the city's Tax Bureau turned up on the doorstep and asked us for more data, especially related to tax declaration reports. Then, on the second last day of 2010, BrightLife China's presence was requested in the building of the city's ICB. After days on tenterhooks, Wings and I, designated by Waits, met two officials there. We sat quietly, intent on every word we heard. I had the embarrassing feeling that we were in the dock, listening to a judge passing sentence though there had been no trial.

The officials, after a lengthy warmup, expounded on a hideous crime of smuggling that had been exposed after government agencies collaborated to hunted down K.J. Co, which was exposed as a huge criminal syndicate; the Tax Bureau's audit of the books of a major K.J. affiliate had triggered the investigation that started more than two years earlier.

Eventually Wings and I grasped that Fred's scheme, involving phony purchases from K.J. and bona fide sales to New Tech, had been a miniature version of this new crime. In fact, New Tech belonged to K.J., and both were registered in Mainland China. Fred had created a third private company in Hong Kong, exploiting BrightLife China to line his own pockets. At the end, the officials gave their verdict, declaring that BrightLife China was guilty of aiding and abetting K.J. Co in its crimes.

A couple of days later, the police officers came again to collect

THE ENVELOPES

further evidence. Though at a distance, Waits and Daisy had their ear to the ground.

———∽∽———

As year 2011 began, Waits and Daisy reappeared in the office, looking fraught. The next day, the four of us — Wings and I, at the request of Waits, and Daisy — went to ICB to receive its formal notice. BrightLife China's unlawful revenue, worth two million yuan, from New Tech Co between 2006 and 2007 — the period before Waits and Daisy joined BrightLife — would be confiscated. During an off-the-record dialogue, with Daisy as interpreter for Waits, the official divulged the police's prosecution against the criminals, and commented that the leader would face the death penalty if he was convicted, as the crime involved a tremendous volume of money and number of companies — some of them had bitten the dust — and covered a huge geographical scope in the bargain. Waits inquired abruptly whether it was possible that Fred Cheung would be brought to book. The official's reply was rather equivocal: theoretically, it was possible. But in reality, it was not doable because the size of the illegal deals put through by Fred was relatively minor. The official actually remarked that BrightLife China should be grateful for small mercies; because he was a foreigner, it would be very costly to get cooperation from Hong Kong's Independent Commission against Corruption to drill down into Fred's personal bank accounts and his own company on that still economically free island, though politically it belonged to China.

Waits ceased to ask questions, but turned to Daisy, smiling wryly. "So, Fred got away scot-free."

"I'm afraid so," Daisy said in English. "And BrightLife is now paying a fortune to get him expunged from its history. But why should BrightLife be the only one made to answer for his sins?"

HASU AUGUST

ICB's decision to seize this revenue made it a terrible day for BrightLife China, filling the four of us with gloom. Only two days later, when we—the task force of us four—met with Mr Liang to be updated on the latest status of our legal battle against Shing Sheng Co, did I latch on to Daisy's strategy, to which she had probably alluded in her last comment in the bureau.

The technical analysis we'd asked for at the end of 2008 had unfortunately failed to determine the date when Fred signed the piece of paper that turned the tide against us. Consequently, in 2009 Shiwu Court ruled that Shing Sheng Co should be compensated for the loss it claimed to have incurred when BrightLife China unilaterally terminated its partnership contract. We were sentenced to pay them a whopping amount, which amounted to double the millions of yuan they owed to us. In early 2010 we'd lodged an appeal against the ruling with the provincial court. And still, as the year 2011 arrived, our fight in court had not come to an end. Mr Liang believed that, in all likelihood, Shiwu Court's verdict would be overruled, though the amount of reparations owed to Shing Sheng Co was still uncertain.

After Mr Liang closed his report, Waits said, "So we aren't going to pay what they're desperate for—no?"

"It's all over bar the shouting," our lawyer affirmed, "even if Shing Sheng decides to appeal to the Supreme Court."

"Mr Liang," Daisy ventured, "what if we give the process a little push? Perhaps, by doing that, we could pull the plug on this nightmare that's been consuming our energy and time."

Mr Liang narrowed his eyes. "What do you mean by 'a little push'?"

Everyone in the meeting was instantly riveted as Daisy calmly told the lawyer about, first, the criminal behavior of Fred, and then the damages that BrightLife China had been ordered to pay.

"As I see it," she said, "regardless of how or whether he'll be dealt with according to law, Fred is now exposed as a liar, and that may cut both ways. We've paid a dear price for it. If we let Shing Sheng know that the authorities are going after him—that the information straight from the horse's mouth is that he has already been investigated by police to a certain extent…"

"Yeah, yeah!" Waits clapped his hands. "Why not make Shing Sheng aware that we know their dear friend's fatal secret? Even if they don't rise to the bait, it won't do us any harm, no?"

"Passing the message to Shing Sheng won't do us any harm, for my money," Mr Liang concurred. "But it will put them between the devil and the deep blue sea."

———∞∞———

Within a week Daisy's proposal, executed diplomatically by Mr Liang, had worked its magic. Now Shing Sheng Co was holding out an olive branch, suggesting an out-of-court negotiation. Mr Liang must've driven a hard bargain, as this was followed in the last week of January 2011 by a settlement that finally wound up our bitter three-year feud. It came as a surprise almost too pleasant to be believed: in exchange for our offer of one million yuan maximum as compensation for their possible loss due to contract termination, they agreed to clear, on the spot, all their debt to us. It was a triumphant day for BrightLife China.

There was no official word on exactly what had at the last moment made Shing Sheng Co change its tune so dramatically, after years of digging its heels in. I'd like to believe, though, that it had invited its own destruction the day it chose Fred Cheung as a confederate.

14

After the roller-coaster weeks from Christmas of 2010 to late January 2011, I thought we'd wiped the slate clean. Finally we could leave Fred's era in BrightLife behind once and for all. During the last two days of January, I let myself mellow out a little, though I did have to attend our Asia-Pacific conference, an annual event organized by Waits to close the business of the old year and kick off the new one. That year, the management teams of every BrightLife subsidiary in the region would meet in Seoul, the home of BrightLife South Korea.

On the final day, we rounded off our business gathering with a warm evening banquet of spicy Korean cuisine to celebrating the year's banner performance: regional revenue had peaked in 2010, with BrightLife China in the lead. We had such a high time at the dinner, between the drinks, jokes, and larks, that most of us were unwilling to stop pursuing more fun somewhere else. As we drifted out of our hotel's restaurant, Wings, who was sharing a room with me, told me she would be back late, as she was going to a lounge bar about which she'd heard much, and was itching to visit. Daisy, standing beside me, winked at her and wished her enjoyment, and then turned to invite me for a stroll along the street nearby.

"Oh, before the dinner," I said, "I saw feathery snowflakes falling, and the pavement was growing white."

THE ENVELOPES

"I think it was only a flurry," said Daisy. "But it must've freshened the air outside. Let's roll."

As we stepped out of the hotel's revolving door, a chill wind stung my nostrils.

"How crisp it is!" I said, pulling the collar of my down coat higher.

Daisy picked a direction, and I fell in step with her. The pavement was icy, and the streetlamps dim. Before long, Daisy's foot slipped, and I hastened to support her, offering my shoulder. Steadying herself, she gave a chuckle of relief. "Gee, that was a near thing." She went on walking, but now at a snail's pace. "It's knocking on the door of my memory of Jack."

"Who's Jack?" I asked casually, keeping up with her.

She was moving gingerly, her head lowered and her eyes fixed on the pavement. "In my life up to now," she continued, as if lost in her own thoughts, "it's my most embarrassing moment. Back to my college days in Boston, on a freezing morning, I was among many people slithering their way toward campus. I was headed for the library, holding a stack of papers in my arms. Right in front of the entrance, I lost my balance and toppled backward, the papers spilling out of my arms. It was cold, but my face was hot with embarrassment. For a while, I neither knew what to do nor felt pain in my buttocks; I just sat on the glassy ground, my head bowed, papers scattered around... Then I saw a hand reach out in front of my eyes. I looked up and saw an unfamiliar but friendly face against the cloudless blue sky, grinning. 'Hey, Miss, how long are you planning to sit there? Don't you feel chilled to the marrow?' That was it. That was how I got to know Jack in Boston, seventeen years ago, in 1994. We've been friends all these years... Phew, I'm wheezing like a bull."

We both stopped to take a break. My mind was far away, spinning Daisy's narration out into an animation on the screen of my brain—Miyazaki's influence on me had never faded away. Raising my head and looking around, I heard Daisy's soft voice. "Gee, this is spiritually beautiful."

Right there, on the street with sparse pedestrians and vehicles, I gazed up at the distant skyline, its silence somehow touching my heart. A multitude of towering crosses, fringed by crimson neon lights, illuminated a part of Seoul that was otherwise engulfed in darkness. As a matter of fact, I was an unbeliever. Those crosses had no profound, sacred meaning for me; they only made a warm, red romance, a glowing foil to Daisy's story of another wintry day, so different with its blue sky and sun.

I said in spite of myself, "How nice this is! It's brightening up our dark walk, just as Jack giving you his hand made your day, and formed an enduring friendship."

"Gee, Jade, what you're saying is inspiring in a way... But I'm thinking about this religion thing. It's supposed to be a moral beacon for one who gets lost in his life."

Feeling the sentiment of pity in her voice, I followed her as she made a U-turn.

"It feels much colder now," she went on. "And it's very slippery. Let's go back to the hotel... Fred just came to my mind. Well, *feng shui* might be what his wife imposed on him. But he believed in Buddhism, according to his family tradition—at least, that's what he told me at one of the lunches he and I had together during my first summer in China."

"I used to think of him as a sincere believer in Buddhism," I said. "If he really is, I'm wondering why he and a man of hubris have much in common."

"He might be more like a man with an inferiority complex," she opined. "He said he did find comfort in Buddhism when his dyed-in-the-wool traditionalist father looked down on him, constantly calling him trash, saying he had no head for the

THE ENVELOPES

business that his family had built up."

"That was cruel," I commented.

"Wasn't it?" she echoed. "He said he fell in love with Latin American music when he was very young, and wanted to play it. But his father was very scornful of his never attending to his 'proper' duties. And in his father's opinion, making music equaled idling about. To defy his father, he went to South America without a dime, and he got some opportunities there that led him to China. He said he'd proved to his father that he was a cat who could catch mice in his own way."

"Unfortunately," I said with contempt, "his own way was a way that couldn't be justified anyway."

"As I see it, he blamed his father."

"Oh, yes," I recalled, "just as he blamed you for bringing him bad luck. Right before he was out of the office, he blamed his wife for the fact that her *feng shui* failed to protect him, and blamed us women managers for biting the hand that fed us. He blamed everyone except himself for his downfall. He might've blamed Buddha too—he didn't even shoot a last look at the 愛 character on his wall. He's a walking example of 'those who swim in sin will sink in sorrow.' Wretched human."

"Gee, Jade, you're getting a little carried away. Is it worth it?" she mused. "I'd rather not make it personal. It's an issue for which the milieu seems to be the hotbed. I'm not in a position to meddle in other people's values. That has a lot to do with their upbringing and education. I'd rather focus on creating a system, independent of any one person's power, that could make BrightLife less vulnerable to wrongdoings. Like fixing an out-of-order traffic light, and, if necessary, adding a secondary traffic police officer to enforce the law. The kind of thing we talked about at my home soon after I started working in China. You remember that?"

"That conversation is still crystal clear in my memory," I said as we entered the hotel lobby.

Instead of going straight to the lift, Daisy turned toward the cafe on the ground floor. "Why not join me in a glass of wine?" she said, beckoning me over. "I'm sure Wings is still having good time in the bar."

Taking off coats, we installed ourselves in cozy armchairs. I watched Daisy ordering the drinks, feasting my eyes on her calf-length boat-neck camel cashmere dress, the wide brown leather belt around her waist, and especially, her beautifully colored, lifelike butterfly brooch—this time pinned near her shoulder. In my eyes, Daisy had always epitomized elegance and refinement...

The waitress withdrew. Daisy gave me a charming smile, and resumed where we'd left off at the hotel entrance. "In accordance with what I said just now, in the past three years, Wings and I have been expending time and energy on instituting processes and procedures to cut down on malpractice..."

"Oh, yes. Perhaps the measures of internal control that you've bulldozed all the departments into taking have caused discomfort for some people, but I think they've worked well."

"Hopefully they're taking effect. I'm gonna level with you, Jade. Even though with these systems, policies, and so on in place, I can't say the company is free of risk. At best, I'm minimizing the possibility of misconduct. There're all kind of temptations out there, and not everyone can resist them." Daisy paused as the waitress returned with our drinks.

Somehow, I found my mind straying to my father-in-law's decision to use his government car for Taohua, which I'd stumbled upon over a month before. What had my father-in-law been lured by?

The waitress walked away. After sipping her wine, Daisy

returned to the topic. "Despite my concern, BrightLife China is lucky to have employees like you and Wings — both admirable, lovable people."

I drank my wine, with a little giggle and a silent protest that she'd bracketed Wings with me, though Wings had really done nothing to leave a sour taste in my mouth.

"You and Wings are quite alike. You're equally brainy," Daisy went on, as if she were reading my mind. "Sometimes Wings seems to show her brash exterior when she's at loggerheads with others over matters of principle. But inside, you have similar values, even if she is scented while you're scentless."

Secretly, I felt a tad abashed. As usual, I took refuge in digression. "Oh, I confess I'm fond of Wings' ever-changing fragrances. But I adore much more the way you dress — smart and preppie."

"Gee, that sounds like an overdone compliment." She laughed.

"I mean it. Look at your butterfly clip. That's a humdinger of an accessory. I've been admiring the way it lands so easily on your clothes for a while. I bet you love it too."

"Yes, I do," she said quietly, bending slightly as if to check it out. "For a reason beyond its beauty."

At my urging, she told me the story behind this "reason," making it short and sweet. "I left Boston in 1996 for an exciting career opportunity in Southeast Asia," she said. "Since then, I've been working in Asian countries. Jack has been living in Boston all the time. Once in a while we've been meeting each other — either when he's on a business trip here, or the other way around. Over time, our meetings made me realize that while I was keeping abreast of the changes in China, in that the city feels like an adolescent going through his growth spurt, Jack was savoring the glamor of Boston, which seemed to him like a maiden just blossoming into a mature woman. We still cherish and enjoy the unchanged bond between us. I feel comfortable spilling my guts to him, whether I'm happy or upset. Anyhow, many years after our parting, it was a trip back to Boston that gave me a chance to see Jack one day, near Christmas. We wandered around some of my old stomping grounds, and then we went to Lord & Taylor's on Boylston Street, for its gorgeous Christmas window displays and a little shopping…" As Daisy spoke, my imagination took wing, so that a sequel to the animation of "Jack offering his hand to Daisy" sprang to life again on my brain's movie screen . . .

When they passed through the jewelry section, Daisy and Jack were attracted to a butterfly brooch of exquisite craftsmanship, wrought in fine glass and silver, and both admired its verisimilitude. The saleswoman helped Daisy pin it to her coat collar. While she studied the brooch's effect on herself in the mirror, Jack watched with amusement.

"I remember you like ornaments in the form of butterflies," he said.

"You've got a good memory, Jack."

"Thanks. And this one is a rare piece of art."

"It is. How I love it!" Daisy smiled, taking the brooch off. "It's a shade too expensive. I'd feel guilty, frittering my money away on it, when I already own several others that are quite similar."

"You absolutely can afford it. Add it to your collection. It's icing on the cake," Jack coaxed. "You don't see this type often. Its shape may be similar to those you already have, but it's distinct in many ways. I'm certain of that."

"It's not a matter of affordability. And yes, maybe I'll pine for it. But Jack, don't egg me on, please." Daisy handed the brooch back to the saleswoman. "I love it, but…"

Jack shook his head with a grin. They resumed walking, and ambled to a coffee shop.

While they were chatting over their hot drinks, Jack asked again,

THE ENVELOPES

"You've really made up your mind? Once we get out of here, you won't have a second chance to buy that beautiful thing."

"Jack, it's over." Daisy enunciated each word. "Skip it, please."

"All right, I'll shut my mouth."

When their coffee break was almost over, Jack excused himself, saying he needed to go out to return a call he'd ignored when they were at the jewelry counter. Daisy finished her drink, waiting for him. After a while, he came back, and together they headed for the subway station.

While they were standing on the platform, Jack said again, "We're gonna get onto the train, and I want to make sure you won't regret."

Though she felt a little conflicted at leaving the brooch behind, Daisy cut him off. "Jack, I've made my decision. Even if I may feel a little regretful later, I won't cry over spilled milk."

They boarded the subway train, and took two seats side by side. Both were quiet until two stops had passed. Then, all of a sudden, Jack held out his hand, which this time was holding a small box wrapped in dark paper and affixed with a camel-colored ribbon. "Before we say goodbye..." he murmured.

Daisy was puzzled. "What's this?"

"It's a Christmas gift."

"Jack, you don't have to..."

"Open it."

When Daisy untied the camel bow, she realized that it was actually made out of two short ribbons, knotted together. Hmph, she thought, the wrapping's a bit tatty, but she quietly moved on to peeling away the paper. Then came out the black-velvet box. She lifted the top, and gasped at what was revealed – the dazzling butterfly laid on inky satin.

"Gee, Jack..." Mesmerized, Daisy was at loss for words.

"Don't say thank you. I don't know how to take it," Jack said smoothly. "I just don't want you to feel regretful one day. I know it's an awful feeling to rue the day you let go of a beautiful thing. Merry Christmas, Daisy."

HASU AUGUST

"You just made this Christmas unforgettable, Jack. I love it!"

"I'm glad you do." Jack added, "Oh, yeah, I'm sorry for the broken ribbons. The saleswoman told me the gift wrapping was centralized, and I had to go to another floor to have it done. But I couldn't let you cool your heels that long, when I was only supposed to be making a phone call. She was nice enough to find these two pieces, and tied it up with lightning speed. I know the color's a bit dull..."

"Camel is a color of tenderness. Jack, thank you. I cannot help..."

In the rocking train, Daisy wound the ribbons into a tight roll and crammed them into a tiny space beside the butterfly brooch in the box

"That's the reason, Jade, why I frequently wear this brooch," Daisy concluded as the image on my mental movie screen faded out. "And as I saw it, the camel ribbons were equally beautiful. They inspired me to design this camel dress and have a tailor make it for me." A faint flush was suffusing her cheeks, thanks to the wine, probably.

"Oh, you've been keeping me astounded since we met," I exclaimed. "Even the way you dress always tells a story. Are all your clothes a result of your originality?"

"Yes, the tailor-made ones, at least," she said with a nod. "I've always been fascinated with designing dresses for myself, and I very much enjoy the whole process, though it's time-consuming. When a new pattern strikes me, usually inspired by a particular occasion, I'll go to the fabric market to find suitable materials, and then discuss my idea in detail with the tailor. I found a tailor in China. He's quick to catch on to my sketches, and sometimes even my vague notions of a design. He's also super good with both needle and sewing machine. For years, our pleasant collaborations have enriched my wardrobe."

"In other words," I said, "to you, tailor-made clothes aren't trappings of wealth, but remembrances of special moments in your life."

"That's correct." She smiled, luxuriating in her wine. After a pause, she added, "A while ago, you remarked that the lit crosses brightened up our walk in the dark. That sparked a brainstorm of designing a warm winter coat with magnified red and weakened black."

"Oh, Daisy, you make me envy your life. And you paint and play piano too?"

"I do have catholic tastes," she said. "Traveling for leisure, painting, music, and of course, dress design… Gee, my life seems to be all about these minutiae."

"Those are fine things in life," I said admiringly, getting a little garrulous; the alcohol seemed to be loosening my tongue. "And they're not exactly in the category of domestic trivia. Oh, speaking of family—probably you're not keen on having one, but it sounds like Jack had a crush on you."

"What led you to that absurdity?" She flushed even more, with a shyness I'd never seen before.

"In the train, what did he say at last? 'It's an awful feeling to, to…'"

"'…to rue the day you let go of a beautiful thing,'" she finished.

"That was it. I think he himself had probably had that awful experience before," I deduced on a whim.

"Like when?"

I grinned. "Like the day you left Boston for Southeast Asia."

She goggled at me, words failing her.

But I couldn't stop analyzing, "Is he married?"

"He had a girlfriend," she recollected. "But their relationship didn't end up in marriage."

"And you, Daisy? Are you attached to a man?"

"I *was*." She shrugged slightly. "But it didn't work out for us."

HASU AUGUST

"See, there's been this invisible connection between you and him all the time, behind the scenes." Well, I wasn't feeling tipsy at all. "It must be because of his deep affinity with you that Jack sensed the regret you might be feeling. And secretly buying you the butterfly brooch was just the medium. People do unusual things, big or small, when they're driven by love, quietly or loudly." Somehow, I recollected that, for my sake, and for that of our baby to be born, Deping, even against his principles, had begged his father for help with his influence. Somehow, I thought of my father-in-law taking care of Taohua with his driver and car.

"Gee, your fertile imagination." Daisy sighed, shaking her head.

"Oh, my husband always scoffs at my amateur sleuth act." I laughed, and drained my glass.

"Talking about your husband, let's getting serious about the *usual*, lovely thing you're supposed to do." She smiled. "You two are planning to have another baby any time soon?"

Then, for the first time, I confided to Daisy — the only person I'd ever told — about my difficulty in getting intimate with Deping, and how I attributed it to the predicament of my body and my soul not being able to unite, ever since the death of my baby son and Taohua's elder daughter.

She lapsed into a short silence. "It might be unwise to keep the issue to yourself," she said finally. "Why don't you and your husband talk turkey? After all, it takes both of you to have a baby."

"How about you? Will you have an open discussion with Jack about his feelings for you?" I replied. "Love is a thing between two people, too."

"Come on, Jade. Those are two fundamentally different things."

"To me, they're the same."

THE ENVELOPES

"Let's not get into this cut-and-thrust, Jade." She waved her hand as if to calm me, but encourage me as well. "If you want to solve your issue on your own, you'll have to relax and liberate yourself from fear and worry... You will. I have faith in you."

I wish I could. I just did not know how I could make myself not see my lifeless infant boy or hear Meihua reciting her essay every time I woke up in the middle of night...

Nonetheless, having poured out my heart to Daisy gave me an ineffable relief that evening, a relief I had not felt for years.

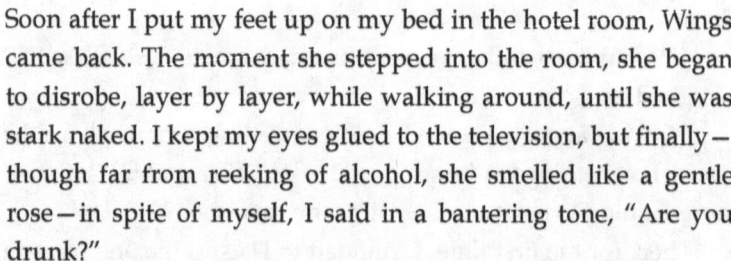

Soon after I put my feet up on my bed in the hotel room, Wings came back. The moment she stepped into the room, she began to disrobe, layer by layer, while walking around, until she was stark naked. I kept my eyes glued to the television, but finally— though far from reeking of alcohol, she smelled like a gentle rose—in spite of myself, I said in a bantering tone, "Are you drunk?"

"I drank," she said. "But don't I look stone-cold sober?"

I stared at the screen, yet not really watching anything. Out of the corner of my eye, I saw her suddenly turn toward me, and I heard her saying with a trace of solicitude, "I like being in the raw whenever I'm in a bedroom. I'm sorry, is that embarrassing you?"

"Oh, why should I be embarrassed?" I denied feebly, keeping my eyes on the screen.

"Then great." She started removing her makeup, sitting at the desk in front of the mirror, her back to me.

In truth, I did feel awkward. When I was a nurse, many years before, seeing naked bodies had been all in a day's work. I never felt awkward holding newborns in their birthday suits or caring for unclothed patients. But now the mature nude body before me was neither a manikin in our medical lab nor a sexy figure in a supporting role in a Miyazaki anime film. It was flesh and blood, alive and kicking in front of me. But why should I feel self-conscious about it? I began to challenge myself, and after a couple of quick glances at her, I turned away from the screen to scan her body. In the soft light, her slightly curved back shone like silk, and her wavy hair brushed her shoulders; her fair, round arm made precise movements, while a bit of the silhouette of her breast appeared indistinctly...

"Are you staring at me?" she asked without turning her head, her voice a shade louder than the television.

"How do you know?" I was rather taken aback, and that was the only riposte I could think of.

"I can feel it. Just the same way that, in a bar, I can sense if a man's watching me." She looked over her shoulder and gave me a cheeky grin. "Tonight, I had no luck seeing anyone interesting among those sleek fellows from various countries, though the place was quite nice and commodious."

"I thought you went there for a drinking spree," I said, startled.

"Drinking at home would be better." She chuckled. "Bars are where I network with people outside of the finance profession — where I expect to find my Mr Right."

"If I may ask, have you met any good candidates so far?"

"You're cynical, Jade," she said, sidestepping my question, her voice low but unconcerned. She seemed to be rather concentrated on her task, doing something around her eyes. "I feel like a zombie, just treading water — I won't just sit there, waiting for a prince to ride in on his high horse. I like being involved in the game of two strangers looking for true love. As you might expect, not everything in the garden is rosy — two strangers can't always find each other. But you can put the search down to experience, at least. The process of seeking the right person is exciting and rewarding."

"Rewarding?"

"Yes—by meeting a motley crew of people with individual aims, I learn more about myself."

"For instance?"

"Well—" She became motionless for a moment, as if considering how to supply an example from memory. Then she continued with her work and words. "Have you heard the bon mot 'For vanity, go to a gym; for casual sex, go to a bar?'"

"Never."

She turned around and gave me another saucy smile, as if on purpose. I was trapped into hastening to add, "But I'm not prudish."

"No, you're not." Shrugging off my redundant self-defense, she went on, "You're just cerebral, and sometimes seem stuck in a groove. But there's nothing's wrong with that, if you like your life that way... Back to one of the experiences I was about to tell you about. I once met a hunky man in a bar. What a dish he was! But he and I were just ordinary friends. One day, he invited me over to his place, saying that he, another female friend of his, and me could have some fun together. I went there. After a glass of mild liquor, he asked if I minded if they had sex to add luster. I said I had no problem with it—I thought they were moving to the bedroom. But, right on the couch, my beefcake friend and the girl started kissing and cuddling ..."

"Good grief!" I couldn't help saying, feeling my own face flush. I did not want to imagine a jot more. This wasn't the theme of *my* animation.

"While they're getting into it," she continued, as if she hadn't heard me at all, "I thought to myself, 'If they feel so free to have a roll in the hay in my presence, why can't I relax?' Then I sat tight and looked at them in action, like watching an intimate movie scene. Alas, their carnal passion was wasted on me, because I soon zoned out. What was happening had actually made me see clearly one thing about myself: for me, love comes before sex. I go to bars to find love, not casual sex."

"What a freak you met!"

"Freak or not, his likes aren't my cup of tea, full stop." She began packing up her toiletries. "And after another incident, I made a rule for myself: in a bar, I never talk to a man wearing a wedding ring. A man who treats his marriage as a charade is not the right person for me, either. I'm not going to be a cop-out or an excuse for a man's failure to waltz through his marriage. I'm not going to be anyone's femme fatale."

Somehow, my father-in-law and Taohua again barged in on my mind. I was quiet while Wings tidied up the desk, passed in front of the television, and went to open her suitcase.

Catching a whiff of perfume, I said from the heart, "You smell sweet."

"You're honey-lipped, Jade. But thanks."

"I meant it. In fact, since the day Daisy and I interviewed you, I've liked your scent," I said, finally breaking my silence after all these years. "But your wearing perfume on that day was unusual to me, because—"

She took the words off my lips. "Because it might give a negative impression to the interviewers?"

"Oh, you knew it. But you didn't care?"

"It wasn't about whether I cared," she corrected, coiling up her hair before entering the bathroom. "It's about my life principle—always to be true to myself, as well as others. If a company turned me down because I wore perfume, that would be a blessing to me. At the first sight of Daisy, I knew that even if I didn't make the cut, it wouldn't be due to my appearance or my scent. To tell the truth, I got two other job offers together, right after that interview. But I liked Daisy, so I accepted the one from BrightLife China. We've been clicking well—there's a meeting of minds between her and me. Okay, could you spare me now? I'm going to wash up."

While Wings was in the shower, I switched off the television and stretched myself out on the bed. I couldn't stop thinking about my father-in-law and Taohua, though. Their cloak-and-dagger behavior was now vexing me badly. I hoped I was misjudging them, and decided to have a talk with Deping about it.

The Spring Festival of 2011 began two days after I got back from Seoul. As usual, Taohua returned to her village for seven days, to celebrate the New Year with her family. Deping and I, after paying a one-day visit to my parents, went to a southern town for a holiday in the warm sun. My father-in-law didn't join us; he and his old gang had promised to get together, he said, after their parting of the ways decades before. He declined my offer to drive him to the train station, stating that everything had been well arranged, and that he hoped Deping and I would pamper ourselves on our vacation, with full privacy and beer and skittles, which, he regretfully felt, had become a luxury for us two.

Deping and I did literally what my father-in-law wished, though we sparred during a stroll on one of our three relaxing days. To avoid the throngs of tourists—though it was still an occasion for family reunions for migrant workers like Taohua, the Spring Festival had become just a public holiday for families, like ours, who spent their daily life under the same roof but yearned for a getaway—we picked only quiet streets to roam along. We happened to pass through a bar street at dusk. None of the bars were open, and on the majority of the doors were notices reading "Closed for the Festival." Far from festive, the street looked desolate. A small group of other people, most likely holidaymakers, were on the street a little ahead of us. They stood reading the notice on one of those shut doors and then walked away, disappointment written on their faces. Probably it was these bars that brought Wings to my mind, and I told Deping about the conversation we'd had in our shared hotel room about her journey to look for true love—well, not all of it; I chopped out a few details that I deemed not repeatable. Deping listened in silence.

After finishing my story, I commented, "Look what a four-year stay in France did to her. Wine, perfume... Have you ever known anyone with such a permissive attitude about sex?"

"My innocent wife," Deping said, in a slightly disapproving tone, "you're making a storm in a teacup. Based on what you just told me, I would say Wings is a much deeper person than someone just doing things that you're not habituated to. Perhaps her critical thinking also owes much to her studying and working in France, as it could hardly be the product of the education in our country, revolving as it does around passing exams. But she's a good sign that our society is diversifying, if people like her come back from developed countries, having been around and seen more of the world. I would say she has her head screwed on the right way. And it's all the more to her credit that she's been able to draw a line between the value of freedom and that of discipline, yet has lived a relaxed life."

I bridled. "Oh, your take on her is so generous!"

"Perhaps," he continued, giving a little pinch to my hand, which was in his, "you could learn from her, and let yourself go from time to time."

"Oh, you don't mind my going to a bar to flirt with men?" I

THE ENVELOPES

jibed.

"My keen-minded wife is willfully twisting my suggestion." This time, though he kept walking, he turned and grazed my nose with his crooked index finger. "How about *you and I* pretend we're strangers, who've bumped into each other in a bar? We make eyes at each other, then I go over to chat you up. Then we have a few drinks. Then we go home, nudge nudge, wink wink..."

"What a pity, steamy Deping," I whispered. "Not a single bar here is open."

"Ho, ho... perfect excuse." He feigned a twinge of disenchantment, but quickly switched to a more serious mood. "Jade, I would say few people are as bold as Wings, to pursue true love in a way true to themselves."

"Seriously though," I said, "not many are as moral as she is either, sticking to the rule of not having an affair with a married man."

"Indeed," he murmured.

He then complained of a little hunger, but we decided to keep walking until we got nearer the hotel, where there were some restaurants with tasty local specialties.

But by now, having broached the subject, I felt I couldn't hold back any longer. The question on my mind had become too insistent. "Deping," I said, "what do you think about extramarital romance?"

"I wouldn't give a one-size-fits-all answer to perhaps please you." His words rang sincerely. "It depends. If someone's marriage is truly a mistake, and if an extramarital romance is the only way to save all the people that a bad marriage hurts, it could be acceptable. But I know you have no tolerance for off-the-rail spirit, let alone adultery. After all, you grew up with Hayao Miyazaki's animations of pure love."

"What if such a romance happens to be played out within your own inner circle? Would you still live with it?"

"Are you hinting about yourself falling for someone?" He halted, turned, and looked into my eyes.

"Oh, I never saw a sign of nerves in you before." I laughed. "Am I the only person you know? Don't block the way, please."

We resumed walking while he let out a loud sigh of relief. "But you're the only one that has the power of stopping my heart."

"You are the same to me, jumpy Deping." Exhaling, I slid my arm around his. "There's one thing I must tell you."

"Thank heaven. Yet it sounds like a bad one," he said, though there was something encouraging in his voice.

"It's about Father letting Taohua use his car and driver…" I told him what I had sporadically witnessed in the past years, ending in what I'd heard from Driver Fu in late January.

Deping didn't interrupt at all while I voiced my suspicion that his father and Taohua had been affectionately involved with each other. My theory, I explained, is that one tends to do unusual things for one's beloved one. That his father gave Taohua time off whenever she wanted to see her daughter was one thing, but his using his car and driver to send her home was something else altogether.

"Your postulation doesn't hold water," Deping finally said. "Father and Mother were devoted to each other when Mother was alive. But Old Man never granted Mother privilege."

"That was because Mother rejected it," I argued.

"Still implausible," he said firmly, but he looked troubled. "Perhaps it was just the milk of human kindness. Taohua lost her elder daughter, and her family is still struggling with their hard life."

"If so, why isn't Father open with you and me?" I challenged.

"Why not let us all help her family?"

"Perhaps Old Man doesn't want to saddle us with the burden," he said, clearly straining for justification. "Perhaps he thinks his doing Taohua a favor like that is a piece of cake."

"Look, Deping, I'm not trying to harangue you. But you're surprising me, if you think Father really believes that the privilege he's granted Taohua is a minor issue. We all know that when it comes to ethics, a miss is as good as a mile."

"You're right about that, Jade. But Old Man, as I know him, must have a better reason for his actions than that he likes Taohua in that way."

"Then what are we going to do about it?" I asked. "Should we have a talk with him about his motive?"

"I don't think there's much we can do for now," he mused. "Let's wait for an appropriate time to find out what Old Man thinks, in order to spare their blushes."

Deping and I got back home on the sixth day of the one-week public holiday. My father-in-law had not told us when he would come back. As for Taohua, she'd promised to return from her village on the afternoon of the last holiday.

On that day, Deping and I had a lie-in until around 10:00 a.m., and then went out for brunch. In the afternoon, we went shopping. We'd almost finished when we realized that we were close to the city terminal, and that it was about the time for Taohua's coach to arrive. On the spur of the moment, we drove there, parked our car, and went to the coach station, ready to surprise Taohua.

Deping and I stood at a short distance as the coach drew up, so we could easily pick out Taohua among the arriving passengers. Soon I spotted her appearing at the coach door. I waved my arm, and was about to call her name when a big hand clapped over my mouth, and another one clamped onto my shoulder.

While I was locked into immobility, Deping's whisper came to my ear. "She's not alone. Do you see Old Man now?"

I caught a clear view of their happy faces while they were alighting from the coach, before Deping dragged me out of sight behind another parked coach. We stayed there until we saw them pass by in the stream of people. Then we came out of hiding and followed them.

They first went to the taxi stand. My father-in-law climbed into a cab, but Taohua didn't get in with him, but only waved as he drove off. We followed her until she reached the bus stop, and then retreated to our car.

I felt mentally exhausted, and speechless, and for a while Deping didn't have anything to say either. "They are taking separate ways back home," he said finally. "Obviously, they don't want us to know they spent the holidays together."

"Welcome to the amateur sleuth club," I burst out. "Good grief! That's the first time I've ever tailed someone like that."

"But it doesn't make sense to me," he mused, as if he hadn't heard me, deep in his own thoughts. "If they're intimate, why did they go to Taohua's village?"

"There're many stops between our city and there," I reminded him. "Do we really know where they've been?"

"No, we don't," he muttered. "In fact…" After a pause, he said, "Anyway, we'll have to bide our time. The whole thing will eventually find its way out of the closet."

I frowned. "That seems like giving them enough rope to hang themselves."

"Maybe—but Jade, I would say we have no conclusive evidence. Taohua's using Old Man's car and driver; they're taking the same coach. Those incidents aren't solid enough proof

THE ENVELOPES

of an irregular relationship. If we make no bones about telling them what we think, it may just get everyone messed up."

"What you're saying is true after a fashion. We don't really have a leg to stand on. As a matter of fact, Deping, at least, it's a wake-up call for us. We should give more attention to Father. He's probably felt lonely without Mother around."

"All in all," he summarized, "let's first pretend we know nothing about what's going on between them. Meanwhile, let's be more considerate to Old Man."

Nodding, I started the engine. "I want to go home now."

15

Once the Spring Festival of 2011 was over, my family life returned to its mundane routine, in large part due to our hectic working schedules. My father-in-law was often out of town on business trips. Though pushing sixty-five years, he didn't seem to be slowing down at all. My husband invested all his energy in lecturing to students in City Normal University and doing pedagogical research. I occupied myself with my office work, as well as my final semester of MBA studies. And Taohua spent most of her time taking care of our family. She said she didn't need to break a sweat to take care of the household chores or cook delicious meals for us. But she was never idle; she spent every spare moment knitting. She could turn out a sweater within half a month, without it affecting her housework at all.

On one occasion, in her room, I discovered by accident a stack of wool sweaters, in various sizes, colors, and design, but all for children. I ribbed her about whether she had a plan to sell her hand-knitted sweaters for a profit, since there were many more of them than Lianhua could possibly need.

"I've found a place in the city that collects all kinds of donated second-hand knitting wool," she said with a sheepish smile, "so I'm knitting it into warm clothes for my daughter and the other children in the village."

I fell silent, embarrassed by my brainless banter.

THE ENVELOPES

Altogether, my father-in-law and Taohua behaved so normally that Deping and I had our moments of doubt. Could we have been mistaken about them? In any case, other than being silent about what we saw, there was hardly anything we could do to ease my father-in-law's hypothetical loneliness.

One day in April, another strange thing happened. We were at the dinner table—though, as so often was the case, not all of us were there; my father-in-law was away that evening, inspecting a power plant site outside the city. Deping was excited about the seminar that he'd organized and had invited Felix Lee to lead on that day; it was the third seminar Felix had led since he started teaching in the countryside, three and half years before.

With gusto, my husband related the adventures Felix had shared with a large group of university students. He waxed eloquent on the absence, in our mercenary society, of the idealistic zeitgeist that had suffused Felix's youth, causing him to devote himself to the arduous cause of providing education for children in a disadvantaged area. He hoped that his students would inspired by Felix's ardor for enlightening those children, and follow his example.

Taohua had been listening intently, with an amused look. Caught up in Deping's enthusiasm, she exclaimed, "Aya, the kids in our village are so lucky, thanks to Mr Lee."

"In *your* village?" I asked, a tad perplexed.

"I wish! Aya, just a slip of the tongue." She giggled, blushing. "I meant *the* village where Mr Lee is. I'll clear the table and bring the fruits now, shall I?" Rising, she started to collect up the dishes.

"It's true, though, what Taohua says," Deping said. "The hundred or so children in the three schools where Felix and his German friend have been pegging away are blessed. More and more migrant workers forced into cities can now safely leave their sons and daughters in the villages with their families to attend these schools."

"I've been wondering—precisely where are these blessed villages?" I asked. I couldn't remember Deping ever having told me. This, it now occurred to me for the first time, seemed odd.

Deping looked a little sheepish. "I have to admit, I haven't been told."

"How come?" I persisted, frowning as I watched Taohua, bowls and chopsticks in hands, walk out to the kitchen.

"Felix prefers not to disclose the schools' location—in fact, that's a precondition for his participation in my seminars. I have no reason to question his decision, just as he's never reneged on his commitment to the private sponsor for the schools when he took the job. But he did pass along some interesting photos that I could use in my lectures. I can show you those ..." He stood up too and walked toward our bedroom.

Taohua and I were already enjoying the ripe loquats of April when Deping returned. He spread out about ten photos on the table. Taohua leaned over to look at them more closely, squinting — she was slightly nearsighted — at each one in turn, as if she was looking for something in particular. Finally, she sat back, picking up another loquat while I looked through the photos. There were a few shots of classrooms, with children sitting in neat rows behind plain desks, looking toward the camera; a line of one-story buildings, a mountain at their back; a playground on which groups of children appeared to be playing a game; Felix and an unknown Chinese in patched but clean clothes teaching classes; Felix's German friend laboring with children in a field... Looking at them, I felt a strange rush of emotion.

"I don't know why," I said slowly, "but these give me an odd sense of déjà vu."

"Which one?" Taohua's voice was oddly sharp. She leaned forward again, her eyes sweeping over the photos.

"Not any particular one," I said, still trying to understand my own reaction. "Just my overall impression. The children's naïve faces, their clear eyes…"

Taohua grinned, leaning back again. "Aya, Miss, all village kids look the same. All villages, too, for that matter."

"Not necessarily." Deping smiled. "Villages on a plain or by a sea look very different from those in a mountain. And rich villages on the coast of our country are a far cry from the poor ones in the inland areas."

"Well, I wouldn't know about that, would I?" Taohua mumbled, starting to remove the empty plates from the table.

Deping moved to the living area and switched on the television for the evening news. It happened that the anchor of Central China Television was reporting on an extraordinary scandal of bribery and corruption. All three of us were drawn to the television, which was showing pictures that made our jaws drop: numerous wads of banknotes that had been found encased in the concrete walls of the bedroom of the mayor of a medium-sized city in China. The corrupt official's name was not divulged.

"Why aren't those people afraid their mountains of notes will fall on them and crush them?" Taohua lashed out venomously when the report was over. "They're not doing any good with all that money, just hiding it in their walls." Shaking her head, she stomped off to the kitchen to finish her work for the day.

That night, I felt a bit uneasy. I couldn't stop thinking about Taohua's words, as well as her body language during our conversation about Felix's cause, and her strange reaction to the 'wall of money' on television.

"Don't fuss, my suspicious wife," Deping said when I finally brought it up with him. "I saw nothing wrong with how Taohua acted tonight, except that she might be not well informed. But, Jade, I have to admit I'm baffled why the location of Felix's schools has to be kept secret."

"Is he just not being candid about it?"

"Felix is a young man of pure ideals. He's not artful..." Deping paused, frowning. "But he never did tell me about how he found his sponsor, either—or perhaps, how the sponsor found him. He said the sponsor was extremely low-key and didn't want to broadcast this pilot project, because the media could get it all wrong. It's the sponsor's explanation to Felix that sounds fishy to me. Perhaps the sponsor wants to keep something dark."

"Such as?"

"I wouldn't know, Jade. It's beyond me. I just have this indescribable feeling."

My husband and I didn't speak further about his sixth sense, or mine, that night. Still, scenes kept playing over and over in my mind, 'starring' my father-in-law, Taohua, and Felix, in various combinations, going right back to the moment when I happened across Felix in our building's hall, right before he left the city for the country, years earlier. And then, despite Deping's dismissal of my suspicions about Taohua's behavior during and after dinner, I was struck by an outré image of intuition. It was not only the revival of my discomfort about my father-in-law and Taohua. Instead, it was as if all these scenes I'd been replaying, like scattered beads, were now being strung together, making *a single* piece, a picture of something that I still could not recognize.

Office life had been keeping me busy after the Spring Festival of 2011, but it was uneventful enough. That changed a couple of

THE ENVELOPES

days after the night we looked at Felix's photos, when something happened that struck a blow to my confidence in Waits.

The television report about loot stashed in a wall had got me thinking. If there were a nationwide system similar to the one that Daisy had forged in BrightLife China, I wondered, wouldn't we see fewer corruption cases? Wouldn't the state be stronger and the whole country better off, just as, these last years, we'd seen our company gaining power in the industry, with happier employees? But events, sadly, soon proved this confidence in Daisy's system and BrightLife's stability premature.

The drama began with Charles's decision to sack George Ni, a sales manager based in a southern city called Haizi who reported directly to him. I'd been called into a meeting with Waits, Daisy, Wings, and Charles, in which Charles told me that his patience had run out with George, who was currently not performing, although he'd once been a highflier, making millions of yuans' worth of sales to Haizi's fire brigade.

"But there's a problem," Charles explained. "The fire brigade hasn't paid us for some of their purchases." He gave a meaningful nod to Wings.

"The fire brigade owes us about two million yuan," Wings stepped in, "which has been overdue for months. My department has tried every way we could to collect the debts, but our requests have all gone down like lead balloons—"

"Wait, wait," Charles broke in. "We have to be clear about one thing: the *guanxi* a salesperson has built up with a government entity like the fire brigade is *crucial* for us to get payment. If we kick George out now, that *guanxi* will be lost, and every attempt to collect will hit a brick wall."

"I still can't comprehend why we can't take legal action to collect a debt like this," Wings objected.

"I've already explained it to you," Charles said gruffly, giving

Wings a stern glance.

"You have." Wings looked Charles in the eye. "And I agreed to hold on to the legal letter addressed to the fire brigade for the moment."

"Yeah, yeah," Waits chipped in, "but our meeting is about what we need to do with George. Charles, what do you propose?"

"Right," Charles replied, turning to me. "Here is my suggestion: to motivate George to help us get the payment, we promise him a commission of ten percent of the total amount the fire brigade owes us. Once the receivable is cleared, we give George his running shoes. We need your support, Jade."

Charles's idea surprised me, and left me speechless for an instant. Waits lost no time stepping in, instead. "Two hundred grand to get back two million yuan sounds okay to me. I think we have no other choice—yeah?"

That Waits was so ready to approve shook me for a moment. But as all eyes turned to me, I took a deep breath. "I'm afraid I can't agree. From a personnel-management point of view, first, it doesn't conform to the company's commission policy. Second, more importantly, giving a nonperforming employee extra pay before dismissing him isn't fair to our employees who *are* performing. And last but not least, we'll be sending the wrong message to the sales force, and even the entire company."

"Yeah?" Waits steepled his fingers, thinking. "Then how about this? We could make it not look like a commission, but something else paid to George."

Surely, I thought, *I've misheard*. After all, Waits was speaking in English, a second language for all the rest of us except Daisy. Realizing that I was almost gaping at him, I averted my eyes. Wings was frowning, her cat's eyes seeming to turn up even more.

I turned to Daisy, and found resolution in her expression,

THE ENVELOPES

although she smiled. "I don't think it's about how it looks," she said calmly. "It's about what it *is*. I don't think we'll do it."

The meeting lapsed into an awkward silence, only broken by the rustling sound of Waits jotting away, as always, in his notebook. Charles was staring at Daisy, his face inscrutable.

Eventually Waits finished writing and closed his notebook. "Okay—Charles and the finance team, please work out a plan for debt collection from the fire brigade. We can't lose those two million yuan. And I'd like to have a further talk with Daisy and Charles now."

As Wings and I came out of the meeting room, I couldn't help probe for understanding. "Wings, what's going on here? I was dragged in but only told half of the story."

She sighed. "Alas, only Charles knows the whole story about George and the fire brigade."

"But what's the reason Charles gave you for not going through legal procedures to get them to pay us?"

"He said legal action would not only damage the *guanxi* with the fire brigade for future business but also spoil BrightLife's reputation in the market."

"It doesn't seem like good logic," I commented.

"Emotional, as expected," she said, nodding slowly and curling her lips. Then she went on, "With our internal control system, we try to ensure our company receives the cash from the credit sales. It works well with the majority of the sales team. But a few salespeople always *emotionally* tell a cock-and-bull story to ask for a higher credit limit rather than using their time and energy to work with us on debt collection. A few surly ones always swear like a trooper, as if a dirty word could scare my team off. And, *emotionally*, Charles labeled me an armchair critic, not knowing one iota of how hard it is for his people to work at the forefront of the business, and declared that my acerbity was more difficult to accept than the obscenities his people scream. When things get illogical, a few people use emotions as a red herring. But that won't prevent me from smelling a rat."

I gasped at her last sentence. "Seriously? You suspect something's wrong?"

"I don't know what Waits and Charles are going to do to George." She shrugged. "But there're a few things that might dovetail, and I'm pawing through my papers for them. Mark my words—if we send a legal notice of delinquency to the fire brigade, that will be the key."

"Is Daisy aware of the issue you're talking about?"

"You think every day she just dips into the management reports? You think the reports are only numbers to her? Daisy is sharp. She sees things and asks tough questions. Haven't you noticed that even Waits could hardly fence with her?"

I decided to have a quiet word with Daisy. It was curious that Waits had endorsed Charles's proposal to give a cash incentive to George, even though he was about to be fired from BrightLife China.

That day, after work, I went to meet Daisy in her office.

She listened to my story, looking thoughtful. Then she put a question to me. "Do you remember Charles fired a salesman less than two months ago, around the end of February?"

"Yes," I recalled. "Sam, wasn't he? As a matter of fact, I remember him very well, for two reasons: he was a salesman who had the privilege of directly reporting to Charles, instead of a sales manager; and we showed him the door because he committed fraud, only eight months into his engagement with us. I handled his dismissal, and made sure he gave back to the company the money he'd pocketed. It wasn't an easy case. He

THE ENVELOPES

actually threatened me, saying he'd burn my car. I called his bluff... But I was happy with his dismissal, in the end."

"Thank you for your hard work on that. But Jade, what you might not know about was the fight Waits and I had, before we reached an agreement on dismissing Sam."

I looked at her, bewildered. After a pause, Daisy continued, "The cashier in Wings' team discovered Sam's ruse of claiming nonexistent expenses via dummy invoices. I urged Waits and Charles to take action immediately, as we have zero tolerance for any employee who cheats at BrightLife. Charles objected that we couldn't afford to fire Sam, because he had strong *guanxi* with high-ranking officials with influence on a major government project that we were bidding for. But what astonished me was Waits' attitude. He said, 'We must succeed in bidding. That amount of revenue will secure our growth target this year. If we fire Sam, he'll join a competitor, and we'll lose opportunities critical to our business.'"

"Oh, that sounds very Waits," I blurted. "All through these years, he keeps saying the same thing—'Our top priority is revenue, because business growth is what we're evaluated on by headquarters.'"

"And unfortunately," she said, sighing, "when we had difficulty achieving that in an ethical way, cheating became a temptation he could hardly resist. Waits and I engaged in a battle of wits. Finally, I pointed out that Sam had been dishonest with us, so how could we know he wouldn't double-cross us in the bidding? Waits had no answer to that, so finally he approved sacking Sam."

"In other words, George's case wasn't an isolated one." I was starting to chafe at Waits' putting the cart before the horse. "And Waits seems to have forgotten the disaster that Fred Cheung caused, which lasted years and only ended a couple of months ago."

"That's what saddens me, Jade."

"But Daisy, I thought we now had a system to flag dishonest behavior."

"No system is a panacea," she said. "It can help detect and prevent risks only to a certain extent. And it may work in the hands of people like your team and Wings', but when it comes to *intentional* malpractice, any system can be manipulated."

"It's demoralizing," I said. "There seems no hope that bad things will cease."

"Hope lies in people. Jade, you and Wings have deterred the management from making improper decisions. And many other employees have been working hard with integrity. There *is* hope."

I was silent, feeling it difficult to swallow my doubts.

"Jade, trust me," Daisy said in her soothing voice. "I understand your frustration. But don't let it overcome you. Take it easy. In my career, I'm looking for someone to work with, not to fall in love with. And you?"

I could not have been more sympathetic to Daisy's perspective on managing emotions at the office. And I felt blessed that my beloved ones at home and I shared the same values, and a life without qualms — though in all conscience, I couldn't swear to that any longer when Wenwu, Taohua's husband, became a local hero.

It all started with the day in mid-May of 2011, when Deping and I returned home from work and found the flat empty, a half-cooked dinner abandoned in the kitchen.

I tried to ring up Taohua, but got an automatic announcement that her mobile phone had been turned off. Suspecting that

THE ENVELOPES

Taohua might've let him know her whereabouts, Deping began calling his father, who answered the second time. He was with Taohua at that moment, he told Deping, in the government car. Wenwu had had a severe accident, and was hovering between life and death. Taohua had received the call about Wenwu too late to catch the last coach from the city terminal, so she'd phoned my father-in-law, who was now escorting her back.

At midnight, the devastating news came. Wenwu had not survived. He'd breathed his last before Taohua and my father-in-law arrived.

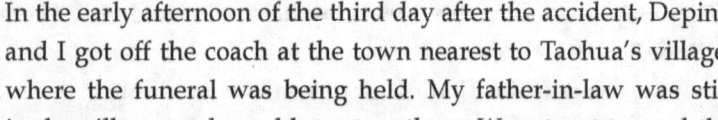

In the early afternoon of the third day after the accident, Deping and I got off the coach at the town nearest to Taohua's village, where the funeral was being held. My father-in-law was still in the village, and would meet us there. We set out toward the village, I led the way, reviving memories of my hike there with Taohua.

On this gray day, town looked no different than it had on that hot, bright summer day almost five years previously, though there were a few more people on the streets now. After the rapid changes that seemed to be taking place in our city every passing day, this little town seemed left behind by the nation's economic boom. The blocks of flats so recently built on my last visit now looked old and worn by the years of harsh weather, but they were still largely empty.

As we passed the elementary school, I started to point it out to Deping. "Oh, that's the shabby—"

I stopped, then cried in consternation, "Good grief! It's fallen apart! Look! Good grief!"

The school entrance was barred, as it had been the last time I saw it, but this time there was a new notice prominently posted on the wall: "Classes suspended, accident under investigation." Through the grilled gate, we could see that the two-story building was still standing, but it was fenced off, the roof and side walls at one corner reduced to rubble.

I stood staring at the building, a feeling of unreality creeping over me.

"Jade," said Deping, breaking into my daze, "could that be the accident that killed Wenwu?"

My father-in-law had told us little about the death of Taohua's husband. But Deping's speculation resonated with me. Perhaps Wenwu had by chance been visiting the school that his daughter, Lianhua, attended when part of the building collapsed. But Lianhua must've been safe, as my father-in-law had said nothing about her.

Deping and I walked along the dirt trail over the hill and then onto the mountain. Thick bushes and tall trees crowded close to the path, which looked dark and dismal on that sunless day. On my last trip with Taohua and Meihua, we'd met no one else as we walked, but on this day Deping and I ran across quite a few people, mostly schoolchildren and the robust elderly, all wearing black armbands for mourning. Some passed us going the other way, while others, carrying wreaths, overtook us. As they passed, I could see remembrance scrolls affixed to the wreaths, the name of Wenwu written in ink brush on them.

Deping increased his pace to catch up with a group of mourners, hoping to get information from them. Left far behind, I walked as fast as I could, recollecting that Taohua had once said her husband was well known among the villagers as a carpenter. He seemed to have been a very popular one, I thought, to judge by the number of people flocking to his funeral...

Deping had paused to wait for me, leaning against a tree. While I caught my breath, he filled me in on what he'd found out. "They're calling Wenwu a hero. He died in the building we saw just now. They say he covered two children with his body when the ceiling caved in. The children, who were unrelated to him, had no injuries."

"Good grief! That's heartbreaking." I bit my lip. "The people in charge of that school must be as blind as a bat. They should've seen how dangerous the building was. How could they let this happen? What if the whole building had collapsed, and all the children in it?... Any news on Lianhua?"

"They said his daughter wasn't attending that school."

"Then why was he there? And what does Lianhua do, if not going to school?"

Deping shrugged and took my hand, and we resumed walking — or, in my case, trudging.

"They also said he was a great man," Deping said. "He made tons of money in a big city, and then came back to run schools for the children living in the mountain villages of this area. That's all I heard. I didn't want to pester them with too many questions. They seemed in a hurry." He paused, and then said, almost as if to himself, "Perhaps Lianhua goes to one of the schools they said her father ran. Something about those seems familiar. Strange."

After that we walked in silence, occasionally encountering other people, who sometimes greeted us and exchanged simple words about the funeral. Somehow, I had a sensation of being led toward the revelation of a mystery, at the end of the trail and out of the woods.

The moment I recognized the adobe house of Taohua's family, memory stirred in me. Through a mist of tears, I thought I could see Meihua, pelting toward home ahead of me and hollering, "Piggy! Piggy! I'm home!"

I gazed at the house, and, around it, the assembly grieving the loss of their hero. Then a surreal figure, his buzz-cut blond hair making him conspicuous in the crowd, popped into my line of sight. Surely it was Felix Lee. Was I dreaming?

I was not dreaming; the next moment I heard Deping whispering in my ear, "What is Felix doing here? No wonder you had a sense of déjà vu when you looked at the photos Felix gave me. And Taohua must've made a Freudian slip."

Our trip to the funeral turned out to be a journey of realization. The disconnected scenes I'd once replayed in my head, my "scattered beads," one by one were strung together to make a single piece: my father-in-law had been operating on the sly, probably since 2007, after Meihua's death. The chance incidents I'd witnessed over the years surged up on the screen of my brain, intercut with the scene and faces I observed at the funeral, as I struggled to find clues to how everyone I'd thought I knew so well had ended up in this place.

Taohua's face, blanched, but showing no mark of remorse nor tears, seemed to float in front of Wenwu's, tranquil with a tinge of a reassuring smile, in a photo on the wall of the living room of the adobe house, used as the mourning hall. My father-in-law looked pensive, as he silently watched Felix and his German friend organizing groups of pupils in orderly fashion for the mourning ceremony. Lianhua stood beside her mother, calmly receiving the condolences people offered her. Five years previously, she had been a ray of sunshine to me, as I struggled to adjust to the way of life in a poor country household. She was much taller now, her bearing just as natural and unselfconscious, yet with a new grace. Though her eyes were red-rimmed with crying, they were still as lucid as I remembered, but now they blazed with an intelligence and tenacity that defied sadness, though it seemed too much for a child of the tender age of eleven. Yet again, the sight of her

THE ENVELOPES

consoled me. Everything that seemed so irrational and confusing might still make sense, if she — with all the schoolchildren in this mountainous area — was the purpose.

At the end of May, in the accident's aftermath, Taohua decided to stay with her daughter, who would continue her schooling in the village. Once we were back home, after much deliberation, my father-in-law finally unfolded to Deping and me the entire "machination" that he'd orchestrated over the past four years, starting two months after Meihua's death. He first told Taohua and Wenwu about his desire to set up an elementary school in their village. Wenwu leaped at his invitation to oversee the establishment and running of the school. Therefore, he, instead of Taohua, abandoned his job in the city and returned to their village, pretending that he'd earned a fortune to capitalize the school.

My father-in-law also instructed Taohua to accept, each time on his specific orders, the envelopes that had been, during working hours, delivered to our apartment. I'd once come upon a strange man leaving, having successfully left envelopes with Taohua, I now realized. My father-in-law was never explicit about the contents of the envelopes only he himself opened. But on the next day, he always passed wads of banknotes to Taohua and asked her to take Driver Fu's car back to her village, and give the money to Wenwu. Finally I understood those scenes in which Taohua, clasping her backpack, got into the car appeared outside my window.

On the other hand, my father-in-law held out teaching jobs to Felix and his German friend, with one condition — they could never divulge the identities of their working partners or give the exact location of the country school to anyone, including Deping and me. The first elementary school was founded in the middle of 2007 to provide free education to Lianhua and her peers in four neighboring villages — after the funeral, Felix kindly showed Deping and me around the spartan but functional classroom there. The second school, at some distance from the first, was created in early 2009 for the children in five other villages. And the third one was in place by mid 2010 to accommodate the offspring of the farmer families in the last group of the villages in the area. With the money channeled through Wenwu, though it originated from my father-in-law, classrooms were built and supplies purchased on a regular basis. Some other supplies were recycled, obtained through a variety of ways — I'd been a numbskull to make my shameful joke about the pile of warm clothes Taohua knitted for the children in those schools. In addition to the painstaking work of Felix and his German friend, Wenwu coordinated, via the *guanxi* he'd developed through his work as a carpenter, the aid of willing teachers working in the government's town elementary school at the foot of those mountains. It had been dilapidated and half empty for years.

My father-in-law's exposé silenced Deping and me for quite a while. I was in a strange frame of mind. My father-in-law Mr Zhengting Dai, a symbol of justice and probity, should've fallen in my estimation, but I just felt what had happened couldn't be true.

But Deping looked composed as he asked, "Why? Father, why have you been doing all these things?"

My father-in-law sat still for a moment, looking thoughtful. Then he said in a slow, heavy voice, "I'm an energy person, but I have a perception that you may think is too pessimistic, or even puerile. Energy is essential to a country's economic growth and prosperity. But in my judgment, energy is hardly the future of a nation... It's people who concern themselves with the limit of

THE ENVELOPES

its sustainability and will utilize it wisely that are the future. It's sad to see fewer and fewer of these people, because in the cities, education is driven by the golden calf, and in the countryside, despite its much larger population, there are far too few schools. I may be regarded as a powerful man, but I feel powerless to help younger generations grow up well educated, in a land where so many things are disappearing. Farmers in the prime of life have been leaving the poverty-stricken countryside for drudgery in cities. Schools are disappearing from the villages. Children there have to move away to get any education. After the old people die, rice paddies will be deserted. Villages will vanish... Is it feasible for a nation of over one billion people to live on imported food? Or will the people face starvation, and the nation disappear?"

"Father," Deping broke in, "did all these thoughts have something to do with Meihua's death?"

"Both my grandson and Meihua's deaths felt like a sneer at the power that many people believe me to have. They came as a rude awakening. For the first time, I felt myself impotent. I was unable to protect even the lives closest to me... I felt sorry for Mama, for you and Jade, for Taohua's family. I felt ashamed of the useless power I possessed... Then I considered those envelopes that people kept trying to leave at my door. I used to turn them down, because I didn't want to return what those people wanted from me... But if those envelopes represented the real value of my power, even if I still refused to give their bearers what they wanted, why couldn't I transform that value into a better life for children in need? They are the future of the nation, after all. Those who would bribe me, indirectly, might actually be making a real contribution to our country." He smiled slightly. "I hit the ground running, once I'd had that thought. For the first time in my life, it felt great to have power."

After a pause, he continued, "My idea took root in the village...

HASU AUGUST

The whole system went smoothly. Wenwu was very efficient. Felix and his German friend are priceless. We got help from others in the area too." He paused again, his face somber now. "But as they say, even the best-laid schemes go astray... That day, Wenwu went to the school in town to discuss borrowing some of their teaching staff. He happened to be in the part of the building that collapsed."

At the mention of the accident, we all must have thought about the hero who had saved two children's lives, for we fell into silence.

I went to fetch some water for my father-in-law. After he'd drunk some, Deping asked, "Father, you knew I was on your side in the education cause. Why did you keep this all hidden from me?"

My father-in-law put his water glass back on the table, and turned to look Deping in the eye. "Son, I admire Mama for her unblemished devotion to education. I'm proud of what you're doing in the right way. But, son, even though it may have realized a tiny part of Mama's dream at a speed she'd never dreamed of, my way is *wrong*. I've left no records, for the money was all cash, and never went through a bank. And I've told no one connected to any of the three schools about where the funds came from ultimately, though they simply know I'm the sponsor. They've never asked about it, either. They've just stuck to their individual positions and devoted themselves to a great cause, just as you and Little Jve have devoted yourselves to doing the right thing in your jobs. Against all the odds, they persisted in giving a world and choices to those disadvantaged children. I didn't want any of you to be part of this, for I *am* guilty. I'm guilty of taking those envelopes. I'm guilty of enticing Taohua and Wenwu, by manipulating their sorrow at their daughter's death. I'm guilty of charming Felix into completely believing me. I'm guilty of ordering Driver Fu to send Taohua back to the village, to avoid the risk of her being robbed in a coach... I'm guilty in many aspects. But let me be the *only one* to be guilty. And son, I hope you can forgive me for my guilt."

"Father, please don't..." Deping choked with emotion.

My father-in-law stretched out his hand and patted Deping on the shoulder. "From day one, I've always known there would be an end to my way sooner or later. But I never expected it to cost a life... I reproached myself for starting all this, and felt an urge to stop it. But it was Taohua who came up to me and said, 'Mr Dai Senior, it was nobody's fault. My man was fated to die in one way or another. I'd rather he died as a hero.' I heard her well. And I'm hanging on in there... for the sake of all the children in those three schools."

That's typical of Taohua, I thought; *she bears her afflictions as a part of her fate, and she survives.* Somehow I recalled the incident I witnessed in the village in the summer of 2006: the snake that stealthily swallowed the kittens; the mother cat that, in her despair, accidentally strangled the baby rabbits she'd mistaken for her children. It was hard for twelve-year-old Meihua to accept the death of the baby rabbits as an accident, and we never succeeded in clearing her mind of hatred for the snake. I felt just like that young girl in my confusion, now. I could not identify what in our society was the equivalent of that snake, the ringleader in a string of slayings among the animals.

16

In the month of June 2011, my father-in-law Mr Zhengting Dai was led away by the government inspection squad to a hotel dedicated to dignitaries in the city. This didn't come as a surprise to him; he'd anticipated that the elementary school building's collapse would soon invite a thorough official investigation, which in turn would likely expose the operations behind the three village schools, for they'd been administered by Taohua's late husband, who was now receiving much attention for his heroic deed. He'd asked Deping and me to stay out of the matter. "Rest assured, I'm braced for whatever might befall me," he'd said, without going into any details.

He was held incommunicado in the hotel for about two weeks, "to assist in investigations," they claimed. Deping and I had to sweat it out. We knew there would not even be a private trial for top officials taking bribes, because my father-in-law planned to plead guilty.

In the meantime, the other matter, at the office, was keeping my nerves constantly on edge. After the meeting in which Waits demanded that Charles and the finance department work out a way to collect the two million yuan the Haizi fire brigade owed us, BrightLife China – as Charles had suggested – for a month took no action against George, the underperforming salesman. At that point, Waits realized that keeping George on had not been

THE ENVELOPES

helpful, and decided to dismiss him. I was the one who executed this decision. As a matter of fact, George had not used his supposedly valuable *guanxi* with the fire brigade as a bargaining chip for anything other than his own severance package.

On the other hand, despite the objection raised by Charles, who maintained that BrightLife China would lose sheer volume of sales, Daisy and Wings (Waits sat on the fence) insisted on issuing a legal collection notice to the fire brigade as a last resort, after it did not respond to numerous requests from our finance department.

In June, after the collection notice had been sent to the fire brigade, demanding it pay its delinquent account, Daisy again invited me to her meeting with Waits. She came straight to the point. "Jade," she said, "the plot thickens."

It turned out that the fire brigade's response to our legal notice had corroborated Wings' suspicions, as she herself had predicted in April, when she remarked to me that the legal notice sent to the fire brigade would be the key. Our letter met a fusillade of refutation from the fire brigade. They felt deeply insulted, they said, pointing out that the accounts we claimed were overdue had never appeared in their books. They did disclose, though, that they had recently purged their organization of several employees for unethical behavior, one of whom might have been George's accomplice. They also threatened to bring both George and BrightLife China to justice for the harm they deemed done to them.

Our contentious meeting was an unpleasant surprise to me, especially as, again, Waits and Daisy disagreed with each other. Daisy strongly recommended that, working either alone or with the fire brigade, we take legal action, holding George liable for our missing revenue and investigating Charles' possible role in the fraud. Waits, on the other hand, urged us to play down the matter, to preserve BrightLife China's business relationship with the fire brigade. We couldn't afford to be discredited in the market, he said, and argued that the company's rapid growth could not have been achieved without Charles.

Caught between these two arguments, I felt quite disoriented. But then I recollected how desperate Waits had been, four years previously, to remove Fred Cheung, saying that it was the perfect time to do it because he and Daisy were new, and had an opportunity to get rid of all past burdens... Suddenly it dawned on me that Waits had been playing the judge, determining whether miscreants should be tried for their crimes — but that he judged not by what was right or honest, but by whether a crime was hurting his top priority, BrightLife's growth. I began to feel that I, as well as other BrightLife China employees with the same values, had been sold down the river by Waits, with his belief in the ends justifying the means.

When Daisy asked for my opinion, I tried to suppress my frustration. "I'm nobody to pass judgment on what really happened. But if one commits a crime, no matter who he is, he ought to stand trial. Isn't that the simple fairness that a society should have? But in a country where a judge might be corrupted, what can we expect?" At that moment, though, I thought of my father-in-law, and wished he could be pardoned for his guilt.

———∞———

In July 2011 my father-in-law pleaded no contest to the charges against him. As a result, he was removed from his position in the Bureau of Energy, and sentenced to ten years of imprisonment. Nonetheless, his impassioned plea for conserving the three village schools that were the evidence of his crime was accepted. The local government took over the schools, which, now affiliated with the elementary school in town, continued

THE ENVELOPES

to provide education to more than one hundred children from twelve villages.

———∞———

Deping and I lived on in the apartment, which we two had bought when the Bureau of Energy privatized its housing two years previously, taking out a mortgage to do so. But life at home without my father-in-law and Taohua felt dismal. It often seemed as if the flat had become nothing more than a hotel room, both of us so often stayed out late working, and made do with separate meals, on his campus and in my office.

I found no escape from my feeling of loss at BrightLife China. Waits held his ground in the matter of the fire brigade, requesting that Daisy drop any further investigation and write off the transactions that had been recorded only in our books. No one knew where BrightLife's goods, passed through multiple manipulating hands, had really gone. Waits suggested Charles could help recoup the loss by bringing in more revenue with his sales team in the near future. Though Daisy stood her ground, Boston headquarters fudged on the case, and as Waits had hoped, it was eventually shelved.

I couldn't tell how much this incident had to do with Daisy's decision, but I was not all that surprised when, in private, at the end of November 2011, she said to me, "I hope I'm not disappointing you, but I'd like to let you know, ahead of the official announcement, about my resignation, which I've already handed in."

For a moment, I could say nothing, as the events of the past years whirled past in my mind.

She smiled slightly. "Just as I predicted, you're not surprised, I see."

"I knew something was brewing," I managed to say at last.

"As I remember, you once said if you couldn't repair a red traffic light that never turned green, you'd find another place to cross the road. Is it that now you've found it irreparable?"

"I'm gonna level with you, Jade," she said. "You've seen that I've been at odds with Waits over work ethics on several occasions. But perhaps you're unaware that I've been rooting for Wings as she probes into what's really behind the surge of sales at the end of each month recently. BrightLife China's incredible growth figures might be too rosy to be completely true. But Waits has been complaining to corporate headquarters about me, angling for them to support Charles' way of doing business. It's ironic that we spend precious time playing this cat-and-mouse-game, instead of working out new strategies for this new phase of development and defining our core competencies for real, solid business achievements. Well, I'm interested in many things in life, but absolutely not in power or politics. And yes, I choose to leave these office-politics games, where I'm a square peg in a round hole... Over four years ago, chance threw Waits and me together, but over time, I've come to feel we're not in the same league."

"I can't fathom what has changed Waits so much," I said. I'd witnessed the rawness of his greed for business growth. I'd had the same doubt about my father-in-law when he began to seem so changed, though I'd since learned his motive for taking bribes.

"Waits has never *changed*," Daisy said. "He's always had his unremitting desire to move up the corporate ladder, and *fear* of losing his status at BrightLife ingrained in his soul. All the time, he's craved wonderful sales figures to please the top boss. It's the circumstances that have changed. Fred's misconduct didn't do any good to him, but as for Charles's unethical way of developing business, it's an ill wind that blows no one good — in the short run, the apparent growth makes Waits look great. The change in his behavior just shows what he really is, and was all along. I understand his type, but I could never persuade myself to become one of them."

I was speechless. My head was spinning around what the true, unchanging thing in my father-in-law could have been, that had made him yield to temptation, and fall. *It could not have been desire for power*, I thought. *It could not have been fear of losing—*

Daisy broke into my thoughts. "Red light in your life again, Jade? You've been on a downer for months, I've noticed. It can't just be due to the 'change' in Waits."

Daisy must've sensed my depression, just as she'd caught my grief at a glance almost four and half years before, on her first day at BrightLife. But I couldn't gather my thoughts into clear and simple words to tell her about my father-in-law's downfall, which somehow hadn't been widely reported in the city's media.

Daisy was leaving. Whatever related to this country—the successes and the failures, the beautiful and the ugly, the likes and dislikes—would soon become a part of her life history...

"Daisy, it is sad to see you going away," I said. "I'm afraid your departure will leave a void in the company."

"No, there won't be a void," she said. "BrightLife China still has people like you and Wings, who have grown professionally mature and independent, with consistent values and ethics. You'll help keep the company on the right path. You've completed your study in the MBA program, haven't you?"

"Yes, I have. But, the company will still be different without you."

"Well, I hope you feel better if I tell you another factor in my decision." She smiled. "In fact, you were right about Jack, during our talk last January."

"Oh?" My curiosity was kindled. "It's true that Jack rued the day that he let you leave Boston for Southeast Asia?"

"Well, several months ago, I went back to Boston, and he and I met again. He confessed his regret that he didn't try harder, on our commencement day, to persuade me to find a job in the States."

"Hooray! He's still in love with you."

"Gee, you just simplified one of the most complicated human feelings." She beamed. "Well, Jack and I agreed there might be a remedy for his regrets about fifteen years ago. I'm going back to Boston."

Daisy's love development was the only delightful event for me that year, and it somehow inspired me; the same day she shared with me her decision on returning to Jack, on the spur of the moment, I took the afternoon off. I drove straight to Normal University and slipped into Deping's lecture theater. There I watched him, still like a conductor on the podium, making his class the most euphonic music for me.

After school, we had a candlelit dinner in a small but cozy place. Somehow, at the table, I found myself waxing lyrical on Miyazaki's animations—those zingy scenes in which the pure love of boys and girls blossomed.

Then, before going upstairs, we strolled hand in hand about the community park, shivering in the chill wind, pecking each other's cheeks, and laughing like lovebirds at puberty. We went home and kissed intimately. And as a natural climax of our affection, we made love, though with my eyes wide open, as my soul and my body were still divorced... For the entire afternoon and night, without any comment about my spontaneity, Deping was a charming companion for me. We were like two children, as if only the love between the two of us counted in the whole world...

THE ENVELOPES

Nevertheless, my life has not been a potted history of that kind of enchanting moment, but a detailed chronicle of afflicting days. I'd rather believe that, about one month previously, right before the Spring Festival of 2012, on that day I now reflect on in this hotel room, my suffering culminated in an illusion in which encroaching red lights left no avenue for me to take, and destroying power threatened the ideal world in my mind. My husband's agony must've also peaked, in the form of a whimpering that I heard for the first time and a feeling of doubt about his own ability to hold the family together. Afterward, he and I held each other tight. Subconsciously, as if to defy all our struggles, we freed our bodies to burn in a flame of passion, our hearts to reach euphoria as the transformation of pain... Now I can see that, in the course of defying and then reveling, my soul and my body rejoined; that Deping and I integrated with each other, emotionally deep and physically productive, and, as a result, my egg and his sperm united.

On the day when my father-in-law came back home on medical parole, while we were chatting, his wish to see those children in the village schools gave Taohua an idea.

Consequently, instead of having Lianhua spend the holidays with us in the city during the 2012 Spring Festival, as we'd originally planned, I drove my father-in-law, Taohua, and Deping to the little town. There, we were greeted by Felix, his German friend, and several villagers carrying a chair-litter, in which they would carry our emaciated old man over hill and mountain to Taohua's village.

The small, austere school, nestled into a basin halfway up the mountains, though closed for the winter holidays, was festooned with red lanterns and colorful scrolls on which couplets were written. A festive spirit was in the air. In the bitter wind, some children—Lianhua among them—were still scampering away on the open playground, enjoying their games.

It was a cold but sunny day. Felix and Deping had run to join the playing children. My father-in-law and I sat under a huge tree, watching them at a distance. The sunlight, passing through the winter-bare treetops, touched us gently. The children's ringing laughter and calls came to our ears, and their spirited movements brought life to the wintry landscape.

My father-in-law chuckled. "Children grow so fast," he said. "They look so much taller already than they did last year."

I looked over my shoulder toward him, and saw his light-hearted smile. The fresh air had blown away the sickly pallor of his face. As if in response to my gaze, he added, "I didn't tell you and Deping that I too came here during the last Spring Festival."

"We knew it, Father," I said. "We happened to see you and Taohua getting off the coach at the end of the holidays."

"You did?" A touch of surprise swept over his face. His calm returning, he went on, "You must've put some careful thought into what you saw, and decided to keep it to yourselves."

Ashamed, I took my eyes off him and looked back at the playground. "Father, I must apologize... I was so silly that I thought you did special things for Taohua out of love for her. I was so wrong."

For an instant, neither he nor I spoke. A cheer of victory from the children filled the interval. But when their hoorays tailed away, and another round of games began, my father-in-law spoke again, his deep, mellow voice calm and steady.

"In fact, Little Jve, you were half right. I did the whole thing out of love...for Mama. Mama wanted to build a school for the children here, to provide them with a fair chance for their minds flying over these mountains. She tried so hard, but I did nothing to help... Little Jve, have you ever wondered, after you die, what will be the evidence of your life, which once existed in this world? Your business cards you kept as souvenirs? Your earnings recorded in the banks? Your homes where you lived? Your children surviving your death? Your tomb lying in a cemetery, to be occasionally visited by your descendants or those who still care for you?"

"Father, I never thought about such a thing," I replied quietly.

"Look at those children on the playground," he continued. "Their unpolluted smiles... And imagine generations after them in the schools here... Aren't they all the evidence of Mama's life? Mama is living on with us, isn't she?"

I nodded slowly, something choking me, everything becoming blurred—the school, the playground, the carefree, blithe boys and girls, in patched clothing and bright sweaters that Taohua had knitted with recycled wool...

Voicelessly, I echoed him in my heart.

Yes. Yes. They are forever the evidence of Mother's life.

———∽∽∽———

I am alone, in this hotel room. Suddenly, the static flat earth on the dormant television screen is changing into animated pictures, accompanied by loud music, the lead-up to broadcasting news. Morning has broken. The new day has begun. I'm still all by myself, but somehow I can feel the new life inside me. I still don't know what to do ...

But I'm dialing Deping's number. He's been keeping a vigil at the bedside of his father, Mr Zhengting Dai, who has only days to live. But I'm going to tell him, when I'm home today, I want to share my realization about the ineffably delightful fruit of our love. I want to make *our* decision on it—even if there might be another tragedy awaiting; even though I will never grow into a

HASU AUGUST

heroine who always triumphs over evil; and I still don't know what will become the evidence of my life...

The call is through. The phone is ringing, ringing, ringing...

About The Author

Hasu August was born in 1968, studied photography in Japan, and management science in the United States. After working in a couple of multinational companies for over twenty years, she started to devote herself to a journey of story-telling, either by words or by photographs, which she had long yearned for. The journey continues, and her passion for it grows. She has lived in Japan, China, the United States, and is currently living in Singapore.

www.ingramcontent.com/pod-product-compliance
Lightning Source LLC
LaVergne TN
LVHW031610060526
838201LV00065B/4795